OF GOLD AND GREED

OF GOLD AND GREED

CHANDA HAHN

ALSO BY CHANDA HAHN

Daughters of Eville
Of Beast and Beauty
Of Glass and Glamour
Of Sea and Song
Of Thorn and Thread
Of Mist and Murder
Of Secrets and Slippers

The Unfortunate Fairy Tales
UnEnchanted
Fairest
Fable
Reign
Forever

The Neverwood Chronicles
Lost Girl
Lost Boy
Lost Shadow

The Underland Duology
Underland
Underlord

The Iron Butterfly Series
The Iron Butterfly
The Steele Wolf
The Silver Siren

The Seven Kingdoms
KILN
RYA
BAIST
CANDOR
ISLA
FLORIN
TOWN OF NIHILL
EVILLE'S TOWER
SION
N
W
E
S

PROLOGUE

"It's useless. You cannot kill me," Greed screamed, digging his claws into the cave wall, ripping through the ancient stone like freshly churned butter.

"I may not be able to kill you, but I can stop you," the dwarf shouted, swinging his heavy axe toward the great black beast as he herded Greed deep into the mountain. The air thinned as the temperature rose. Sweat beaded across his brow, running into his eyes, causing them to sting. He dared not wipe his face, for Greed would surely strike. A beast he had let roam the caves for far too long, it prowled his homeland, lurking in the dark, gaining strength until he was too powerful. For this was his ancient enemy. One that he had battled many times before. Each time he encountered Greed, his enemy left him with a scar.

But even though he himself was long lived—he was aging, and his enemy was not—time was no longer on his side. His reflexes were slower, his vision fading, and he favored one arm over the other.

Yet, he was the last defense. The one who could keep the monster at bay. The last of his line of the Stiltskin family. He was the only one strong enough to lure the creature out of Ter Dell and across the boiling abyss, deep into the volcanic mountain . . . and he was the only one strong enough to survive it.

A geyser of steam erupted from one of the hidden vents, filling the mountain tunnel with smoke, and he lost sight of his prey. When the steam dissipated, the hate-filled red eyes of his enemy had disappeared.

"Come out, Greed, so I can send you back to Hell!" the dwarf shouted, raising his great double-headed axe. The wood handle creaked beneath his desperate grip.

Scratches echoed throughout the cavern, making it appear like his enemy was everywhere at once. The scraping sounded in front of him, but he wouldn't fall for it. Not again. If the noise was in front, that meant the attack was coming from—

"Aargh!" The dwarf spun, swinging the axe upward at the last second as a great maw filled with yellow teeth almost swallowed him. His axe grazed scales but might have slid off water for all the damage it did. Greed retreated into one of the many tunnels that ran through the Ragnar Mountains.

"Pitiful dwarf. Why do you fight so hard?" Greed's voice was distant as he slithered between the different caverns. "Your people are gone. There's no one left. All because you failed."

The axe grew heavy in the dwarf's hands as the guilt of his past creeped up on him. It was his folly that caused the destruction of the dwarven city of Ter Dell. The hundreds of lives lost. He was the one responsible. He had succumbed to Greed's dark influence, and the innocent had paid the price.

"You should just let me eat you," Greed coaxed. "I can

make the pain go away. The memories will cease, and you can have eternal rest."

He missed the hidden attack. The claw appeared out of the shadows, swiping at his midsection. The enchanted chain mail did little to stop the cursed talon. Pain ripped through his stomach. He pressed a hand to his side, and it came away red with blood. He was old, too slow, and he should have blocked that blow.

The dwarf retreated down a small dark tunnel that ran toward the main vent of the volcano. His blood leaving a slick, wet trail behind him. The heat was intense. His skin burned; his lips cracked. But he pushed on, travelling downward. He couldn't give up. They did not nickname him Steel-skin for nothing.

"I smell your blood," Greed said, his voice slithering out of the darkness. "It is much, for one such as you. Let me quell it once and for all, with my teeth." A crack followed his words.

He could hear the beast snapping his jaws, his lips smacking together as it imagined eating him.

The stone floor swam before him, and he stumbled. A little farther. He grasped the cave wall for support, leaving a bloody handprint. The roof brushed his head, and he had to duck. Pushing one foot in front of the other, he knew he was going to his death. He was okay with his life ending, as long as his death meant something.

The tunnel he was in came to an end, opening to reveal an enormous cavern filled with gold—gold shields, coins, crowns, swords, chain mail. Enough gold to feed everyone in the kingdom multiple times over. Most of it once belonged to the dwarves. With their kingdom decimated, they had no use for it. He had to convince the human king to come to his aid; to fight their common enemy. It had almost bankrupted the kingdom of Kiln, but it was the only way to stop Greed.

He slowed when he saw the familiar throne tossed among the pile of treasure. Taking one step at a time, he approached the golden chair. A tear slipped down his weathered cheek as he remembered the great dwarf king who once sat upon it.

"I will get revenge for you, my friend," the dwarf promised the dead king. The blood now flowing freely from the wound in his side, he was slowly succumbing to the death blow. He patted the arm and turned his eyes to the only entrance to the cave and waited.

A black scaled claw reached through, gripping the edge of the too small tunnel, trying to widen the opening. There was no way for Greed to enter in his current size.

"What is that I smell?" Greed howled like a bloodhound that caught scent of his prey. "Is that gold?"

The dwarf smiled wanly. There was a reason this creature was called Greed. It was attracted to that desire, that *want*, that which caused people to covet. And what better physical representation than gold? It was the perfect lure to trap a beast so aptly named.

"I wa-nt! I ne-e-d," Greed scratched at the tunnel as he tried to widen the entrance.

"Your fat butt can't fit, old man," the dwarf wheezed. He coughed and blood bubbled up between his lips. "Maybe if you weren't so big."

Smoke filled the tunnel as the creature shrank and became ethereal. Black mist moved into the tunnel and red eyes gazed out at him from the center of the burning smoke.

Come closer, the dwarf thought. *Just a little closer.*

"The avarice taste is sweet on my lips."

Greed's ethereal form hovered over the pile of gold. In this shape, he couldn't tell where the head was. He could only tell when those burning eyes looked upon him.

"I thought the gold would be a fitting headstone for you." The dwarf raised his axe high in the air.

"What?" Greed turned in confusion as the axe sliced through a rope that was linked to a hidden lever attached to a pulley system. The ground shook as a giant boulder rolled in front of the cave entrance, blocking them in. Another lever activated, and a rumble started deep in the mountain.

Greed laughed. "Do you mean to trap me? You fool, I will rip through the rock in seconds."

"Yes, tis true. But I know your secret." The dwarf coughed, and he wiped his mouth. More blood smeared his sleeve.

"You lie."

"I know that which you crave—is also your weakness."

The dark shadow flickered in and out as if scared.

The dwarf looked up at the hidden shafts directly above them. The thick rumbling sound grew louder as trap doors opened and molten lava rained down onto the gold.

"No!" Greed shrieked and pawed at the hoard, trying to gather it as it melted.

The dwarf, with his mighty axe in his hand, swung it through the air. It sliced through Greed's corporeal form and caught, pinning him to the gold. He struggled against the golden axe, but it was no use. The room was quickly filling with lava; the heat melting the gold—and melding to

Greed's body. The thing tried to pull away, but he was trapped.

The dwarf threw more gold on him. Everywhere it touched, it melted against Greed, slowly encasing the creature within.

"That which gives you power also binds you."

"You fool. Release me. You will die too," Greed begged.

"I've fought you countless times in my lifetime. Now, I will guard you in my death." The dwarf gave one last rattling breath as the heat became too much for even him to bear.

"Rumple!" Greed screamed as he sunk deeper. "I will escape. This can't hold me forever."

"No," Rumple wheezed. He crawled onto the throne, pulling his axe across his lap. He leaned back as the chair slowly sank into a pool of molten gold, adding to the gilded prison that would confine this demon. "It just needs to hold you long enough. Until another can take up my mantle. And there will be another like me. One who will fight you and defeat you when I could not. I promise."

Greed's voice rose in a pitiful wail, echoing against the walls, "No-o-o."

The mountain quaked in response, collapsing inward, burying them both in a chamber of gold before it settled.

CHAPTER ONE

"**R**hea, it's time," Mother said, her face grim as she inspected my trunk. She latched the strap, then tested the strength of the worn leather. "There's no use waiting any longer. To delay could mean great travesty." She gave it a last tug, resting her hand on my luggage that was strapped to the back of the waiting transport.

"The magic mirror has gone silent before. Maybe it's having another temper tantrum," I said numbly, referring to the mirror that hung in our sitting room that we used to spy on the neighboring kingdoms.

Mother's piercing eyes left little room for argument. Now that the cruel sorcerer Allemar was gone, there was only one name that was still whispered in fear on the breath of children. And it was my mother's name—Lorelai Eville. To the world, Lady Eville was one of the most feared sorceresses: cruel and unforgiving. To me, she was my adoptive mother. One who had taken pity on the golden-haired child left on her doorstep. She had raised me and my sisters to be powerful, fearless, and coldhearted like her. With me, she succeeded at two of the three. My heart was more lukewarm than frozen, and I let my head do the thinking more than my heart.

"Not like this," Mother said firmly. "The mirror was created in Kiln, a gift from my father before he died. It's my link to my home. It can always see home." Her eyes fluttered. She was doing everything she could to hide her pain. "Something is wrong there. Something powerful has taken up residence in the kingdom and is blocking my scrying. You need to find out what it is and eliminate it."

"Eliminate *it*. It sounds like you already know what it is?" I asked.

"I'm not sure. I dare not speak it out loud until I know more."

"What about sending Honor?" I asked, referring to my sister who spent more time roaming the country with Lorn, our Elven friend. She was on her way to becoming a master spy and hunter.

"This isn't a job for Honor. You were always supposed to go to Kiln. Your magic will be stronger there, unlike here." She opened the door to the transport wagon waiting outside our home.

I balked. *My magic was a joke.* I was the bookworm. I excelled at alchemy, potions, and forging charms. Magic that had proven outcomes for correct steps. Magic that could be taught. I wasn't born with talent, or magical gifts like my sisters. Gifts that were passed down from their talented lineage that always led back to a powerful ancestral tree. My tree was barren, the sparse fruit just adequate. Which made me feel lacking in this powerful family of sorcerers. My very normal parents, Nell and Martin Free, were millers, and with the loss of their workshop to debt collectors, they were relocating to another kingdom when I was a baby. They died before ever reaching Sion. I appeared in a handbasket on Lorelai's stoop, bearing nothing but a necklace with a silver charm made from a rare ore found in the Ragnar Mountains.

I grasped the charm for comfort as a soft note rang out. A note only I could hear. I cast a look at the brown padded bench seat inside the transport, the inter-kingdom carriage. Currently, there were no passengers, but that didn't mean we wouldn't pick up any on the way to Kiln. The driver, with his oversized hat, seemed oblivious to our conversation. He'd probably witnessed hundreds of goodbyes just like this.

Lady Eville backed away to stand by the front stoop. Our home, an old guard tower, with an added main house and workshop, loomed high, casting a shadow over the front yard. With all of my sisters gone, spread out across the seven kingdoms, it seemed too spacious and lonely. Is this how the villagers saw our tower? Foreboding and dark? Most gave us a wide berth after my sister, Meri, killed one of the mayor's sons in self-defense. We avoided town at all costs, and so its people shunned us. Now our home was no longer filled with my sisters' laughter as they cast spells and curses over each other. It was filled with silence and sorrow.

Maybe it was better that I was leaving.

"You know what you need to do," Lady Eville said. It wasn't a question.

I nodded, swallowing thickly. As I stepped onto the wobbly ledge and slid onto the bench seat, the transport door closed behind me. Turning, I leaned out the window to gaze at my mother. Her lips pinched together, and I saw the barest hint of a tremble, but she cut it off. Her raven black hair was pulled back into a bun, and I noticed the slightest streaks of silver. How long had those been there?

She buried her hands in her apron pocket and looked north toward the direction I would be travelling.

"You could come with?" I whispered. "Visit your old home."

Her eyes narrowed, and her breath hitched. She shook her head. "No, I won't go back there. There are too many memories. But Eville Manor still stands. I've seen to that. You can find refuge there while you plan your next steps."

Lady Eville was born in Kiln. Her house was quite wealthy, and she had been engaged to the Prince of Sion, but when her family lost their fortune, the prince spurned her. They were not treated well at the high court, and her father died in her arms after suffering a heart attack. She had retreated to this remote location to heal her bitter and broken heart while diligently watching over the seven king-doms. Some women healed a broken heart by investing their time and energy into a new hobby: gardening, sewing, quilting. Our adoptive mother healed by raising and training seven powerful daughters, each of us specializing in the magical arts. It was a deadly weapon that could defend or cause harm, dependent on our moods. We were pointed like a compass of power and revenge to wherever our mother wanted us to go.

And for me, my compass pointed north to the Kingdom of Kiln. High in the snowy mountains, filled with goblins, dwarves, and gold. Something dark was brewing in the kingdom. Her magic mirror told her so, and she waited as long as she dared. It was time to send me in her stead to hunt out the problem . . . and do a little digging while I was there.

"Rhea, when you get there, seek out Grimkeep." She pressed a piece of paper into my palm, his name written in her handwriting. "He is the only one I trust. Speak not about your intentions. Do you understand? It's been too long since I've returned. I do not know the political climate of the kingdom since the mirror has gone dark. But at one time, King Goddrick was a kind ruler." The slightest pink rose in her cheeks as she spoke of him. She reached up to brush a strand of my honey-brown hair behind my ear. Then her gentle touch became firmer as she rubbed at the soot marring my cheek left behind from my earlier project. "Really, Rheanon, you couldn't keep yourself clean for even one day," she chastised. "They're going to think you're a dwarf with how dirty you always are."

I tucked my fingers under my palms, hiding the soot from working in the forge as I frantically tried to replace my diminishing supply of magic charms, having only finished a candle mark ago.

I winced and gave her a tiny smile. I wanted to say more—wanted to stay here forever—but before I could get the words out, she signaled to the driver and the transport shot off with a crack of a whip, sending me flying backward into the cushion. In a swirl of dust, I left the only home I've ever known, and I tried to keep the tears from welling in my eyes.

"The Ragnar Mountains are just ahead," Herst, the driver, yelled back to me.

After two weeks sitting in the carriage, my back and bottom had gone stiff and numb in that order. I had given up on trying to stay clean, as the shades that pulled down did little to keep out the dust of the roads. I used every opportunity to clean myself up as we stopped at the various waystations that spread across the kingdoms. As we passed through Candor, I held back the desire to make a visit to my sister Eden, for I knew if I stopped, I wouldn't want to continue my journey north. I would find a reason to avoid my duty.

Then the dusty roads turned to mud, the warm fall air slowly chilled as we headed into the mountains. I pulled a scarf out of my satchel and wrapped it around my neck and face as the temperature slowly dropped, pulling on mittens as well to keep my hands from freezing. A light snow fell, and I hung out the window, squinting up at the snowy sky, each flake falling like a puff of a dandelion head.

But the beauty of the snow was paltry compared to the landscape. He drove the horses around a snow-covered copse of trees and a great mountain seemed to sprout out of the white earth like a pillar rising to the sky. And not just any mountain, a dormant volcano that was critical to production of the mines. Even now, I could see great spirals of smoke that trailed from the various magic-made fissures to release the pressure of the volcano. Farther east, nestled in the mountain range a safe distance away, was a castle made of enchanted stone.

I knew that a great colony of dwarves once lived under the Ragnar Mountain. Their skin was thick and could withstand the heat as they dug deep, forging their highly sought-after armor and weapons, but that was over a hundred years ago. Something had gone wrong. The entire underground city was destroyed. The few dwarves that were left moved closer to the castle or settled on the lower plains.

I shivered, dropping the shade back into place and

pulling my thin cloak tighter around my body, snuggling further into the darkness of the cabin to stay warm. The northern part of Kiln was nothing but snow. The kingdom spent most of the year cloaked by a white frozen blanket, and its people still thrived as they relied on the magic of salamanders to stay warm.

The transport slowed as we came into the small village of Verdan. I couldn't hold back my excitement at the change in the scenery. The houses had peaked roofs painted in various bright colors. Women walked the streets wearing fur hats and muffs over thick, colorful wool coats. Many of the villagers used sled pushcarts to do their work, and children with ice skates on their feet let their oversized dogs pull them around on the streets.

The transport pulled up to a small inn no bigger than a house. Light spilled from the windows and smoke billowed out of the chimney, creating a warm and inviting environment. A placard covered in snow had a silhouette of a goat, announcing our location, the Goat Head Inn. Herst dismounted, walked the horses around to the inn's back stables, and I cried out in delight when I saw the furry creatures that were happily eating hay in their stalls.

Reindeer.

"We'll stay here for the night, and tomorrow I'll swap out the horses and rent the reindeer to take you the rest of the way. They'll be sure-footed and safer on the mountain pass."

I nodded, not unhappy with the decision at all. I had already stepped out and had made my way over to the first stall, reaching my hand forward and letting the reindeer sniff me. His fuzzy lips brushed across my palm, searching for food.

"Sorry, I don't have any treats for you, girl," I said. The very domesticated reindeer leaned forward as I brought my hand up to scratch at the base of her antlers.

"Seems you know your reindeer," a voice cracked with age spoke from over my shoulder.

I turned in surprise to see a faun, whose bark-colored horns curved back over his head like a ram. He wore a gray wool jacket over his torso, and his hair was a mix of brown and gray, matching his long beard, while spotted fur covered his hooved legs.

"I know what I've read in books," I said. "All the males would have already lost their antlers for the winter."

"Correct. Very good for an outsider." The faun handed me a carrot and immediately the reindeer snatched it out of my hand. "Holly, knock it off," the faun teased the reindeer. He turned to address me. "I'm Fezik Fleetfoot, and this is my inn."

"Nice to meet you, Fezik. I'm grateful for your hospitality." I shivered as I stood out in the open without a thick cloak.

"Well, you're going to freeze to death if you don't get inside. My wife, Taffy, will have my head if I don't see to you." With the agility of a goat, Fezik jumped onto the back of the transport to unlatch my trunk.

"No need to bring the entire trunk in. I only need a few things." I released the strap and opened my trunk, shifting the items around. "Hold these." I handed him a stack of books and a set of chisels and then more books as I grabbed an extra nightdress.

Fezik raised a curious eyebrow. "Most ladies pack essentials, like clothes. You're the first I've met that cared more about books and tools than undergarments."

"Books *are* the essentials," I grumbled, snagging my prized chisel set from his hands. I placed it back in the trunk and gathered the rest of my belongings. I had packed it all without mother knowing. I'd panicked earlier, thinking mother would have looked inside to see that I had only brought one spare dress and nightclothes. The rest was stuffed with everything out of my workshop, and books. Lots of books. Which I was now regretting, having underestimated how cold Kiln would be.

"Nothing in there is going to keep you warm against the blizzard."

"I may have slightly underestimated the weather in Kiln—a bit." I pinched my fingers together.

"A bit?" he laughed.

"Okay, a lot."

Fezik chuckled. "We have a wool, fur-lined cloak that a guest left behind. You can have that until you get to the market tomorrow to shop."

"That sounds wonderful."

Fezik took me through the back door of the inn, handing me the cloak that was hanging on a hook. It fit perfectly, and I thanked him, appreciating the warmth. Following him, we came into the kitchen. He gestured for me to sit down at the table. When I did, his wife turned in surprise and gave me a warm smile. She was golden in hair and fur, her horns shorter and turned outward. "Welcome to Goat Head Inn." She pushed a bowl of soup and fresh bread toward me.

"Thank you." The soup was vegetarian, filled with mushrooms, leeks, celery, and a few tubers I wasn't familiar with. "This is delicious."

She grinned and set down a wooden cup filled with a spiced cider. "This should warm you up from your travels."

My gaze drifted through the kitchen and I took in the height of the lowered sink and tables, perfect for the shorter fauns. Lavender, basil, mint, and oregano hung on the drying rack above the table. The aromatic smells reminded me of home. Just beyond the kitchen was a sitting room and a bigger table for more lodgers. I seemed to be their only guest.

"May I ask you something?" I stirred the soup with my spoon, unsure how to broach the subject.

"Why did we call it Goat Head when we are obviously *fauns*?" Taffy guessed my question before I asked.

I nodded.

She laughed. "We get that question a lot. When my ancestors first settled here generations ago, the locals had never seen a faun. They kept referring to us as 'goat heads'."

"But isn't that insulting?" I asked.

"Only if the person chooses. Words can bring harm if you let it. Instead, we embraced the moniker, and it has brought fond memories over the years. Besides, I call my husband a goat head when he's stubborn. Which is often, of late."

I smiled, but the smile fell from my face when the wood floor beneath my feet rumbled. The drying rack shook and dried bits of lavender rained down from above. Teacups on the shelves rattled until one slipped off and broke on the floor.

"What is that?" I gasped, covering my head as a shutter fell from the window.

"Earthquake!" Taffy grabbed my hand and led me outside into the snow.

All around us, the townspeople screamed and shouted as they ran out into the streets. Untethered horses were spooked and ran amok, while dogs barked and children cried as the rumbling didn't slow but gained momentum.

Herst grabbed my elbow and pulled me farther away from the outbuildings and into a clearing. His keen eyes weren't watching the people, but the mountain.

A great crash ripped through the air as the roof on a nearby barn couldn't handle the strain, and it collapsed. The shaking finally settled, and we were left to face the wreckage.

"Taffy!" Fezik cried out as he rushed to his wife's side. They embraced and turned to look up at the mountain.

"It's happening again," she whispered.

"Hush," Fezik chided. "It was nothing."

"No," Taffy argued.

"What's wrong?" I asked.

Taffy turned to me, fear in her eyes. She straightened her shoulders and warily went into the inn to assess the damage.

Fezik spoke up. "I must check on the others. There may be injured. I'll be back."

I looked at Herst. "Do you know what she's talking about?"

He shrugged. "Don't know. Sounds like local superstition, if you ask me."

But it didn't. It sounded like they knew more than they were willing to admit. Even though the earthquake was over, the fear it left behind in its wake was as thick as molasses. Most of the main buildings were still intact, other than the barn that collapsed.

"You should come back inside. The worst is over," Herst said.

I stared up at the dark mountain. To where we would head toward tomorrow, and I didn't think it was over. I had a feeling. The problems were just beginning.

CHAPTER TWO

"That's mine," the tinker man shouted, his high-pitched voice piercing the bitter air, causing a flock of birds to scatter.

Early morning risers filled the market as the cold winter didn't deter or slow down work. Life still carried on despite last night's earthquake scare. As I was walking through the quaint town, I was attracted to the commotion coming from a nearby tinker's stall.

The tinker stared down at his accuser with tired eyes, his face weathered, his bushy eyebrows peeking out under his worn red hat. His clothes were patched, covered with black dust, and his gloved fingers were clutching an object to his chest possessively.

"Calm down, I wasn't stealing it. I just need to see what's in your hand," a dwarf said to the old man.

"Ah, Grimkeep. Just let me keep it," the tinker whined. He pawed at the small golden cup. The rest of the tinker's stall was filled with various objects. Lots of tin cups, pots, a spinning wheel, skates and sleigh parts, and assorted half-finished projects.

"Not if it doesn't belong to you," Grimkeep growled. His thick fist slammed into the wooden table. "That looks like a goblet from the forbidden hoard. Have you been digging in the Ragnar Mountains?"

The tinker shook his head and retreated farther to the back of the stall.

"Doren, if it is, it isn't safe for you to have it. It's cursed."

"No, it's not." Doren clutched his find. It seemed the old tinker wasn't necessarily right in the head. Whether it was from the cursed object or dementia, I wasn't sure.

Grimkeep turned a frustrated sigh my way. It was my first chance to see the dwarf up close. He had a thick brow, deep red hair, and his beard braided with little beads depicting various runes.

"Maybe I can help," I asked. Stepping forward, I focused my attention on the cup in his hands. It was without a stem or base; simple in design. I searched for a similar tin cup in his wares and found one. "Distract him for me," I whispered.

Grimkeep nodded and went on a verbal rant about how it's not nice to steal from the mountains.

Kneeling down, I quickly drew out a spell diagram in the snow, being very careful that my sigils were perfect in every way, then placed the tin cup in the center. I was going to use a glamour charm, but to work, glamour had to work on a healthy mind, and I wasn't sure what the state of mind the tinker's was in. This would be a gamble.

With the final sigil in place, I backed up as the ground glowed slightly and the tin cup was now in the shape of the gold cup the tinker had.

A few gasps came from behind me, and I turned to see that a crowd had gathered. They'd watched me weave my spell. Whispers followed. Many turned away in disgust. A few called me names like witch and devil. A man in a dark uniform slipped away without a sound.

"You shouldn't have done that," Grimkeep whispered. He brushed his foot through the snow, destroying the evidence of my spell. His eyes following the man in black who ran farther into town.

"It's a little late for the warning."

Grimkeep growled ominously at the crowd and reached for the axe on his back. He did it slow, as if threatening them. The crowd scattered. Grimkeep spit at the ground in disgust before addressing Doren. He reached for a dented kettle and waved it in the air. "Hey Doren, how much for this thing?"

No longer feeling threatened, the tinker moved forward to conduct business, tucking the cup in the outer pocket of his tunic. Grimkeep sidled up to the man. With deft hands, he dropped my charmed cup into the left pocket and turned around him, slipping the one out of his right pocket.

"I'll take it." Grimkeep put a few coppers into Doren's hand while hiding his pilfered prize. From a distance, we could hear men yelling and horses riding toward us. "Come with me." Grimkeep gripped my elbow and forced me to follow him down the closest alley, pushing me behind a stack of crates. I was about to speak, but he reached up and clamped his hand over my mouth.

Just as he did so, men in black uniforms came down the street. They stopped at the tinker's stall and questioned him. I couldn't hear their exchange, but I could see the old man's confusion. The leader, a tall man in black armor, was intimidating. He wore a large black helmet in the shape of a beast with horns, keeping his eyes hidden. With massive strength, he lifted the tinker's table and flipped it over. The goods spilled into the street, and the horse trampled the silverware into the muddy snow. A terrified Doren handed over the golden cup.

The black knight took the cup, tucked it into a pouch at his waist. Though his gaze was hidden, but I could feel the darkness within as he searched the streets. He jumped on his horse and waved his men on.

Grimkeep cursed under his breath. He released my elbow and growled. "Just as I feared. They'll keep searching for you."

"Why?" I muttered, rubbing my elbow in nervousness.

"The king's blades have rounded up anyone that has shown any talent toward magic. Just last week a woodcutter's daughter was taken in the middle of the day," Grimkeep said. He turned, his boots crunching through the snow as he slipped between the buildings, taking the side roads until we came slipped in the cover of a lean-to across the street from the inn.

"Again, why?" I asked.

"I suspect it has to do with this." Grimkeep tossed a coin to me, and I caught it midair.

As soon as my fingers closed around the coin, I felt it— the darkness. My stomach roiled, and I dropped it into the snow.

"Why did you do that?" Grimkeep asked. He reached down with a gloved hand and held the coin toward me.

I backed away. "It has a strange aura about it."

His eyes narrowed. "Very good. Now tell me why?" He held the coin open in his palm, and I was reluctant to touch it. "You're gifted, Rhea, but you need to know how to use your gifts."

"I never told you my name?" I asked, startled.

"Dwarves live a very long time. I've known Lorelai since she was a babe. I knew her daughter Rhea was in alchemy and earth magic. It's a bit obvious since I've seen no one else do what you just did." His thrust his fist out again. "Now, daughter of Eville, use your senses. Tell me about this coin."

My breath hitched as I obeyed. My fingers brushed against the icy surface, and I became sick to my stomach. A rolling feeling rushed through my body, but then it settled, and I had a desire to possess the coin. I fought it, even as my fingers closed around the treasure against my will.

But Grimkeep wanted to know more. Clearing my mind, I tried to break down the components of the coin. Images flashed through my mind.

Pain. Rage. Darkness. Cave. Gold. Death.

I pulled away.

"It's cursed," I said in disgust.

Grimkeep's lip tightened. "That it is." He held out the tinker's gold cup. "And now this."

I prepared my mind to receive the same onslaught of feelings as I touched it. I sucked in my breath and waited.

"What do you feel, Rhea?" Grimkeep urged. "Does it come from the same place as the coin?" he asked fearfully.

"No," I sighed, as the metal warmed with the heat of my hands. "It's just painted metal."

He looked relieved. "That's good. I wasn't sure with how Doren was acting. I thought for sure he got his hands on some of that cursed treasure."

"What treasure?" I asked.

"The cursed treasure of Rumple Stiltskin, one of the greatest dwarf heroes of our time."

"Then why was he cursed?"

Grimkeep scoffed. "*He* wasn't cursed. The treasure was, or it had become cursed over time as a great enemy's evilness seeped into it. Over the years, as the earth shakes and winter thaws, pieces of the treasure have washed down the mountain and into the rivers. Vandals and robbers have been trying to mine the mountain and find the hoard, but everyone that goes in doesn't come back out. The mountain itself is cursed; the tunnels filled with dangerous creatures and goblins. But pieces of the cursed gold still make it to the surface and go into circulation. When it does, madness follows. It's my sole job to protect the cursed hoard."

"Then what's with the soldiers?" I asked.

Grimkeep frowned. "Those are the king's men." Grimkeep rolled the coin over his knuckles before tucking it into a belt pouch. "The king's been obsessed with gold as of late, forcing his men to mine deeper than they should in search of it, but their mines have all dried up. There's no more riches to be found in the mountain. I have a suspicion that his men are trying to find the hoard. If they do, they could unleash a far greater evil onto the land."

My mouth went dry in awe as I listened to Grimkeep's rough voice pull me into the story. Goosebumps ran up my arms and I had a feeling this was why I was here.

A horse neighed, and I ducked farther into the lean-to as more of the king's army rode down the streets. A scrawny soldier dismounted just outside the entrance to the inn and headed inside. He must have found out where I was staying.

I had nowhere to go now. "What do I do?" I asked.

"Don't worry, Taffy and Fezik won't give you up.

They're loyal to my cause. But you need to leave. Lie low for a few days. I have to check on something, then I'll find you." He turned his back to me and headed out into the street toward the soldier's hitched horse.

"But how do you know where I'll—" I started.

He turned and pointed at me. "I have my ways." Just as he finished speaking, he sunk deep into the ground as if the earth swallowed him whole. He reappeared at the guard's hitched horse. He released the reins, then slapped it on the rump, spurring it to run back toward the center of town.

The soldier, hearing the commotion, rushed out of the Goat Head Inn, and took off running after his horse, screaming and cursing. Grimkeep gave me a last wave before using earth magic and sinking beneath the surface.

I whistled under my breath, having previously forgotten that dwarves had access to different magic. Grimkeep's clan clearly had the ability to travel through the ground. Others had powerful jaws, like iron or super strength, and could wield weapons five times heavier than a human. But what he had done was create a diversion for me.

Running across the street, I ducked into the inn through the front door just as Taffy came out of the kitchen, her eyes wide with fright.

"You need to go. They're looking for you." She wrung her skirt in worry.

"It's okay." I held up my hands. "Grimkeep is leading them away."

"They'll be back. You're not safe. The knight in black armor is one of the king's blades. And *that* one never gives up on his prey. You must go. Fezik is helping Herst convert his carriage and hitch up the reindeer." Her words became clipped as her anxiousness rose.

We went out the back door, just as Herst finished hitching the last reindeer. Not only did they switch out horses, but they had lifted the transport cart and attached metal runners, turning it into a sleigh.

"You ready, girl?" Herst called to me. "I heard you made quite an impression on the locals already." He opened the transport door, and I jumped inside while he climbed into the driver's seat. He was about to snap his whip and set us off down the street toward the exit when we heard the guards returning. They gathered in mass outside the inn, blocking our escape route.

There was no way we could sneak past them. The snowfall was picking up, and I could smell a snowstorm was on its way, but a full sled with reindeers trying to leave town was going to gain attention.

"Now what?" Herst mumbled.

"I'll take care of it." I slipped out of the transport and pulled my hood up over my hair. Reaching into the satchel, I felt around for the unique charms I carried. Rubbing my fingers over each rune, I searched by touch until I found the ones that would help me.

What I wanted to do was walk into the middle of the street and call down thunder and lightning like Maeve or Rose, or sing and cause a storm to wipe them out like Meri. Instead, I had a bag of charms I had enchanted. But would I have enough for the distraction I needed?

"When I give the signal, you go," I called over my shoulder to Herst.

"I'm not leaving you."

I laughed nervously. "That's the last thing I want you

to do, but trust me." The words felt hollow, as if I didn't even believe them.

Under the lip of my hood, I saw the bladesman turn his mount toward me. His horse was stocky with a thick coat, a born and bred steed for these harsh winters. It looked like it could easily run down Fezik's reindeers.

The bladesman held up a black gloved hand and pointed.

"You there! Stop!" a soldier yelled.

"I'd rather not," I said simply, a smile creeping onto my lips.

"By order of the King. You are commanded to come with us."

"I don't take well to orders, or commands." Pulling a stone out of my pocket, I flung it into the street. As soon as the charm hit the snow, it turned into an enormous snarling wolf.

The bladesman's horse reared in terror, and he struggled to keep it under control. The other soldiers' horses began to scream and run.

"Now!" I yelled. The transport bolted out of the alley, and I took off running to catch it.

The blade regained control just as I leapt onto the sideboard.

I waved cheekily and tossed the second charm right at his feet.

A black and white diamond-backed Sion adder rose out of snow. Its hood flared as it prepared to strike.

The blade's steed reared, and I thought this time it would surely take off running. But this was a horse trained for war. Instead, fire lit in the horse's eyes, and it screamed and stomped on the snake.

My smile fell as my glamour disappeared when the charm disintegrated beneath the horse's deadly hooves. Under the black helmet, I could almost imagine his creepy smile as he spurred his horse after us.

"Faster, Herst!" I yelled as the reindeer bolted up the road.

"Can't! We're carrying too much weight."

Still clinging to the sideboard of the carriage, I glanced at my trunks that were tied down and I felt a deep sadness. I needed to lighten the load. The transport turned too close to a tree and branches threatened to pull me from my precarious perch. My fingers dug into the top rail, and I inched my way toward the back and reached for the strap.

Herst cast a glance over his shoulder. "What are you doing, miss?"

"Losing some excess baggage."

I reached across for the buckle, unlatching my trunk off the back hitch. My chilled fingers struggled with the leather, the adrenaline causing me to fumble. I didn't think I could do it without more leverage. I placed my foot on the immobile wheel as I shifted my weight until I was on the back of the transport.

The bladesman was bearing down on us, only a few horse lengths away. The buckle slipped free and flapped in the wind. I lifted the lid and shuffled the contents, searching for the heaviest of my beloved books. I chucked them with a frenzy at the blade's head. He dodged them, right and left. One hit his shoulder, a second clunked against his helmet with a thud.

I reached for my tools and let them fly, but he dodged them. With a renewed fervor, I grabbed my nightdress, the wind ripping it from my fingers, carrying it right into the horse's face where it wrapped around his head. Blinded, the horse veered off the path and into the woods. I knew it wouldn't be for long before he was back on our tail.

I was out of missiles to launch, and I sighed in frustration. The trunk teetered, and I sent it crashing into the road with a single push. I felt the sleigh rise, and we slid faster over the snow. Crawling back around the side, I opened the door as we went over a bump. I slipped and my feet flew out from under me, catching air. I clung to the upper roof rail as my face slammed into the side of transport with a grunt.

The storm blew the snow sideways. The sky was white, and visibility was becoming scarce.

It took three tries before I got my feet back onto the sideboard and fell headfirst into the interior cabin. Just as I landed, a tree took out the open door, ripping it from the hinges, leaving a scattering of dried pine branch needles in its wake.

I stared through the gaping hole, my breath heaving as I watched the white woods beyond. Waiting for the bladesman to come crashing through the trees.

But the reindeer continued to run.

Herst slowed, and rode off the trail, pulling the reindeer behind the cover of large snow-covered brush.

"Quickly!" he called to me, and I jumped back out into the snow. He pulled a broken pine branch that had caught on the side transport and rushed to wipe away the sleigh tracks that led to our hiding spot. Even though we couldn't see them, we could hear the horses bearing down on us. Herst went back to the reindeer, doing his best to calm them and keep them quiet while I kneeled behind the brush.

"I see their tracks. This way!"

I cursed under my breath. I gave a worried glance to Herst, and he held up his finger to his lips.

It wasn't enough. Our tracks were visible thirty feet away. I would have to do something more. I stood up.

Herst began waving his hands for me to get down, but I ignored him. My legs trembled with nerves as I attempted one of my least powerful spells. One that barely worked for me. But I was out of options. Cupping my hands into a V shape, I raised them to my lips and blew. The snow swirled like a cyclone gathering in an already chaotic storm.

In Nihill, I struggled to cast a single fire spell without a charm. Here the magic rushed to me, eager, and I felt flooded with power and confidence. I almost fumbled, so overwhelmed by the ease of it. Quickly, I directed the spell in front of us, giving us more cover by creating a white wall of snow.

The lead horse came into view, cresting the small hill that led to our hiding spot. It was the bladesman, and behind him were three of his soldiers. The spell would only hold as long as I stayed focused and kept my breathing even. One hiccup, a single gasp, or a blink held too long would break the spell, and we'd be revealed.

The storm was on my side, gaining strength. The wind blew my hair into my face, whipping it into my eyes, causing them to sting as I struggled to keep us hidden. But it also casts its wrath right at the men.

They squinted as they tried to continue forward, the snow quickly hiding the tracks that Herst missed. One man shook his head, covering his eyes with his hand to block the wind as he scanned the snow. He opened his mouth and yelled at the king's blade, his words carried away by the storm. The men were ready to give up. The bladesman wasn't ready to stop the hunt.

My lungs were bursting as I tried to hold him back.

My lips were numb, my fingertips like ice, and I could feel my spell slipping. The swirl of snow around us lessened.

The bladesman's head swiveled as he saw the giant snow-covered bushes. He pushed onward, urging his mount forward. He was almost to us.

Wrong way. I tried to force my thoughts into his using compulsion. Again, a spell that I could never accomplish at home. *This is the wrong way.*

In the storm, the bladesman's dark armor stood out like malice on a blanket of purity. He turned his head, and I saw the silhouette of his helm. It was a horned dragon.

That black head focused on our hiding spot, and I sensed his gaze zero in on me. I felt naked in the storm under his penetrating stare.

I used more magic and pushed it into my voice, letting my words carry on the wind with the compulsion. *Go back. Your prey is getting away.*

He shook his head and looked over his shoulder at his retreating men. Whether it was my spell or the storm, I didn't know, but he turned and rode after them. I stood frozen in my spot. Unable to move, for fear of the bladesman returning for me.

A hand grabbed my shoulder, and I jumped.

"It's me, Miss Rhea," Herst whispered. "This is our chance. We need to go. The storm will only get worse."

I sighed and relaxed, patting his hand. "Yes, let's go before he comes back."

CHAPTER THREE

With the side transport doors missing, I became a victim of the storm's violent wrath. I felt worse for Herst, who was bearing the brunt to get me to my destination. In Nihill, our winters were short and mild. Nothing like the monstrous howling wind and blinding snow that we were trying to navigate through in the Ragnar Mountains.

The carriage struggled up the mountain path; the snow getting deeper with each passing candle mark. I shivered in my seat, pulling my wool cloak closer to my body. We stopped.

"This is it . . ." Herst sounded unsure as he looked at the map. "I think."

I stepped out of the transport and took in the snow-covered forest beyond. This is where my mother's childhood home was supposed to be—but there was nothing here.

Herst pointed to the map and the gray stone mile marker that sat about waist high. "This is where she said to bring you." His breath left white puffs of frozen air after each word. "Sorry, Miss. I must have taken a wrong turn. We could continue north. There's another settlement there. Returning to Verdan would mean taking a chance of running into that black knight again. We have to make a decision soon."

I chewed on my inner lip as I debated. Yes, of course, I would rather wait out the storm somewhere nice and warm, but that was supposed to be the manor house.

I looked at the stone marker and knew we were close. "I'll stay," I said.

"You can't be serious, Miss. It's too dangerous," Herst argued.

The wind picked up, causing the snow to blow sideways. I squinted and turned my head away from the blast of freezing air, and as I did so, I caught a glimmer. I blinked. It was gone. Was it a trick of the light?

Stepping a few feet past the stone marker, I reached out with my senses.

There.

It happened again. I could see a stone pillar about ten feet high. It would suddenly appear, and then quickly disappear. I reached out into the air and should have touched nothing, but my hand brushed against cold iron.

An illusion.

I smirked. Of course, Mother would protect her home from unwanted intruders. I should have expected that.

Stepping back, I breathed out the revealing spell under my breath.

"Revelare."

The air shimmered and revealed a ten-foot arched gated entrance.

Once, the name Eville stood out across the top of the iron in great flowing letters. But age and time had taken their toll, and an L and E were missing, spelling out the word EVIL instead.

I smiled at the subtle nuance. *If only they knew.*

"What in the stars is that? Where did that come from?" Herst asked in a panicked voice, crossing his chest when he saw the great evil gate looming over him.

"It was always there. Just hidden by the storm," I said, pointing to the marker. While I'd used magic in front of him, he hadn't made mention of it. It was still in my best interest to play dumb. "Just where my mother said it would be. Now let's go."

Herst hesitated, debating on whether to follow me through the gate or leave me. "Okay."

Even with the reindeer, it took us another full candle mark before the manor house came into view, and I couldn't believe what I saw.

A three-story gray stone manor stood tall against the looming winter forest. I assumed it was once white stone but had turned from years of grime. Dead ivy clung to the sides, hiding beautifully arched windows. Even from a distance, I could see that many were missing panes of glass. Beyond the manor house, there were outbuildings, stables, the servant's quarters, and even the garrison for Lord Eville's private troops. There were the remains of an over-grown garden and hints of an orchard. Small houses lined the property for the tenants that once farmed the land. But without a Lord or Lady to govern the property, it had slowly gone to waste.

Lord Eville had lost his fortune when his merchant ships went down at sea because of Sirena, the sea witch. Unable to pay his debts, the Lord had lost everything of value, his honor, and eventually his life when he had a heart attack at court. He died a beggar, pleading with the prince to honor the betrothal to his beautiful daughter. The princes laughed in the face of the penniless man until they saw Lorelai's beauty and reconsidered. Each begged her to be his bride, but she saw through their cruel and selfish hearts. That's when Lorelai, my adoptive mother, swore to never return home. Now decades later, the past still haunted this once beautiful manor, and I wondered what secrets lay within.

"Well, I'll be—" Herst said, as he tied up the reindeer and came around to help me out of the transport.

We both took a moment to stare up at the manor house in awe. "It's like something out of—" I began.

"A nightmare." He brushed his hand across his mouth.

I frowned. It was in bad shape, but I'd seen worse.

"These snowstorms have been known to last quite a few days. I just don't feel right leaving you alone in a place like this. Who knows what could have taken up living inside?" Herst tried to plead his case for me to leave.

"It's fine." I rested my hand on my satchel. Inside were all the possessions I had to my name, which included a few coppers, one glamour charm and the spindle made of an enchanted thorn.

"But you don't have any supplies."

"I'll manage." I lifted my head high and gripped my bag closer.

Walking up the stone steps, I paused at the old mahogany door and the elaborate door knockers that had turned dull from age. My hand reached for the door. Running my fingertips over the iron, I could feel a slight hum of magic that made my body tingle. It was sealed with a ward of protection.

"Lochen," I whispered.

The lock clicked, and the doors swung inward, revealing a checkered tile hall and a dimly lit interior. I did not want to go in there. Stars, it was creepy.

"Are you sure you'll be safe, Miss?" Herst peered over my shoulder, and then retreated as if he'd seen a ghost.

"I'll make do," I said with more confidence than I felt. Something scuttled across the floor, and a chill ran down my spine. *Was that a rat?*

Herst shuffled on the steps before pointing north. "A few miles that way is a guard tower, if you run into trouble." He brushed the snow from brim of his hat, pulling it low over his eyes. He shivered and waited for my decision.

With the enormous rat still in the back of my mind, I was too nervous to speak. I nodded, my teeth already chattering loudly from the cold.

Herst removed his hat, revealing his peppered white hair, and plopped it down on my head. Immediately, I felt a warmth flow through my scalp and the wind stopped nipping at my ears. He pulled it low, tightened my scarf and patted my shoulder.

"I hate leaving you like this. You remind me of my daughter." He took a deep breath. "Don't go outside during the storm. I've seen ones like this. It's going to get worse before it gets better. During a white-out, you can get lost and freeze to death steps from your home. Also, this mountain is cursed, and the monsters that roam it at night are deadly. Stay inside."

I nodded, pulling my bag closer to myself like a shield, his words making me want to turn back around and get right back in the transport.

"I'll be fine," I said bravely.

"Okay, be safe." Reluctantly, he retreated down the steps, hopped onto the transport and called out to the reindeer. They took off, eager to continue.

As Herst left, a sudden bout of loneliness hit me at the thought of facing the next few days alone in a dusty manor filled with giant rats.

I summoned a mage light that floated over my shoulder, creating a glow. The mage light was bigger than any I had ever summoned at home. My magic really was stronger here. I swallowed my trepidation and entered the house where an Eville sorceress was born.

CHAPTER FOUR

"Well, this was anticlimactic," I muttered after touring most of the first floor. The main hall was off a large dining room that could easily seat over twenty people. The kitchen had a built-in fireplace with three large wood worktables. Most of the porcelain dishes and silver were gone. With each room I explored, my heart broke a little more as I saw what had been taken and what was left behind. It wasn't until I came to the sitting room that I felt my heart skip a beat. The once beautiful room with floor to ceiling bookshelves had been ransacked. All the books that were worth money had likely been sold off or stolen.

A great fireplace stood along the far wall with bookshelves on either side. A single intact mirror hung on the wall opposite the window. The wallpaper around the mirror faded, revealing shadows of the numerous paintings that once hung in the room. A lone high-back chair with a broken leg lay abandoned on its side in the middle of the floor. A chair that I recognized—for it had a mate. The other was in our tower back in Nihill.

My mother's chair.

A coat of dust covered everything in the room and

thankfully, this room still had its windows intact. I didn't get to explore the second floor of the house because the sun was quickly setting, and I knew I needed to get a fire going. I trekked out into the cold, collecting wood I could find in an old shed. I would have to work on finding an axe and chopping down a tree to create a larger supply the next day.

It would hopefully be enough to get me through the night. I took the pieces back into the sitting room and laid them across the grate. I wasn't worried about how wet they were. My magic could help dry them out. I found a book that was beyond repair, sun-damaged from years of lying open on the floor, the pages faded and unreadable. It hurt my heart to destroy it this way, but they were no longer useful. I tore a few pages out of the book and crumpled them between the dried-out wood.

"Fiergo." I whispered the fire spell, and it enveloped the paper into a fiery blast.

The kindling burned, spreading to the wood with an intensity before settling into a soothing crackle. Holding out my frozen hands, I let the heat seep into my fingers, and I flexed them, letting the pins and needles feeling fade away.

Night had fallen, and the wind picked up, creating an eerie rattling sound against the panes. It was the perfect time to try scrying so I could find the source of disturbance that was blocking my mother's magic. I focused on the mirror hanging on the wall.

The mirror had a slight crack in the ornamental frame, and I wondered if it would withstand the magic needed to power it. There was no better time than now to find out. Normally, we would need blood to activate a calling spell and it would be used to direct to a certain person. But I was going to scry.

I took a second to take in my appearance. My honey brown hair took on a golden hue in the firelight's reflection. Several unruly strands had slipped out of my braid, giving me a wild look. My hazel eyes shifted with my mood, changing between a grassy shade or muted brown. This evening they were a bright green. My suntanned skin was blessed with freckles across my nose, giving me an impish look. I pressed my lips together, wishing they were thicker. But wishes were self-serving. One shouldn't wish for what they couldn't have. Looks weren't everything.

Running my fingers across the glass, I leaned close and breathed onto it, leaving steam on the reflective surface. Quickly, before it disappeared, I drew the few sigils needed to turn the mirror into a vessel for magic.

The sigils glowed and then disappeared into the glass. The hair on the back of my neck rose as I felt the magic gather, rushing toward the mirror like a river running downstream. There was so much magic in Kiln, the land was practically seeping with it because of all the ley lines that crossed through, deep underground. Magic that I could feel and hear. It sang to me. The power gathered, and then I felt it turn away as if avoiding the mirror.

I frowned. Mirrors were finicky, and when infused with magic, could sometimes take on multiple personalities. Memories of the previous owners would imprint themselves on the mirrors. Sometimes you'd get a helpful mirror. Other times, it might be selfish or deceiving. I would often see my mother speaking to the mirror in her home. I had a feeling—though I wasn't sure—that the person she was speaking to was her father.

When the mirror had pulled enough magic from the land, my reflection disappeared, and it took on a frosted glow. It was ready for the test.

"Show me Honor," I commanded.

The frame glowed once before turning dark. I thought it wasn't working, but then I saw a shadow. The shadow morphed into a shape, and she appeared.

Honor. The sister closest in age to me. We were both turning nineteen this year. I was a fall baby, and she was a spring. We didn't celebrate our exact birthdays because neither of us knew when we were born.

Honor's dark hair was bound back out of her face. A black cowl covered her, making her blend into the background. She slipped through the woods, passing from shadow to shadow. No wonder I couldn't see her.

Honor spoke, and I could tell by the subtle nuance of her lip movement that she was speaking to Lorn in Elven. She gestured with her bow, then pulled back the drawstring, aimed and released. She grinned and ran toward her catch.

I didn't have the stomach to see what creature she shot down.

But Honor froze mid-stride. She ducked. Her shoulders stiffened and her eyes searched the sky, then the forest, before turning around and looking right into my eyes through the mirror.

Her brows furrowed, and her lips formed my name. "Rheanon?"

I inhaled, thinking she saw me. Then shadows moved within the glass as if a heavy cloud settled over the mirror. This wasn't good. It was just as my mother feared. An anathema covered the land. Anytime the mirror had gone dark on a kingdom, it meant trouble wasn't far behind. But what was the source of this darkness?

Mother said my magic would be increased when I arrived. And I'd seen the results already. *Dare I tap into the ley lines to magnify the mirror?*

Once, I created magical rods to amplify our mirror at home. My sisters called them antennae because it caused our mirror to look like a shiny beetle. But I didn't think I would need them if I tapped right into the magic of Kiln.

Kneeling, I pressed my palms to the floor and sought with my senses, seeking the magic. It was deep beneath the mountain, but I found the closest line of magic. I coaxed it to me, but the more I swept it toward me, it seemed to slip out of my grasp like water running through my fingers.

Slowly it came, and I tapped into it. My vision merged with the ley line, and I followed it. It was like being in a dream, slipping in and out of consciousness. I followed the magic to the source and found a void deep within the mountain.

"What is this?" I murmured. As I studied it, I saw another ley line that had been redirected and converged into the darkness and nothing came out. The darkness was swallowing the magic like a leech. This seemed to be the source. I would need more time to study it and to determine how to cast it out. Whatever it was.

My hands were shaking. It was draining, following the trail of magic. And even though it was giving me strength, there was something odd about the ley line. The magic tasted off. Like a well that had been spoiled. I was wary of staying connected for too long. Just as I tried to disengage from the vision, the void shifted, as if noticing my presence.

My heart pounded as I tried to pull my consciousness back. A strand of shadow shot out of the void and seized my wrist.

I cried out as a sharp pain hit me in the chest, the darkness ripping at the source of my magic. My soul. I fought it, pulling away, but it hungered for my power. It had tasted my magic, and I knew it was trying to drag me into it. I could feel it try to pull me into the void. The black strand solidified into a black sticky goo and encased my arm and shoulder. The more I struggled, the farther up my arm it traveled.

"No!" I shouted at the darkness. "You cannot have me!"

A deep chuckle came from it. Ancient. Old and powerful. Goosebumps ran across my skin as it spoke. "You are mine."

It pulled again, and I recognized the same sensation I'd experienced with the cursed treasure.

Terror gripped me. My mouth went dry, and I knew that if I couldn't disengage right now, I would die.

Even though it was a vision, it was a fight for my life. The black curse of magic now trapped both of my feet and worked around my hips. I tried to use my magic to fight it, but it only swallowed me faster.

"Help!" I cried out, screaming into the ether. "Help!"

A golden blast of fire ripped through the air and cut through the strands. The fire, white and purifying, made the darkness retreat. The dark goo, once disconnected from the void, dissipated into smoke.

Quickly, I pulled my consciousness back into my physical body. The return was brutal as I slammed into myself and fell backward onto the floor. I lay there, breathing hard, holding up my hands and envisioning the darkness that had moments ago almost swallowed me whole. I knew it didn't physically touch me, but I couldn't shake the feeling that I was still in danger. If it hadn't been for that fire spell . . . or was it a spell? I didn't know. But someone, another sorcerer maybe, had come to my aid at the last minute. If they hadn't . . . I shuddered.

"What are you?" I spoke aloud, thinking of the dark void.

I could feel its greed; the insatiable hunger of that monster and I had a feeling it wouldn't be the last time. I would face the eater of magic. I wasn't sure if I could survive my encounter a second time. Painfully, I sat up and winced. My head was throbbing. I tried to stand, but my legs wobbled.

My nerves were shot, and I was exhausted, my mind swept up in the fear of the unknown. I didn't have the energy to search for bedding.

I pulled the high-back chair closer to the fire, tucked a few books under the broken leg that was four inches too short and curled up in the chair. I was scared to leave the protection of the warm fire. I loved books, and sleeping in a room surrounded by books—even if there were few—was comforting. After what I'd just experienced, I needed all the comfort I could get.

Against the crackling warmth of the fire, bathed in a sweet glow of light, I drifted into a fitful sleep.

A loud crash awoke me from my dream, and I sat up. My heart pounded wildly in my chest. The fire had dimmed.

The coals were barely alive, and the room was immersed in darkness. The storm howled fiercely outside. I had thought I imagined the noise when the sound came again from out in the main hall.

Something was in the house. The giant dog-sized rat? No . . . the giant dog-sized rat, *and* all its friends.

Then I heard the creak of a door opening and shutting.

Rats can't open doors.

Which meant a person.

How? I thought. This place was warded and impossible to find. Then realization hit me. I'd never replaced the spell. I clenched my teeth together in frustration at my stupidity.

Tiptoeing toward the open sitting-room door, I slid behind it and looked through the crack into the hall. It was empty.

For a moment, I wondered if I had let my imagination get the best of me.

Then a gigantic shadow passed by, and I almost screamed. I clamped my hand over my mouth as the human-like shape moved toward the dining room. There was no way about it. There was an intruder in my mother's home.

I reached for my magic, and I hesitated. Would that *thing* find me again if I used it?

That doubt had me reaching for the heaviest book I could find. I slipped back behind the door, holding the volume of ancient herbal remedies above my head.

The stranger moved toward the sitting room. I held my breath as the tip of a blade came into view first, followed by a hand. My arms trembled from the weight of the tome as I waited to strike. My breath caught, and I could feel my heart thudding loudly in my ears. Surely, he could hear it too.

A log shifted on the fireplace, and the stranger turned toward the sound. I stepped out from behind the door, swinging the book downward with all my might, aiming for the back of his head—and I missed.

He was lightning fast. He grabbed my hand and twisted, pulling my body toward him. I flew through the air and landed on the wooden floor. My breath knocked from my lungs. I gasped as the knife came down toward my throat, stopping to press lightly against my skin. Torn between struggling and not, I held still as he tapped my neck with the tip.

The man was clothed in darkness, backlit only by the dying fire. I couldn't see my attacker, only the long knife and the hand that held it. I waited for him to strike. Instead, he looked at what I clutched in my hands.

"Did you really try to attack me with . . . a book?" he scoffed. "I'd hardly call that dangerous."

Was he making fun of me?

"Books are a weapon in the right hands." My anger rolled through me, and I closed my eyes and concentrated. I didn't do well in stressful situations. My reaction times were slow, my thoughts jumbled. I was a planner, not a fighter. My previous hesitation about using magic dissipated.

"Fiergo," I whispered.

The fire roared to life, and he turned to glance over his shoulder, giving me enough leeway to snake my arm up and press a finger to his forehead, calling forth a sleeping spell that was activated by touch.

"Somnus."

The man collapsed on top of me in a spelled slumber, the knife clattering to the floor.

"And to think, I learned that from a book," I wheezed from under his weight as his head dropped forward over my shoulder. I inhaled at the mixed scent of winter woods and leather, his breathing deep and even. I tried to push him off me to no avail. The man was huge.

"Why do you have to be so . . . muscly?" I grunted as I tried to shimmy out from under him, which only caused his face to move toward my neck. I froze as his lips grazed my skin in a sloppy kiss.

Heat raced through me in embarrassment. I smacked him hard with an open palm, shoving his face far away from mine. With another awkward shove, I could roll him over onto his back and slide out from under the man. I kneeled and ran my fingers down his side, searching for hidden weapons. I found none other than the knife that was still abandoned on the floor.

When I knew I was safe, I studied his face and once again struggled to control my breathing as I took in one of the most handsome faces I had ever seen. By the glow of the fire, it highlighted his angled jaw, covered with the scruff of a few days' growth. His hair was a midnight black with the slightest curl, and he bore a faint scar on his chin. His broad shoulders were hidden beneath the dark fur-lined cloak that was still damp from the snow.

But it was the knife that gave me pause.

A knife with a golden hilt.

Was this part of the cursed treasure? I didn't really want to touch it to find out, but I had to. I closed my eyes and tapped it with a finger, quickly withdrawing it. Nothing happened. With a sigh, I pressed my fingers to it a little longer and waited for the onslaught of darkness I had felt before. It didn't come. It was just warm.

With that worry out of the way, I needed to focus on my other problem.

Knowing my sleeping spell would only last a candle mark, I used the time to prepare for his awakening. I dragged his sleeping body across the floor toward the fireplace and into the broken high-back chair, binding his hands behind his back with the rope from the curtains, and waited for him to waken.

Standing in front of the newly stoked fire, the sheathed dagger in my hands, I practiced my poses, trying to seem intimidating.

My hand on my hip—the knife casually laying across my hip. I sighed in frustration.

Crossed arms—the dagger tucked under one of them. No.

How about a fighter's stance, holding the knife in front of me threateningly? But I wasn't the scary sister. I was the bookworm. *How do I look threatening?*

I raised my chin and tried to glare down my nose, but each pose only seemed more ridiculous.

After substantial time had passed and the man still hadn't stirred, I became suspicious. I kneeled next to him, taking in the slack head that was tucked against the frame of the chair. The tightening of his lips gave his ruse away.

He wasn't asleep. He was faking.

His leg swept out, knocking me off my feet.

I cried and fell to the ground a second time.

The same time he swung out with his leg and lunged, the chair fell over, having been balanced precariously on a stack of books. He kicked against the restraints, and I grabbed the knife, unsheathed it, and pressed it against his neck.

His eyes opened, and I was lost in the intensity within. Swirls of golden amber met mine with a warmth that tugged at my stomach.

I struggled for words. "Move and *I'll* die. No, wait. I mean, move and *you'll* die."

His enchanting eyes disappeared beneath closed lids as his head fell back and a deep chuckle shook him, filling the room with his laughter.

I didn't think it was funny. Just embarrassing.

When the laughter disappeared, the man's lips came up in a smile, highlighting the scar on his chin.

"Well, since I would hate for a beautiful girl such as yourself to die, I won't move."

Heat flushed my cheeks, and I fell under his spell. "Flattering will get you everywhere."

"Don't you mean nowhere?" He cocked his handsome head in response.

"No, that time I *meant* what I said. It *will* get you everywhere. Just . . . not with me." I smiled, sheathing the knife, tucking it into my belt. I moved toward the fireplace and struck what I thought was an intimidating pose.

"The other pose suited you better." His voice was warm, deep, and sounded like the earth rumbling.

I frowned and took in the situation. I had a strange man, tied to a toppled chair, and he was teasing me. I had every desire to leave him there for the night.

"Who are you?" I asked, changing the subject.

"Just someone seeking shelter from the storm. I saw the smoke from your chimney and followed it here. When I saw the state of the manor, I assumed that the surly sorts inhabited it, like vagrants and thieves." He gave me a smug look. "But then, to my surprise, I find someone much more dangerous, and who has quite a swing with a book. You knocked me out good there. Didn't even see it coming."

I stared at him wide-eyed. He assumed the reason he'd passed out was because I'd hit him with a book and not a spell. I thought it was better to let him think that.

Then he moved the whole chair, and it wiggled on the floor. "Do you mind untying me? I think I'm losing feeling in my hands."

Those golden eyes studied me, and he became quiet.

"No, you're a stranger."

"Well, that is easily remedied. I'm Kash. Pleased to meet you."

His gaze left mine, and he focused on the fireplace. It was the way he looked at the blazing flames, with such longing and desire. After a long moment, he pulled those swoon-worthy eyes away to meet mine, and they consumed me with fire.

"What do they call you?" he asked, pulling me away from my daydream.

A simple question, but one that seemed very intimate suddenly.

"Rhea,"

"Ray-uh," he repeated. The way my name fell from his lips made me shiver.

"It doesn't matter the formalities. You could be lying to me about your name. You're a stranger and an intruder. You are not welcome here."

"You would deny someone shelter during a snow-storm? Ouch!" he said, pretending to be wounded. "You really are heartless. Besides, I'm the one tied up and helpless. Speaking of help . . ." Kash swung his head around to take in the room: the broken curtain rod and the blue curtains piled on the floor. The almost empty bookshelves, the lack of furniture, the threadbare rugs, and the twenty-plus years of dust that layered everything. Even after our scuffle, each of us had gray dust covering our clothes. "I think you need a better housekeeper. Even goblins make fewer messes, and that's saying something," he said.

"Why you!" Out of anger, I stepped closer to kick his leg.

Kash acted. He wrapped his free leg around mine and swept me backwards, knocking me down onto the floor. This time, I wasn't able to catch myself, and my head smacked the floor before everything went dark.

CHAPTER FIVE

When I awoke, it was to the pounding of a splitting headache. He individually tied each of my wrists to the arms of the chair. The barest hint of light poured through the dirty sitting-room window, letting me know I had been unconscious for a while. Kash was stoking the fireplace. He had set up the chair, and just like I had done, balanced the broken leg on three books.

Trying to mimic him, I kept my eyes closed and watched him through lowered lashes.

"I know you're awake, Rhea," Kash commented without even turning around.

"How?" I blurted out, blowing my ruse.

"Your breathing changed."

While I was unconscious, he must have gone out and found more firewood because the pile by the fireplace had grown considerably. At least he hadn't used more books to feed the flame.

"There's no way you can hear my breathing from way over there," I fumed.

"I happen to have exceptional hearing." He turned, giving me a lingering look before returning to add another log to the fire.

I cursed at him under my breath, and his shoulders stiffened. "I heard that."

I narrowed my eyes and glared at the back of his head, hoping to bore a hole into it. He turned to the side, and a swoop of his hair fell into his eye.

"Whenever you stare at me, your breathing becomes shallow," he added.

"Does not," I said breathlessly.

He turned to me, pushing the stray hair back out of his face. His gaze dropped to my mouth, watching as I unconsciously held my breath. The corner of his mouth rose, and he shook his head. "Does too."

Inwardly, I seethed, digging my bound hands into the armrests of the chair. Where I had made the previous mistake of tying him around the chest to the back of the chair, which he seemed to have weaseled out of. He had bound each of my wrists separately to the chair's armrest.

"Let me go," I demanded.

"Not yet." Kash stood, easily towering over six feet. He walked over to the window and looked out at the still raging snowstorm.

"What are you going to do with me?" I asked.

"I don't know," he said simply. "It's almost morning." Gray light poured through the panes, illuminating his features. He closed his eyes and raised his face to the light, as if soaking it in. He was doing the very thing I did whenever I had spent too long in the forge or the workroom, working on a spell. "It will be safer if you stay here."

He then walked out of the room, closing the doors behind him.

"How dare he?" I fumed and struggled against the bindings. The rough rope dug into my skin, chafing them.

But I wouldn't give up. I could try to light my bindings on fire but would more than likely set my whole body ablaze.

Leaning forward, I tried to use my teeth to pull at the knot, but it was under the armrest and at an awkward angle. Shifting my weight, I forgot again about the broken leg, and it teetered over.

"Ack!" I screamed as I fell to the side, my head jostling forward and hitting the floor again.

I was beginning to hate this chair.

The stone floor was cold, colder than I had expected, and as I lay there, the chill seeped into my bones. My teeth chattered as I worked at my wrist. When the chair hit the floor, the right arm broke off, freeing my hand. Quickly, I worked at the knot and freed myself from my bonds.

But now what? Would he have really left the door unlocked?

He did. I pulled it open and stepped out into the hallway and right into Kash's broad chest.

He grasped my upper arms firmly, but not enough to hurt. "I was going to congratulate you on your escape, but that took longer than expected. We should work on your knot skills." He released me and turned away, giving me his back, once again proving that he didn't see me as a threat.

My hands itched to grab another item and conk him over the head, but his apparent disregard of me hurt.

"Just promise you're not going to hit me with a book again," Kash tossed out over his shoulder.

"Can't promise that," I said between clenched teeth. "Your head makes *such* a nice target."

Kash chuckled but continued to walk away from me.

He headed into the dining room. I followed like a

sulking puppy, watching him warily in case he tried to steal anything. Like I had done the day before, he moved through each of the rooms on the lower level, stopping to take stock of the kitchen.

"There's no food in here. I checked."

Ignoring me, Kash stomped around on the floor until he heard a loud creak. He looked up at me and grinned, bouncing up and down on his find. Kneeling, he felt along the floor until he found a hidden ring. He brushed the dust away from the floor, revealing the faint glow of a preservation ward as it brightened and then faded away.

"Jackpot." Kash pulled the door and looked down into the black pit.

"You'll need a light," I admonished as he went down the stone steps and disappeared.

Apparently, he didn't.

Glancing at the cellar door, I had the briefest thought of locking him in the cellar.

"Don't even think of shutting me in," a gruff voice came from below.

"How!" I gasped.

"I just had a feeling." He laughed.

"You know nothing about me," I snapped.

Kash appeared seconds later, holding multiple canvas sacks. He dropped each one on the table and opened them. "Look what I found."

There was flour, sugar, salt. He went back down again and returned with bags of potatoes, apples, and more.

"I have no idea how none of this hasn't spoiled," he said and grinned.

I did. All of it stayed perfectly preserved because of a preservation spell guarding the cellar.

Kash tossed me an apple, and my stomach growled in response. "And this will help keep our bellies warm." He held up a bottle of wine.

Kash made his way around the kitchen, searching through cupboards until he found two not-chipped cups. He popped the cork off the wine and poured some in a cup and handed one to me.

"Truce?" He held the cup in the air. "No more attacking or tying each other up, no matter how fun it may be." He winked at me. "Just let me stay until the storm passes and I'll be on my way."

"How do I know you won't attack me when my back is turned?"

"If my memory serves"—he tapped his fingers on the table—"you were the one who attacked me."

"You had a knife." I pointed to the blade still tucked in his belt.

"Yeah, well, you didn't see the giant rat I saw earlier." He held his hands apart to show its size. "It was *huge*."

I bit my lip to hide my grin. "I saw it, and you're right. I'm sorry. I *was* the one who attacked you first."

"You're forgiven." He took a sip of the wine and I followed suit.

"Where did you get that?" I asked, pointing to the dagger.

"Family heirloom," he answered as he patted it.

"Really?"

"Yep, can't get rid of it even if I tried."

I was tired of his games. He didn't want to take any of my questions seriously. I left the empty cup on the table and stormed out of the kitchen. Making my way to the main hall, I took the stairs to the second level. I was too exhausted yesterday to explore the house further, but now seemed like the perfect opportunity. Maybe I could find something larger to smash against his skull.

Like a brick.

I didn't know why I expected to be left alone on my journey, but I heard footsteps follow me. Turning abruptly, I had meant to tell him off, but Kash was right behind me on the step below. When I turned, we were eye level and once again, my breath caught in my chest.

He leaned forward, bringing his face close to mine. I instinctively leaned back, but almost fell. His cheek brushed past my face and stopped as if a lover were whispering in my ear. His voice rumbled, "You smell like. . . smoke."

Taking a strand of my hair, I gave it a cursory sniff. It smelled like smoke, but that's because I was sleeping next to a fire. Kash was grinning like a fool. He seemed to love riling me up.

"That's not a compliment you give a lady."

"When I see a lady, I'll be sure to compliment her." The comeback was quick and so was my temper.

I pushed his chest hard.

Kash flailed his arms, going wide as he teetered on the steps, leaning backward. A moment of fear flashed across his face, and I instantly regretted my actions. I grabbed his shirt and pulled him roughly toward me. Kash's face crashed into mine painfully, his jaw striking my forehead.

I sucked in my breath and winced. As soon as Kash had regained his footing, I retreated farther up the stairs, cupping the spot on my face that would surely sport a bruise later.

"Thanks," Kash called up to me from his spot in the

middle of the stairs. "For saving me." He grinned, running his hand through his hair.

"I was the one who almost killed you."

"I wouldn't have died."

"You could have," I argued.

"It takes more than a fall down the stairs to kill me." He flashed me a debonair grin, meant to disarm me.

"Good to know," I said coldly, narrowing my eyes in the perfect imitation of my oldest sister, Rosalie, in an attempt to be threatening.

Kash pinched his lips together, and I knew he was doing his best to hold back another round of laughter at my expense. "It's like watching a puppy trying to growl."

"I'm really starting to hate you."

"No, you aren't." He ran his hand through his dark curls. "Besides, being mean doesn't really suit you." He stepped onto the middle landing.

"You don't know that," I snapped, feeling defeated. "I could be mean if I tried."

"No, you can't. Trust me. I know evil, and you're not." As he spoke, the sun rose, the rays coming in across the area rug, alighting on his boots. Kash stepped backward, avoiding the light. His face paled, and he looked over his shoulder toward the exit.

"What's wrong?" I asked, sensing his sudden change in mood.

"Nothing. I just have to take care of something."

Kash gave me a curious look before frowning and gently running back down the stairs and into the sitting room. A loud creak echoed through the hall, and I looked toward the front doors just in time to see Kash leave with his cloak. The heavy door slammed behind him with a solemn thud of finality.

I followed him to the door, opening it to see his form disappear into the storm. How had he gotten so far away already? Where was he going? Would he survive? I debated going after him, but I didn't trust my survival instincts. It would be best to stay close to home.

The morning passed slowly; the howling snow and wind didn't let up. Instead, it seemed to get worse. The day wore on and Kash didn't reappear. So instead of fretting over the handsome man's whereabouts, I worked on staying busy by exploring the west wing of the manor. Most of the rooms were decorated in the same faded blue wallpaper with white roses. In some rooms, the wallpaper had aged more than others and was curling off. Most of the tapestries were gone, as well as the curtains and paintings. Each room had one or two pieces of furniture inside of them that could be salvaged if I had the tools. But that would have to be for another day.

The rooms with broken windowpanes were covered in snow and freezing cold. I needed to find the things necessary for survival through this winter storm.

Priorities first; warm clothes and more fuel for the fire.

Herst was right. This storm didn't seem to let up, and my extra garments had blown somewhere over the mountain range. As much as I hated to admit it, I was also worried about Kash. The stranger was more of an inconvenience than a threat. He had many chances to kill me, but he seemed more amused by me instead. I would figure him out later.

On my continued search, I located a locked room. After spelling it open, I found it to be relatively untouched by weather and wear. Heavy trunks were stacked on top of each other, and miscellaneous crates were packed with valuables and what looked like portraits covered in clothes to preserve them. Someone had the foresight to hide them from the creditors.

Digging through the trunks, I found many silk dresses for parties and shoes that matched. Holding up a soft purple dress, I couldn't help but press it to my body, to feel the fabric against my skin. This had to have been my adoptive mother's. Digging through more of the trunks revealed even more elaborate ball gowns, riding dresses, and matching headpieces and hats to match.

All of them were styled for a young woman of marrying age, with delicate lace along the sleeves, or embroidery and pearls along the collar, all in bright pastel colors. I couldn't even imagine my spinster mother wearing this gown. I couldn't imagine that she had a life before choosing to wander the kingdoms with a magical menagerie, then settling down in the desolate town of Nihill, making and mending her own clothes. How far she had fallen.

But I understood her hesitation to return, for ghosts walked these halls in memories. When I stood up, I knocked over a portrait. Setting it upright, the sheet slipped off, and I couldn't help but lift it up to study the familiar face before me.

A young woman wearing a lavender riding dress and hat, her black hair falling loosely down her back. She stood next to a beautiful white stallion that towered over her but seemed protective. Her smile was brilliant and carefree.

But it was the man next to her that gave me pause. He was burly, with a thick beard and the same dark hair. His eyes were green, and he wore a dark suit. He stood on the other side of the horse, holding the reins. It was easy to see the love he had for his daughter. Lord Eville and his daughter, Lorelai.

Feeling like I had intruded where I should not, I set the portrait upright and picked out fur-lined boots. None of the dresses in the current trunk would keep me warm, but after moving to a second trunk, I found warmer winter gear, similar to the style the women in town wore. Much of it made of wool or lined with fur cuffs and collars. I found thick wool mittens and an angora scarf.

Gathering my borrowed goods, I changed into the warmer boots and a warm burgundy dress with soft fur-lined cuffs. As I stood in front of the mirror, I did a little turn, surprised at the hidden pleats and folds in the skirt meant to give added layers. I slipped my hands into the deep-lined pockets and instantly fell in love with the dresses of Kiln. I ran my hands through my hair, brushing out the tangles, letting my locks fall over my shoulder. I paused and wondered if this was what my actual mother looked like.

Shaking my head, I pushed the thought aside. I may not be the daughter of Lady Eville's womb, but we were the children of her heart.

"Come on, just a little further," I muttered as I struggled to pull down a wood crate I'd found in a supply cupboard. I got a hammer hanging on the wall and could see a glass jar filled with nails. Standing on my tiptoes, my fingers could barely touch the bottom of the crate. Looking around, I found very little to stand on other than an old empty barrel.

Rolling the barrel over to the shelf, I balanced it against the wall, and scaled the rocky curved side. It wasn't the most stable of positions, but I just needed the extra few feet to get the container off the shelf. Now I could reach it, and I pulled toward me, but it was heavier than I expected. I shifted my weight to compensate, but the barrel rolled under me. I slipped, falling down, and sliced my hand open on the edge of the crate as I crashed chin first into the barrel. The crate broke, scattering the nails across the floor.

"By the stars," I grumbled as I tried to stop the bleeding from my hand. It wasn't a deep cut, but it was a nasty bleeder. Finding a scrap kerchief, I bandaged my hand as best I could. Then I began the long and arduous process of picking up the nails and the broken crate, knowing I could use the wood to board up the broken windows.

It was hard to tell the exact time with the gray sky, but by what I assumed to be afternoon, I had boarded up most of the windows on the main floor and headed to the second floor. My hand was throbbing, and my stomach was growling because I had forgotten to stop and eat.

The newly patched window rattled in anger, but little air got through. I went back to the sitting room and continued to stoke the fire with the pile of wood Kash had provided before he left. I made a few more trips upstairs to the west wing and brought down every spare blanket to create a bed near the fire. Thankfully, water was plentiful. I only had to scoop snow and warm it up. I grabbed an apple and ate it, letting the sweet juices dribble down my chin, savoring each bite.

As the sun set, all hope of Kash returning faded. I

settled in to prepare for a night alone, and worry crept its ugliness into my thoughts.

I tried to find out what was wrong with the kingdom. But so far, I'd been swamped with survival, and I hadn't even attempted to contact my mother. What would she say? What would *I* say? Guilt flooded through me as I looked around at the once magnificent home that was in embarrassing shambles.

My old room in the tower seemed opulent in comparison. Pulling the dusty blanket close to my face, I curled up and watched the fire dance in the grate as I ate another apple. Tomorrow, I would try to make bread and take better stock of what came out of the cellar. Now that the supplies had left the protection of the warded cellar, they would spoil.

CHAPTER SIX

The smell of roasted meat slowly brought me awake. My mouth was watering even before I opened my eyes. My stomach let out a greedy and loud churn.

"Somebody's hungry," Kash whispered.

Sitting up, it surprised me to see him sitting cross-legged on the floor next to me like we were old friends. Over the fire, he was roasting a rabbit on a makeshift spit.

"Where did you go?" I asked accusingly.

He nodded toward the rabbit. "Hunting. I have to admit, it's been a while since I've tried my hand at setting snares." He pulled a leg off the rabbit and handed it to me.

I passed the burning leg back and forth between my fingers until it cooled off. I took a bite, moaning in pleasure.

"But the storm; it's dangerous to go out right now," I said, licking my fingers.

Kash nodded. "Storms are common, and life must go on despite the setbacks. It's a chance we all take every time we set out. We wonder if we'll return."

I devoured the rabbit's leg while he talked. Kash took the rabbit off the spit and cut away another leg.

"Aren't you going to have any?" I asked, taking the second leg.

"I've already eaten my share while you were snoring away." Kash's voice was low as he gestured to the bones that were tossed in the fire from the previous rabbit. "This one's for you."

My stomach dropped this time, not from hunger, but from something else. A new feeling.

"I do not snore," I said between mouthfuls.

"Like a dragon with a cold. I'm surprised you never knew." He tapped the knife against his boot, his grin highlighting a hidden dimple.

I watched him warily, trying to judge whether he was telling the truth or teasing me. Instead, I let it go.

The wind roared loudly again, and I glanced out the window. "How much longer is the storm going to last?" I asked worriedly.

Kash cocked his head and closed his eyes as if listening to the wind. "Three more days at least."

"Three days." I dragged out the words with a sigh. "What am I going to do for three more days?" I said to myself.

"It looks like you kept yourself pretty busy boarding up windows. The lower floors are already warmer." Kash grabbed my bandaged hand and slowly unwrapped it, revealing the ugly gash. "How did this happen?" His thumb rested on the inside of my wrist and my heart raced.

"I can take care of it." I pulled my hand away, but he tightened his grip. He reached for his pouch and pulled out a metal tin. Using his fingers, he smeared some of the cream on my gash.

I leaned down and took a whiff. "Linseed oil, yarrow, and clove?"

"Very good. You know your medicines."

"I should, I burn myself enough to know all the tricks."

"Burn?" Kash turned my hand over and revealed many of the burns and scars on my hands from working in the forge as I perfected my alchemy. My skin wasn't smooth and delicate like a lady, but instead marred by my studies.

This time when I pulled my hand out of his, I tucked them under my thighs, hiding my scars.

"So what should we do until the storm passes?" He pressed his chin into his hand and grinned at me.

My head snapped up, and I looked at Kash. It was odd that he would assume he'd get to stay here for that long.

"You mean I have to put up with you for three more days?" I pretended to be affronted.

Kash grinned. "You know most people would be thrilled to have me for company."

I don't know why I assumed it was *women* he was referring to. I rolled my eyes.

"I'm enjoying my evening with you. We could play a card game. I promise not to cheat too much." Kash pulled out a deck of cards that I had found in the kitchen earlier.

"That doesn't instill much faith."

Kash shuffled them and gave me a crooked smile. "It's not cheating if I'm giving you fair warning that I'm going to cheat."

"It *is* cheating," I laughed. "Stating your cheating is still cheating."

"No, it's not. Because everyone cheats at card games. I promise I'll let you win."

"Then what's the point of playing? If you're going to cheat and sometimes let me win," I smirked.

"The point of playing is to win the prize."

"Now there are prizes?"

"Imaginary prizes," Kash bit his bottom lip to keep from smirking.

"I feel like I am being bamboozled." I was laughing so hard, my side was hurting. "You're going to cheat to win imaginary prizes."

Kash leaned forward, and I looked up, our faces so close I could feel his warm breath on my cheeks. "Well, it doesn't have to be imaginary prizes." His voice dropped, and so did his eyes as they focused on my mouth.

Heat rushed to my cheeks, and my lips parted as I inhaled.

My physical response startled Kash as the cards slipped out of his hands mid-shuffle, and half the stack flew into the fireplace.

"No!" Kash tried to save them, but he kept pulling flaming pieces of paper out of the fire.

"It's fine." I placed my hand on his shoulder. "I'm not a skilled card player, anyway."

Kash entertained himself by flicking the cards he had left into a bowl.

Earlier that day, I had found a few books and placed them near the fireplace for me to study. I pulled one from the stack and opened it.

"Where are you from?" he asked. "It's obvious from your accent you're not from around here. You have very little supplies, and you weren't prepared for our frequent winter storms."

"It's that obvious?" I sighed, closing the book.

"A little." Kash pinched his fingers together. He leaned forward and lifted the cover to reveal the title of the book I was reading. "And you're reading a book on our history."

He was very observant. "I'm from Nihill. I grew up there and only recently came to Kiln."

"Why?" he asked. "No one travels to the northern Ragnar Mountains in the middle of winter, unless they're crazy."

"Maybe I *am* crazy."

"Or maybe you're after the gold," he said, lowering his voice.

"Gold?" I asked, feigning ignorance.

Kash's eyes glittered. "It's well-known that these mountains have secrets. Many believe the stories of a hoard of gold buried here." His hand brushed the handle of his knife.

"Do you?" I asked.

"Of course." He stared into the fire.

"Well, I'm not here to hunt gold. I'm here for another reason."

"What's that?" he asked.

"I'm here until"—I paused, remembering my mother's warning—"someone comes for me."

"Oh, who is he? A fiancé, betrothed?" Kash hedged.

"No." I blushed. "A friend of the family."

"Ah." Kash leaned back on his side on the floor and took to playing with a few pebbles that had come loose from the brick fireplace, pushing them around.

"Do you have family or siblings?" I asked.

His mood darkened, and he was reluctant to respond. "Family is what you make of it."

He was being very evasive, and I hated people that never answered a direct question.

"If you don't give me a straight answer, you're going to find yourself out in the storm again," I snapped.

Kash's golden eyes met mine. "I'm not proud of my past, nor my family. Speaking of it always causes trouble wherever I go. So I'd rather not." His congenial demeanor was gone and replaced by a firm, commanding tone that surprised me.

"Well, where are you from?"

"Here. Just further up the mountain. Far enough that I can't make it by foot during the storm," he said in a clipped voice.

I wanted to ask him where to, but even though we had fought and not killed each other, I had to remind myself we were both perfect strangers. He knew nothing about me, and I knew nothing about him. And the way our conversation was going, we were going to remain strangers.

Kash grabbed a spare blanket and curled up by the fire, tucking his hands behind his head to prepare for sleep.

"What are you doing?" I asked, my voice rising in pitch.

"I'm going to sleep. I'm exhausted." He stretched out his long legs and crossed them at the ankles.

"Not here, you're not."

Kash leaned up on his elbows and gave me an exasperated stare. "Rhea, I'm tired. You're tired. It's cold out. This is the warmest place in the manor. Just rest. I promise not to knock you out or tie you up." After he said his piece, he leaned back down and turned on his side, giving me his back.

I stared at Kash for close to a candle mark, and I couldn't tell if he was asleep or not. But I gave him plenty of time to doze off into a deep sleep. Grabbing up the blankets I slept on, I tiptoed out of the sitting room. There was no way I was going to sleep in the same room as a stranger, even if he did feed me. It wasn't safe. My mother taught me not to trust strange men, and Kash was by far the strangest I had met.

Bundling the blankets to my chest, I ran up the stairs to the west wing and into the one room I knew locked from the inside. I needed the safety of the wall between us.

Unfortunately, it was a room that was still missing a pane of glass and the temperature was below freezing. It was the first bedroom I'd found, with the peeling blue wallpaper and the fourposter bed that sat directly under the window. I turned the key in the lock and to be safe, placed a ward on the door. One that would shock any intruder. I crawled up on a rug at the far end of the room, opposite the window, and wrapped the blanket around me, wishing that I had thought to recharge my charms during the day—or that I had the forethought to carry wood to more than the main sitting room.

I shivered as I pulled the blanket over my head to block out the bitter chill, letting my breath create a pocket of warmth. But try as I might, I kept falling in and out of fitful sleep. My dreams were chaos as I floated in and out of consciousness. I dreamed of the storm.

The next morning, I awoke to find that I was warm despite the freezing room. Pulling the blanket off my head, I was confused to find that another had been placed on top of me. Looking around the room, the door was locked, and the key was still in the keyhole.

I must have been mistaken. I must have taken three blankets with me in the middle of the night. That must have been it.

When I went back down the stairs, I found the sitting room empty; the fire had dulled to a flicker, and it hadn't been tended to in hours. I added more wood and walked through the manor, searching for Kash. Realizing that, once again, I was alone.

Unsure how to process his sudden departures. What was he doing? Would he come back? And then my heart fluttered as I realized I wanted him to.

I spent the rest of the day working on bread and letting it rise. Thankful once again for my mother's foresight to place a preserving charm on the kitchen cellar.

The scent of freshly baked bread filled the kitchen as I let it rest on the table.

But all my baking had depleted the wood bin, and it needed to be filled to get through the rest of the night. As the sun continued to set, I knew I needed to face the coming darkness and the fact that Kash very well would not return. I had to rely on myself.

Wrapping my cloak around my shoulders, I braced for a blast of freezing wind when I opened the door. And blast it did.

The snow stung my eyes, and I could feel it melt on my cheeks, and then instantly freeze. This wasn't good. It was freezing, and I'd have to move fast. Thankfully, Kash had found a cart to haul the wood and left it by the front door. Inside the cart was an axe.

"Praise the stars," I said in relief as I picked up the long handles of the cart and lifted it. Pushing it around the side of the house, I saw a trail into the woods where the snow wasn't as deep, indicating Kash had used that path.

I stopped at the first tree that seemed easy to cut through and would provide adequate firewood. Growing up in the country, I wasn't without basic skills. All my sisters knew how to cut wood. It was easy if you chose your target wisely. I never picked a tree thicker than my leg. I could cut through it easily and chop it into small pieces and carry it back easily without burning through too much energy. The ash grove I stumbled into was perfect.

I spent the next few candle marks cutting down the white barked trees. When I had loaded up my cart, I wheeled it around to face the manor house, but all I saw was trees. I needed to go farther and then I'd see the path.

But I had lost track of the time and the sun had set.

I wheeled the cart in the direction I thought I had come from, but I didn't see the house. I couldn't have traveled that far away. I dropped the cart and turned in a full circle, refusing to believe that I could get lost so easily.

The snow had not let up and all I could see was a mix of gray and black shadows in the distance, but then one shadow moved, and I froze.

What was it that Herst said about monsters that roamed around in the woods?

"I hate rats and I hate monsters," I whispered. There was something standing and blending into the tree line. It moved again and seemed larger than any human.

I bolted. Running in the opposite direction as fast as my feet could carry me. I didn't know what it was, but I knew I didn't want to stand around and find out.

I ran blindly. My hands out in front of my face as I rushed through snow covered boughs, ducking under dead branches. One branch hooked my cloak and ripped it from my neck. I choked back a scream and slid down a large hill on my bottom, soaking my dress, terrified to look behind for fear that the creature was within the distance of tearing my face off.

Running across a frozen stream bed, my foot crashed

through the ice, echoing all around me. Sounding out an alert to where I was. My breathing came in gasps, and I clawed my way up the embankment on my hands and knees, slipping in the snow and face-planting twice. When I crested the top, I ran straight into a something warm.

I screamed and kicked it in the shin, hard.

The monster groaned in pain. "Rhea?" Kash gasped.

I opened my eyes and saw Kash huddled over, a bundle of wood tied to his back.

"I'm sorry," I cried out, feeling embarrassed that I'd attacked him. "There's something out there. It's chasing me."

Quickly, he stood up, ignoring the pain in his leg. His dark eyes scanned the forest, and his head snapped to the left, as though we weren't standing in a snowstorm. He still knew the layout of the land.

I shivered in my drenched clothes.

Kash wrapped his arms around me, his hand on his knife. The sound of a breaking branch had him spinning to confront the monster.

A buck with a magnificent set of antlers watched us warily before bouncing off through the woods, a beautiful doe at his side.

"Well, there's your monster," he chuckled.

"I'm s-sorry." I shivered in Kash's arms.

He blinked. "What were you doing out in the storm?"

"Getting firewood. We were almost out."

"I told you I would take care of it." He sighed.

"But how did I know you would keep your word? Y-you just disappeared . . . again."

Kash grabbed my elbow and pulled me through the storm until we were back at the manor again. Were we really so close? I felt foolish as I stood in the foyer, shivering and dripping wet.

With a groan, Kash dropped the bundle of wood on the floor. "Quick, to the kitchen."

I didn't budge.

"Now!" he barked.

I jumped and rushed in, where it was already warm with a roaring fire. Kash had already returned earlier while I was out getting firewood. Three skinned rabbits were roasting on a spit, and a kettle of water was boiling. It looked like he'd been able to get the water pump working. He rolled out a big copper tub.

"Get your boots and socks off."

While my frozen fingers fumbled to undo the laces, he filled a bucket with water out of the well pump and dumped it into the tub. Repeating the actions until it was filled halfway. He added the hot water from the kettle and reheated it over the fireplace. Placing his hand in the water, he realized it was still too cold. Using tongs, he took a searing coal ember and dumped it into the water. It sizzled, the wood crumbling in the tub's bottom, turning the water black but heating it more than the kettle could.

I stood there shivering, crossing my arms over my chest, staring at the odd scene before me.

He tested the water again and looked up at me with worried eyes. "Get in," he ordered. I stepped into the tub and immediately I hissed in pain as the heat of the water brought feelings back to my toes. Thankfully, it was a large enough tub that I could sit in it comfortably with my knees up to my chest.

Kash reached a hand into the water to test its temperature, and it brushed against my leg. I slapped it away.

"Don't," I warned.

"It's only looks warm. I need to heat it again."

"I can take care of it myself."

Kash narrowed his eyes. "I find that hard to believe. You wandered out into a storm and fell into a river. You could have frozen to death."

Unfortunately, he was right. As he was speaking, the chill was taking over again as my frozen clothes quickly dropped the tub's temperature. He reached for another burning ember, and I didn't feel like having my clothes covered in black bits of charcoal.

"I'm more capable than you realize. If you would just leave me alone," I pleaded.

Kash shook his head. The muscle in his jaw clenched as he debated what to do. Finally, with a sigh of frustration, he left the kitchen, slamming the door behind him.

I laid my head back on the edge of the tub, snaked my hand down the outside of the metal, and pressed my palm against the base. I smiled as I traced a sigil on the outside wall to heat the copper. The tub glowed, and the water bubbled and steamed within seconds. With a contented sigh, I released the spell and ducked under the water, rinsing my hair, letting the heat run over my scalp.

When I came up and wiped the hair out of my face, I was staring into Kash's frustrated glare.

"What in the world was that?" he asked.

My eyes widened, and I sunk into the water, as if it could protect me from his questions and the accusation in his golden gaze.

He pressed his hands against the copper tub and pulled it back. "It's hot."

"Of course it is."

"It's like one of the hob's saunas. You did this?"

"No, it was your ember," I lied.

"Don't lie to me. I watched you touch the side, and it glowed bright orange. You heated the tub."

This was such an awkward place to be discussing my abilities, and I didn't enjoy feeling attacked and cornered.

"You spied on me? What if I was going to get naked?"

He slouched. "I went to get you dry clothes and was bringing them to you, and then I saw you do—whatever you did."

"So what if I did—whatever you think I did? What are you going to do about it?"

Kash's mouth dropped open as he tried to follow my questioning. I couldn't help that he made me nervous and fumble my words so much. He shook his head, kneeling next to the tub.

"Careful, or I may melt your eyeballs next. I mean, if I could do what you think I did," I warned, trying to be threatening.

He chuckled. "I'd want to know what else you can do." He reached out and flicked the water into my face.

I gasped as he surprised me. In retaliation, I kicked out my leg to send a wave over his boots.

"Hey!" He scooped more water and tossed it into my face.

I coughed and wiped it away, my grin turning into an evil smirk. "You realize that this can only go one way. I'm already wet. You're the one in danger here." I brought my arms back, attacking with all the water I could, sending arc after arc of water into his face.

"Fine, I concede. You win. But when you're done. We need to talk." Kash's warm eyes pleaded with mine. He leaned forward, shaking the water from his hair, before leaving me alone.

Once dressed in the extra gown Kash left for me, I tended the food on the fire. My hair was still damp, and it created a long, wet 'V' down the back of the dress. Using the same water, I did the best I could to clean out my old clothes and hung them to dry by the fireplace.

A knock came at the kitchen, and I called out for Kash to enter.

"Come—" I barely got the word out when Kash rushed in, heading right for the fireplace.

"It's not burned."

I pointed to the rabbits I had placed on a large serving platter. "No, they're not."

He sighed in relief. "Good."

I gave him a pointed look. "You expected me to let them burn, didn't you?"

"I didn't know what to expect, truthfully. You keep surprising me." Kash leaned over the long wooden table and pulled at the rabbit leg, and it separated easily.

Sitting on a stool close to the kitchen fire, I ran my fingers through my wet hair and tried to untangle the knots while letting it dry.

Kash stopped chewing as he focused on my long hair. "It's like molten gold."

Holding up a honey brown strand, I examined it. "In this light it is."

He swallowed. "So beautiful." I wasn't sure if he was referring to me or my hair.

I paused in my detangling, and our eyes met over the table. It was such a unique, and at the same time, homey scene. We were odd partners, forced to survive in each other's space. At times he was abrasive, other times quite charming, but he was still a stranger in my home. I was the trained sorceress, and yet he was the more dangerous of us because he could disarm me with a smile.

I grew uncomfortable again at how easy it was to let my guard down, and I knew I mustn't. Clenching my jaw, I broke eye contact first, which felt like a slap. Turning my gaze onto the fire, I winced as I pulled a little too hard on my hair as I attacked a snarl.

"I'm sorry," he said.

"Go ahead," I said coldly. "Ask your questions. Just know that I'll only answer if I feel like it."

Kash took a deep breath and looked around the room. He was thinking of a question and then his expression changed.

"How long have you been able to—" He gestured to my hands.

"Since I was five. My mother tested each of us to see if we had an affinity for magic. My sisters have a natural talent. Mine was slow to reveal itself. I had to rely on charms and books and learn the hard way. But it wasn't until *recently* that I've had success with basic spells."

"Can you break a curse?" His golden eyes met mine, revealing a deep sadness within. One that he hid behind his smooth words and jovial demeanor.

"Breaking a curse is hard. There's almost always a counter, or requirement to break it. That or you need the original castor to release the curse. Is the castor still alive?"

Kash sadly shook his head.

"Oh. What kind of curse are we talking about?"

"I don't know. It seems to get stronger, not weakening at all as time goes by."

"Would you be willing to go into detail?" I prodded.

Kash looked down at the table. His fist clenched, and he sighed. "I will not burden you with the details, for there is very little hope."

The deep mourning sadness in his voice made me reach out to comfort him. I touched his fist, and he looked up in surprise. His tightened fist loosened, and I held his hand in mine.

"I promise that if you tell me, I will do everything within my power to help you."

Kash looked down at our hands. He moved his fingers until they were interlocked with mine. His thumb brushed the back of my hand and he smiled wearily. "If only it were that easy."

"It can be, if you trust me enough," I said gently.

Kash's voice deepened, and he shook his head. "If you knew my secrets, you would hate me, and I can't bear for you to hate me."

Kash rose to move away, but I tightened my grip on his hand, refusing to release him. "We all have a past that we're ashamed of."

"Yes, but I can never outrun mine, no matter how hard I try." Kash carefully removed his fingers from mine. "You can't help me."

My confidence took a shot with his last statement. What was I doing here? Even Kash didn't take me seriously or believe in me. I wasn't a hero, or a savior, or even a good sorceress. I slumped forward, pressing my hands to my face, instantly feeling defeated.

A heavy warmth covered me, and I looked to see Kash kneeling before me, his hand on my head. "Hey, it's okay.

My problems are my own." His hand dropped to my shoulder, and his fingers brushed against my neck.

I inhaled at his touch; my breath caught in my throat again at how close he was to me. I blushed, knowing he could probably hear me holding it.

"We really need to work on that," he whispered.

"On what?" I asked.

"On your attraction to me." The corner of his mouth lifted, revealing his dimple.

"I'm not attracted to you," I rushed out.

I couldn't think as he leaned closer, his eyes lowering to my lips. I wasn't breathing now, and I became lightheaded.

I blinked and looked away, unsure of what to say or do.

"Rhea, look at me," Kash pleaded.

My eyes locked onto his lips first, and I definitely wanted to press mine to his. It was harder than I thought to meet his warm eyes, and I was instantly lost. I could feel myself slipping, losing control, my mind racing and trying to think of something witty to say. But scared I'd mess it up, I just kept silent.

"It's okay, because I'm struggling too." His hand slowly cupped my neck, his thumb stroking my cheek. Butterflies fluttered in my stomach, and I felt like I would pass out.

"With what?" I asked, feeling unsteady.

"With not kissing you right this moment."

My lips parted, and I released the slightest gasp.

"Screw it. I'm cursed anyway. You can hate me later," he whispered before his lips brushed against mine in the softest of touches. I held my breath for the millionth time.

"Breathe," Kash whispered, coaching me.

With his permission, I exhaled and smiled. He pulled

back just enough, and I could see his eyes twinkling with mischief. This time it was I who leaned forward, initiating the kiss, taking him by surprise. The kiss started slowly, but it flamed the slow-burning coal in my heart, and it lit, burning with the desire of a thousand furnaces.

When he pulled back, we were both out of breath. Kash brushed his thumb across my swollen lips.

"I underestimated you, Rhea," he groaned, pressing his forehead to mine. "You *really* are dangerous."

He stood, pulling me up with him, our hands still clasped together. We headed out into the main hall.

"It's time for you to go to bed," he ordered, pushing me toward the stairs. "And lock your door."

"Why?"

"To keep unwanted intruders out." Kash gave me a slow smile. "Or don't."

My heart raced as I ran up the stairs to my bedroom and locked the door behind me.

CHAPTER SEVEN

I came downstairs the next morning after spending way too much time in the mirror playing with my hair. I braided one side, pulling it back and pinning it, letting the rest of my locks run down my back. I pinched my cheeks to add color and stared at my lips for far too long. My heart fluttered, and I went down the stairs, eager to see Kash and his devilish smile, only to realize that the front door of the manor was slightly ajar. The gloomy light streamed through, and a set of footprints led off the steps and into the woods.

I closed the door, the beating of my heart slowing down as disappointment followed. He left again. It was not how I imagined the morning after my first kiss. I had hoped we would spend breakfast together, holding hands, talking while I stared at his contagious smile. I had it bad. My first crush and first kiss, all in one. With each passing candle mark, my heart ached even more with the desire to see him.

As the day wore on, I skimmed the books left in the manor. I made soup with the leftover rabbit, bits of dried herbs, and the potatoes that were only just beginning to grow eyes. Even moving around the kitchen, I would frequently stare at the place we sat and shared a kiss.

I found myself gazing out the windows, searching the snow for a shadow of Kash returning, hoping he would enjoy the hot meal I had cooked for him and the fresh bread I had baked. *Is this what it was like to be in love?* My head was in the clouds, my heart unable to keep a steady rhythm, my lips aching to press against his again.

But despite all my longing and wishing, I knew he wouldn't return until the sun had set. I sat on the stairs facing the door, watching the last ebbs of the overcast sun's rays disappear, time passing as the shadows moved across the marble floor.

He didn't return. The sun had set and Kash still didn't come home. *Home.* I chastised myself. This wasn't Kash's home. He didn't live here. He lived . . . I didn't know where he lived. What if he already had another home . . . and a wife?

My thoughts continued to spiral, and I worried on my thumbnail, biting on the edge.

Nonsense. He wouldn't have kissed me if he were married, right? But what if he regretted it and wasn't coming back? What if he realized it was a mistake? He seemed comfortable in the snow and storm. There was nothing keeping him here. My shoulders slumped and my head lowered onto my arms as the night wore on.

He still hadn't come back.

Despite telling myself not to cry, I couldn't hold back the sting of tears and I fell asleep curled up on the stairs.

"Rhea." Kash's gentle voice broke through an uneasy slumber. "Why are you sleeping on the stairs?"

I blinked and rubbed at my salt-crusted eyes.

He touched my face and swore. "Your skin is like ice." He swept me up in his arms and carried me to the kitchen.

"You didn't come back," I said lamely. "I was worried."

Kash kneeled by the fire and took a flint out of his pocket and quickly had it going again. Heat warming the room and my frozen toes.

"I see you made dinner. It smells wonderful." Kash lifted the lid on the pot, his face wrinkling. "But it looks questionable."

I let out a long sigh. The soup had thickened and looked like greasy mush. "I can fix it." I stood to go to the pitcher to add more water. "It just needs to be reheated."

"Sit, get warm. I'll take care of it." Kash looked different. There was something about his demeanor that immediately alerted me to the problem. That and he was wearing different clothes than he had been the last time I saw him. These clothes were clean, pressed, and had the slightest detailed trim. As he passed me, he caught me staring at the intricate design worn by those of nobility.

"Who are you?" I asked coldly, my eyes taking in the shiny boots, the leather belt, and the rich black cloak. "Those aren't the clothes of a peasant."

Kash stopped stirring the soup, his shoulders slumped, and he looked at me, guilt filling his golden eyes.

"I can explain," Kash said softly.

"Where do you go during the day?" I continued, my hurt bursting with pain at the secrets that were slowly tearing us apart. "It's like you're avoiding me."

"It's not like that. I mean it is. I *am* avoiding you." He

took a deep breath, his shoulders straightened. "It's complicated." He reached for my hand.

My anger rose at his admission, and I yanked my hand back. "It's not, really."

People had avoided me my whole life because of my family. I never expected to find someone that cared for me, and to learn that he didn't want to be with me hurt. It hurt more than I wanted to admit. I turned so he couldn't see my eyes fill with tears of rejection. I quickly wiped them away.

"Rhea, I want to tell you something. I—"

"Hellooo!" a high-pitched voice hollered from the foyer, echoing through the manor. Kash pulled away, reaching for the knife that was never far away from him.

"Stay here!" he commanded and tiptoed toward the kitchen door. He pressed his body against the wall and peered around the corner before slipping into the next room.

Stay? I inwardly fumed. I grabbed a heavy pot and headed out the opposite servant's entrance, taking the back halls that would bring me around to the other side of the manor.

Running on tiptoes, I made excellent time to the west side of the manor and took a glance at the intruders. There were two. One extremely huge with ruddy brown hair that brushed his shoulders, a giant axe on his back, the other small and feminine.

They were both covered in snow and were stamping and shaking it into the foyer.

"Why did you convince me to come here?" the female whined. "I don't like this white stuff. I'm freezing my tail off."

"You don't have a tail anymore," the one with the axe said. His voice deep was filled with affection for his companion. "And the white stuff is called snow."

The female pulled her hood back to reveal long lavender hair with eyes that were deep and exotic. She stuck her bottom lip out. "Well, I don't like this *snow*. Make it go away. It tastes like—"she licked her lips again—"like nothing. I'm not going back out in it." She stormed across to the stairs and crossed her arms, giving him a stern look.

The man was no longer listening. He had tensed, his hands held at his sides. I don't know how I knew, but he sensed us. Just as I was about to step out of the shadows. Kash slipped behind him and pulled his knife.

"Move and you're dead," Kash threatened.

"Same goes for you," the man answered, his own knife pointed into Kash's stomach. With his cloak pushed aside, his arms were riddled with long white scars. He was an obvious fighter, possibly a mercenary.

The lavender-haired woman didn't even care about the commotion. She was removing her cloak and heading into the sitting room toward the warm fireplace.

"You're alone now," Kash added.

The man shook his head. "Velora knows I can take care of myself."

In a flash, both men spun away from each other like partners in a dance. They returned and faced one another, weapons drawn, glaring and slowly circling.

Stepping out of the shadows, I made myself known. "Marco, I would hate to tell Maeve that you got blood on the marble floor."

Hearing my voice, Marco turned and dropped his

knife. He bowed and placed a fist over his heart. "Sorry, Miss Rhea. Maeve sent us. She thought you might need help."

I shook my head and wondered if Maeve had gone crazy. Was she really expecting them to help me, or was this her way of playing a prank on me by making me babysit Velora? Or—and I hated to consider it—she really thought I couldn't do this on my own.

As if hearing my thoughts, Velora floated out of the sitting room and gave me a look. "Can you make the white stuff go away?" she asked prettily, and then shivered.

"Sorry, Velora." I smiled. "I'm not strong enough by myself to dispel this. It's best to let the storm run its course."

I wasn't sure, but I thought I heard her harrumph and make a comment on how Maeve could probably get rid of it.

During the exchange, Kash had made his way over to me, tucking his knife into his belt. "You know them?" he asked cautiously.

"They're um, sort of friends of the family."

I knew little about Marco except that Maeve vouched for him. Velora was a mermaid, and her social skills were a bit lacking, having lived in the sea all her life. I found her reaction to the snow to be quite comical.

"I have to also assume that Maeve told you how to get here?" I asked Marco.

He scratched his chin and held out a charmed string with a lock of hair. "She gave us a tracking spell."

I rolled my eyes. "Of course she did." Maeve had used the glamour charm I gave her and reversed it into a tracking spell to find me. She was smart.

Having Velora and Marco in the manor seemed to have put Kash on edge. He didn't know what to make of the newcomers, and he kept edging himself closer to my side.

"Come, eat. We have food," I said, stepping away from Kash.

He noticed I avoided him and frowned.

At the mention of food, Marco perked up and Velora squealed in delight.

We showed them into the kitchen and poured them soup into porcelain bowls I had found upstairs hidden in a trunk. Kash pulled his stool close to mine, leaning close, while Marco kept his hands on the table where we could see them at all times.

Velora leaned over the stew and gave it a sniff before wrinkling her nose. "You ruined it."

"What?" Kash seemed offended. "How?"

"She likes her food raw," I guessed.

Kash reached for his knife again, his eye narrowing in suspicion at what kind of creature she could be. Marco mirrored his actions and placed a protective hand in front of Velora.

I had to settle Kash down and reveal a secret I wasn't sure if Velora wanted known.

"Relax, she's not an onwae," I whispered, referring to the shape-shifting dark fae creature that hungered for human flesh. I placed my hand over Kash's as he gripped his knife under the table.

"Then what is she; for she definitely isn't human. I can tell there's something *off* about her." He leaned toward me whispering, his shoulder brushing mine.

I glanced to Marco in a silent question, and he nodded.

"Velora is a mermaid," I said. "*Almost* as dangerous as an onwae."

Kash's knife lowered. "What?" He glanced at the curious girl. Velora was oblivious to the dangerous fight about to break out on her behalf. She was picking through the soup with her spoon like it was the most disgusting thing ever.

"Do you have any butt?" she asked curiously.

A snort came rushing out, and I clapped a hand over my mouth. Kash's lips tightened as he tried to not laugh.

Marco smiled and said, "I've got your *butter* right here." From the folds of his bag, he produced a jar.

Velora ignored the soup and used her spoon to dig in and eat a spoonful.

I tried to hold back a gag but could feel my shoulders heave, and I had to look away.

After the mystery of Velora's background was solved, we spent the rest of the evening in mild conversation. Marco shared that he'd grown up in Eldor and had once trained with Gridlock of the Goldiron Clan. They were a clan of dwarves that were strictly mercenaries for hire. Marco wanted to return to visit, and Maeve heard they were coming to Kiln. She begged for them to check on me.

"Have you heard the location of any more of Allemar's apprentices?" I asked, referring to the sorcerer my sister Maeve had fought against and defeated in Florin.

Marco seemed uncomfortable. "I don't know. I was Aspen's friend, not Allemar's lackey. But I know that even Allemar refused to come to Kiln. There was something here that even he was afraid of disturbing. An old magic."

Marco's warning made me shift on the stool uncomfortably, feeling sick to my stomach as I remembered how the sentient being I encountered wanted to devour my magic. Dare I reveal what I saw? Would they believe me? I had to try.

"I felt it when I was scrying the kingdom. I've encountered nothing as powerful as that entity."

Kash stared into the fire, deep in thought. "There *is* something stirring beneath the mountain, causing it to become restless. Earthquakes, avalanches, and bouts of madness have erupted throughout the towns. It has many of the locals frightened, and even the king is worried."

"Then what is the king doing about it?" I snapped. "I don't think kidnapping people is the way to solve the problem. Or is that just a rumor?"

"It's not a rumor," Kash said. "The king sends his blades to find *anyone* with power and bring them to the palace." He looked directly at me in warning.

"Why?" I asked.

"I don't know why." Kash rubbed the bridge of his nose. "But if that's the case, then the best course of action would be to keep you hidden here. If you leave the manor, I cannot guarantee your safety."

"So, I do nothing?"

"Exactly, you will be safe if you do nothing."

"But what about the others?" I asked.

"I don't care about the others." Kash's fist hit the table with an angry thud. The muscle in his jaw twitched as he tried to control his anger. "Only you."

My heart thrummed in my chest as I knew it was the wrong thing to do. "I can't do nothing. I need to get inside the mountain."

Kash shook his head and leaned back on his stool. "You won't survive."

"Why?" My mouth suddenly went dry, and my fist curled around the fabric of my skirt.

"It's a labyrinth of tunnels. Very few know their way through them, and ever since the fall of the dwarven city of Ter Dell, goblins have overrun the passageways."

"You've been inside them," I said, realizing how confident he sounded.

"I have," Kash said, his voice dropping to a whisper. "And I barely survived getting out. I would hate for you to experience the same fate."

"You don't understand what's down there. I need to find a wa—"

"I *know* more than you think!" Kash's hands clenched into white-knuckled fists. His eyes met mine, and I felt his frustration. "And that's why I *forbid* you from going."

I stood up so fast; the chair scraped against the tile floor, startling Kash.

I turned to Marco and the nonobservant Velora and gave them a tight, polite smile. "Excuse me; I'm sorry that I'm not a more gracious host. Please stay as long as you like. Most of the rooms are empty. Pick one." I waved my hand at the floors above and moved out of the kitchen.

Kash could see I was upset. He followed on my heels as I headed upstairs.

Kash grabbed my wrist, pulling me to a stop. "Rhea, don't be angry. I'm only trying to protect you."

"Protect me from whom, Kash? Or from what?"

"Obviously things that you don't understand," he vented. "You've only just come to Kiln. How could you possibly understand the complexities of our kingdom's problems and solve them when we've been trying to for years?"

"You have no right to tell me what I can and cannot do." I pulled away, but he didn't release my wrist.

"Rhea, no matter how powerful you are, you are no match for the king, or his blades. So don't try anything stupid."

"I don't think it's the king or his blades I need to fear—but you," I snapped.

"Rhea, what are you talking about?" Kash's voice broke as he realized I was driving him away.

Giving my hand a hard shake, I escaped his grasp and stormed upstairs to my room to think. I stared out the window, watching the wind scream and blow snow against the panes. In the distance, trees swayed in the wind, their branches like maidens bowing to the moon.

For the next few candle marks, I waited, plotting, and planning and I kept coming to the same conclusion.

I knew I was supposed to wait for Grimkeep, but I felt there was something wrong. He would have come for me by now if he were able. I couldn't wait for the storm to end. I needed to forge my own way, and not rely on others. Especially not Kash. He couldn't know what I was doing, for it seemed he only wanted to stop me.

When I opened the door to leave my bedroom, someone fell inward with a heavy thud, and I jumped back in surprise.

Kash had been sitting, leaning against my door, and now he lay sprawled on his back, blinking up at me.

"What are you doing?" I asked, my fists resting against my hips in exasperation.

"Guarding you." Kash stretched his hands above his head to cushion his neck not even attempting to get up from the place where he sprawled on the floor.

"From what?" I frowned.

"From the scary one," he said.

Just then, Marco came up the stairs and entered the bedroom across from mine. "Not that one." Kash turned his thumb down the hall as Velora slowed and gave Kash a chilly look before slipping into the room next to Marco's. "That's the scary one."

I couldn't hide the chuckle. "I don't need a bodyguard. I can take care of myself."

He shrugged. "I can't help it. I feel responsible for you." Kash got to his feet and leaned on the doorframe to my room, towering over me. "I'm sorry about what I said earlier. Will you come down and sit by the fire with me?" His breath was warm on my cheeks, and the way his eyes dropped and focused on my lips hinted that it wasn't just talking he wanted to do.

I felt myself moving toward him, wanting to be close, but I stood firm. I didn't trust him—or more likely, I didn't trust *myself* with him. "No, I'm tired. I'm going to go to bed."

"Okay." He nodded, his eyes roaming over my face. The corner of his mouth twitched, and he had a mischievous smile. "Be sure to lock your door . . . or don't," he added, his voice husky as he spoke the last two words.

Before I could fall under his spell, I slammed the door in his handsome face and turned the key in the lock. I could hear his low chuckle, and it made my stomach tie up in knots. The floorboards creaked as he settled in to protect me. My hand reached for the handle to open the door and let him in, but a stray thought changed my mind and made my blood run cold.

Was Kash my protector, or my prison guard?

That night, my sleep was awful. I tossed and turned and punched my pillow a thousand times as I tried to come to terms with my plan. I would follow him, find out his secret, no matter the cost. Even if the answer meant losing him forever.

My heart already mourned his loss when a soft knock at my door brought me out of my sadness.

I slipped out of bed and opened it to see a forlorn expression on Kash's face. His hair looked like he spent the night running his hands through it with worry. There were rings under his eyes, but the apprehension lightened when he saw me.

"Rhea, we need to talk." His voice was soft; pleading. "Each morning I have to—"

"Stop," I interrupted. "I don't want to hear it." I took a deep breath. "I know. . . you're going to leave again. That's fine. I've come to terms that you have another life that doesn't include me. And I decided, I don't want to know what it is. I don't want to know what you do. What happened between us was an accident. Let's never speak of it again." I took a step back from him, already trying to create the distance, as it would emotionally help me disconnect.

Kash stepped inside my room, closing the space between us. "Is that what you want? Or what you *think* you're supposed to say?"

Could he hear my heart racing? My shallow breathing? Could he detect the lies falling from my lips?

"I know you've been lying to me. I just don't know why. And I can't stand liars."

"Is it a lie if I'm forbidden from telling you?" His lips turned down. He raised a hand to brush his knuckles against my cheek. "Is it a lie to say that I am conflicted day and night, with duty verses my heart? That I want to tell you everything, but I'm unable to, knowing that the truth would only drive you further from me? That these last few nights have been the only joy my heart has seen in years?"

As he spoke, the sun rose. The wood floor warmed under my feet. Kash cast a look behind me at the rays and he sighed as if in pain.

"You need to leave," I whispered, knowing he did.

"I do," he groaned, taking a step closer to me. "But I promise I will come back to you. Every night. Just stay here and I will always find you."

I was proud when I didn't hesitate, keeping my eyes locked on his as I nodded. "Okay."

Kash sighed. His relief clear. He leaned forward and brushed his thumb across my lips as if giving them a goodbye kiss. "Till tonight," he promised.

"Till tonight," I lied, giving him a smile that didn't reach my eyes.

Kash seemed to believe me. He gathered his wool cloak and knife from the pile on the floor and headed down the hall. I followed at a distance, stopping at the top of the stairs, and watched as he donned his cloak and left the manor.

As soon as I heard the door close. I grabbed my own packed satchel and cloak and slipped out after him into the storm.

I lost him. I couldn't believe that a trained sorceress like myself lost Kash so easily. I followed the dark shape of his cloak against the white and green backdrop of the woods. But Kash was running, and I couldn't keep up with his longer gait. When he went over a hill and out of sight, I focused on following his footsteps in the deep snow, leading up a narrow path on the side of a mountain . . . until I came to a downed tree.

I studied the green boughs and made a note of depth of the snow covering the tree, or the lack thereof. To the right, the top of the tree hung off a long cliff, and on the left was the mountain. The tree grew sideways out of the dirt wall. Moving toward the roots, I found the spot where the tree was broken and studied the break. The sharp fresh angles in the wood, obvious signs of an axe striking the trunk. Heat broke out along my neck as fear raced up my spine. This wasn't an accident.

Someone brought the tree down on purpose. Did Kash know I was following him?

As quick as my short legs allowed, I crawled over the downed tree that was a mess of broken branches. The wet snow made the climb difficult, and my leg slipped downward across a broken branch. A sting of pain told me I hadn't escaped unscathed. I hissed, pulling my leg up. I could feel the warm trickle of blood flow down my calf to my stocking.

"Don't look," I told myself as I meandered along my backside until I was safely across. Once there, I hobbled and pulled up my skirt to look at the deep gash in my thigh. I took my scarf and wrapped it around the wound, pulling tight and knotting it. I needed to move quick, get out of the storm, for now I was injured and cold.

I followed the path around the mountain. Until the road widened and flattened out. The path diverged and headed into the woods. The longer I traveled, the harder it became to find the road. Every step I took sunk deep into the snow, my leg trickling blood. Two miles seemed like two hundred. I knew I had to be getting close to the guard tower until I spotted a red spot against the white ground.

"Oh, that's not good." It was blood. Next to a small footprint. I stepped backward, scanned the trees, and followed the prints. They were mine. I was walking in circles.

I was lost.

It was too late. Snow had covered the path. I could try a finding spell or a tracking spell, but I needed an object of the person or item I was tracking. Why didn't I have anything of Kash's to track?

It's because he took all his belongings with him every time he left.

The wind picked up to a loud whistle that blasted my ears. One foot in front of the other, I carried on. Searching the skies for a pillar of smoke, a sign, anything that said I was heading toward civilization. Snow stuck to my lashes, and the wind made my eyes tear up, the wetness freezing to my cheeks. My toes were so numb the charms did little to warm them up. I could no longer feel the throbbing of my leg wound. With each breath I took, my lungs rebelled as the frozen air burned in my chest. Worse was the extreme exhaustion that was overtaking me.

I only wanted to sleep, but I knew sleep meant welcoming death.

Must keep going. I needed to find shelter, or the guard tower.

A shadowy figure stepped out of the tree line ahead of me, and my knees trembled as the dreaded bladesman appeared. His breath billowing out in puffs of white clouds. I stilled, hoping that the bladesman didn't see me.

A rumble deep in the ground made me freeze. I kneeled and pressed my hand to the earth, sending my magic into the mountain, searching for the cause.

What I found terrified me. So much *hate*. I'd heard tales of the mountain's anger, but never had I seen it in person. I trembled as I looked up the mountainside, knowing what I would see: the white wall of snow rushing at a frightening speed. Striking down trees and boulders like they were twigs. The avalanche swarmed the mountain, and I turned to run.

The blade saw the same thing I did. He started barreling toward me, and I knew I was doomed. I spun, slipping in the snow, running blindly as fast as my frozen feet could carry me down the mountain.

I screamed as the blade grabbed me by my cloak and tried to lift me into the air. I could hear the rumble as the avalanche roared toward us, and I couldn't decide which was the lesser of the two evils—being captured by the king's bladesman or overtaken by an avalanche.

Making my choice, I swung my arm up into the helm. I kicked and used my arms to push myself away from his body. The cloak ripped in his hands, and I slipped down a steep embankment, slowing myself when I grabbed the root of a tree. The blade stood under a rocky outcropping right above me where he was protected and safe from the oncoming avalanche. I glanced over his shoulder and saw the rush of white. The bladesman kneeled, reaching for my hand. All I had to do was grasp it and he would pull me under the outcropping.

But I stared up at the dark mask and shivered. I gritted

my teeth and prepared myself. Within seconds, the avalanche hit me in the side like a hammer, knocking me over, head over heels. I tumbled in a frozen blanket of snow further down the mountain. The weight slowly crushed me, my breaths becoming shallow, and I let out a last burst of magic and prayed I was strong enough for this one last spell.

CHAPTER EIGHT

Darkness surrounded me. Sweat trickled down my back from the intense heat that enveloped me. In the bleakness, my ears picked up a faint echo. Scratching followed by the deep sound of heavy breathing. Something very large. The seconds between each breath became shorter. The earth rumbled and shook as a blast of fire came rushing out of the darkness toward me. I held up my arms and screamed as the fire consumed me.

Fire burned my skin, blistering where it licked across my body. Then the fire's wrath turned bitter, the burn biting. I was no longer sweating but shivering.

I blinked as I tried to make sense of the very real hallucination I had caused by my current predicament.

A scratching sounded from above again. I barely registered the noise inside my coffin of ice, the last magical barrier I threw around myself to protect me from being crushed to death by the avalanche.

The noise continued to follow a pattern of scraping, shoveling, and then a clink as the shovel hit the ice enclosure.

"What the . . .?" the voice mumbled. "Never saw this before."

Through narrowed eyes, I saw a blur of gold and red through the wall of ice. A lantern drew close, and the light refracted around me, bathing me in a warm glow. I was too cold to move, too cold to even react beyond closing my eyes against the brightness.

A knocking hit the ice. "Hello in there. Are you dead?"

I shivered, my lips struggling to form a word. Any word. "N-no," I stammered.

"I'll get you out."

My rescuer was nothing more than blobs of color that moved through the ice wall. My eyes struggled to focus as I heard a clink followed by a loud crack as the ice broke around me. A cold breeze rushed in, sending goosebumps along my skin, but it was the sweet air that rushed into my lungs that had me almost crying with relief. My spell was not that well thought out. I had created a coffin of ice to protect me, but it had very little in the way of air. I would have suffocated if he hadn't found me. I couldn't break out or use a heat charm, or I would have still been crushed under the snow.

Hands reached in, grasping my arms, pulling me out of the ground. A warm fur was draped across my shoulders, and I tried to stand, but immediately my knees gave way and I stumbled.

A muscular arm grasped me around the waist and the other under my legs lifting me into the air. My head fell back as I looked into dark eyes, my consciousness fading to the sound of his voice.

"I got you. Ol' Molneer's got you."

I awoke, warm, covered in furs, and surrounded by the scent of clove and burning wood. The crackle of a fire and the soft clatter of dishes told me I was in someone's home.

Sitting up, I took stock of the rounded stone walls, the soft braided rugs that covered most of the floor, and the dwarf leaning over the fire. A log shifted in the hearth, and it sent an array of sparks up the stone chimney that disappeared into the ceiling where stalactites clung. We were underground. There were no windows, just large cave openings and a round door.

The dwarf noticed my perusal and watched me from across the room. His narrow eyes disappeared behind dark bushy eyebrows, and his smile was hidden behind his long, braided beard which he scratched as he watched me. I sensed no malice from him, only curiosity.

Molneer gave a little poke with the stick. Black beady eyes appeared within the flames and a hint of a tongue flicked out as Molneer spoke. "Tell Freya she's awake."

The eyes blinked once slowly, before turning in a circle and disappearing into a ball of flame.

A fire salamander. I had heard of them but had never seen one in person. My sister Eden had made friends with one. Of course, I shouldn't have been surprised at their existence so close to the volcano. There were many creatures here that didn't exist in the town of Nihill. I couldn't wait to explore the kingdom and find out more about the differences.

"That was quite the protective spell you cast. Knocked you out for two days straight. Wasn't sure if you were going to wake up or not." He stood, pulling a wooden box from the mantle and retrieved a bone pipe from inside. He preceded to fill the pipe with tinderweed and tamped it down.

"Two days. I've been asleep for two whole days?"

What had transpired during the two days since I'd

been gone? Did Kash realize I was missing? Would he even look for me? Two whole days without a word. Would he even care? What about Marco and Velora?

"Almost did you in, though. Didn't think it through all the way, did you? If I hadn't been alerted to your spell, I might not have found you." Molneer gestured with his elbow to the white ward crystal on the fireplace, similar to the ones we had guarding our house against attacks. His seemed warded for magic. But why would a dwarf need a ward against magic?

"We don't get many like you up here. Once before, long ago, but she hasn't been back in years . . ." he trailed off.

My cheeks flushed with embarrassment, and I wondered if he was referring to my mother.

"Thank you. I didn't know what else to do. I've never dealt with an avalanche before."

The dwarf lit his pipe and took a long draw, releasing puffs of smoke into the air. A sweet smell of cinnamon and herbs filtered across the room toward me. "Won't be your last one either. The mountain has a temper." The dwarf rose and moved to my cot. "But what, may I ask, is your business on this mountain?"

"I'm Rheanon, and I'm a friend of Grimkeep."

"Ah, that's my cousin!" He slapped his knee in excitement.

He extended his hand toward me. "I'm Molneer of the Drikard clan."

Reaching across the white fur blanket, we shook. His hand was smaller, but thick, and could easily crush mine.

Molneer's grasp tightened, and he turned my wrist, reading the calluses on my fingers and the scars on my skin.

"I recognize those burn marks." He dropped my hand, the beard rising to reveal two middle teeth that overlapped slightly in a grin. "You work the forge, do you?"

"I've forged a few charms and weapons. Grimkeep said he would come to meet me in three days, but that was a week ago." My voice filled with worry.

"He hasn't returned yet from within the mountain. Could be gone for days, weeks even."

"Can we go after him?"

Molneer shook his head. "Nay, too dangerous for you. Only he has thick enough skin to withstand the heat and the pressure of the mountain. He should return shortly. But that isn't your concern now." He rubbed the back of his head and looked around his small home, obviously not set up for company. Least of all company of the female kind that may be here for days or weeks on end. "You used a lot of magic on the mountain. It caused quite a stir. Many people noticed."

My cheeks flushed. "Sorry. I didn't mean to."

"Don't feel bad. You did what you needed to do. But the problem now is my hands are tied." Molneer leaned back in his chair and puffed on his pipe. Smoke circled high into the air as he drew on his pipe, his eyes closed in thought. "The king knows you're here," he muttered. "You made that quite obvious with your burst of magic. The entire world felt that. The blades are already searching for you, and they will eventually find you. But I've got a plan, and a good one too. I'm gonna hide you right under the king's nose." He drew on his pipe some more and I had to wave the smoke away. It seemed the more clouded the room became with smoke, the easier it was for him to think.

His eyes opened, and he grinned. "So I've already

figured out the perfect disguise. You need freedom to go where you please but be easily overlooked. Hide in plain sight per se, and I think Grimkeep would be proud of me for thinking of this. I can't hide you in my home forever."

Molneer moved to a cooking pot over the fireplace and drew me a portion of soup. "Here." He handed me a bowl and spoon.

Not realizing how hungry I was, I took a huge spoonful. It was thick, meaty, and seasoned with vegetables that were foreign to me. The flavor was not lacking although it was the spiciest thing I had ever tasted.

"Good hmm?" he nodded, sipping from his own bowl.

My eyes watered. "It's good." I tried to clear my throat before taking a smaller sip.

"It's my mother's recipe. Guaranteed to put hair on your chest."

An unladylike sputtering noise came from my lips as I coughed. "I should hope not." I pounded my chest to keep from choking.

Molneer grinned, his brown eyes twinkling with mischief. "Hairy chests are a prized attribute amongst the dwarves. Even our women have been known to have them."

I couldn't deal with his teasing. I was laughing so hard, I almost spilled the soup.

"Now you know that's a lie if I ever heard one," a harsh reply came from the doorway, interrupting our commune.

Turning, I saw a tall woman, her lips turned downward in a frown, her arched eyebrow displaying how unamusing she thought the comment was. "Unless you're referring to your hairy backside."

Molneer quickly quieted down, her stern chastisement enough to bring him in line.

The woman's faded blonde hair, peaked out from under a white lace cap. A white apron covered her deep red servant's dress.

"Ah Freya, my love. You got my message."

Freya sniffed and shifted her weight, giving Molneer her back. "I'm neither your love nor a dog that you can summon."

"But you came, that counts for something." Molneer moved into her view and wiggled his bushy eyebrows at her. His obvious attempts to woo Freya were falling on deaf ears.

"Not for you," she huffed. "I came because I needed to check her leg wound." Freya turned to give me her attention. "Are you feeling better?" she asked hopefully. "I'm Freya, the one who bandaged your leg."

I reached for the wound and was surprised that there was only minor pain. I stood, placing weight on my leg, and felt nothing. "It is, thank you. I'm Rhea."

One eyebrow arched. "Rhea—?" she dragged it out, waiting for me to fill in my last name.

"Just Rhea."

Freya's eyebrow dropped, and she nodded. She took quick stock of the situation, glancing around the room for my belongings.

"Is this all she has?" Freya picked up my satchel.

"It is," I answered.

Her lips pressed together in maternal warning. "It's a good thing you came when you did. We are a bit short staffed at the moment."

Molneer was already slipping his coat on to head back

into the storm. He pulled a red stocking hat low over his ears and called over his shoulder as he opened the door. "Take care, my dear."

"Not your dear!" Freya snapped back, but Molneer was gone. The door slamming closed behind him.

"Grrr, *that* dwarf is so infuriating." She stomped her foot in anger before smoothing back her hair. She blinked a few times before remembering where she was. "Oh, come along."

Folding the fur on the cot and placing the empty bowl of soup on the table, I followed Freya out the door, surprised when I was met by more stone halls lit by torches. The air was warm, almost humid despite being underground.

Freya turned left out of Molneer's home and headed up a tunnel that almost immediately forked, and she took the right path. There was an old mining cart with a switch. Freya got inside and gestured for me to do the same.

"Where are we?" I asked, settling in, and holding onto the edge of the cart.

Freya released the brake, and we started along the track. "Below the castle in the old mines."

"But I thought Molneer said that we couldn't go into the mountain."

"We're not in the mountain. Not really. More like the sub level chambers of the palace. This is home to the salamander breeding dens, and where we keep our coal reserves. On the coldest of nights, we need more than just the salamanders." The cart came to a platform, and we slowed to a stop inside a metal cage. Freya put on the brake and reached for a second lever on the platform. The cart rumbled and rose in the air by a mechanical system.

"This is amazing!" I leaned over to look at the machine that was climbing up a shaft higher into the mountain.

Freya didn't seem overly impressed. "It's just our coal cart system. I wouldn't even be in them, but it's the fastest way to reach Molneer's home. Dirty little dwarf can't take a room in the palace like the rest of us. He still wants to live underground." She shuddered. "The dwarves are the only ones who dare tread deeper into the lower levels of the mountain."

"Why is that?" I asked.

"It's dangerous, and we don't dare wake what sleeps within."

"What is it?"

Freya turned slowly to gaze at me. "A demon," she warned.

"What kind of demon?" I asked, testing the waters.

Freya blinked in surprise. "Stars, you are the strange one. Most girls would have shuddered in fear or mocked a fainting. You seem almost eager."

Dropping my gaze, I closed my mouth and pretended to be chastised. After the platform locked into place, she opened the cage door and we stepped out into a furnace room that was as hot as a sauna.

Sweat formed on my neck as we quickly exited, passing by shirtless hobs who were shoveling coal into the furnace. Giant copper boilers filled the room with pipes that ran up the walls and into the upper floors of the palace.

The hobs were different from our garden hob, Sneeze-wort. These hobs were muscled with brown skin that was dry and cracked from the heat. They tied their long ears back out of their face, and their noses were black from coal dust. I would have felt sorry for the creatures, except on the other side of the furnace room, there was a natural hot spring and a few of the hobs were swimming in the water. Others were laid out with a towel over their heads, enjoying the heat from the furnace. Just like the garden hobs preferred life outdoors, mountain hobs preferred heat. This was probably a wonderful life for them.

Freya caught my curious staring as we passed by a group of roughhousing hobs. One dunked another under the water. "We still use salamanders for heating our rooms and cooking fires, but nothing beats having instant hot water."

I agreed and followed her up a flight of stairs to a wooden door.

"Here we are." Freya pushed open the door and stepped into a wide-open hallway. The hall we were in happened to be near the kitchen. I could smell the bread baking in the ovens, and the hint of spices simmering. I closed my eyes and took a deep breath, trying to identify the exotic scents. Cardamom, curry, and cinnamon. The three Cs of exquisite cuisine.

"Let's go. I'll show you to your quarters and get you settled in."

As I followed behind Freya, I had the first chance to take in my surroundings. Because the castle was built into the mountain, the western side of the castle's light came from high windows or glass-paned ceilings, whereas the eastern side was filled with floor to ceiling verandas that were open to the fresh air. I hoped that wherever I stayed that I would have an open window.

I was wrong.

The servant's hall was tucked away in a windowless

tower. Light streamed through well-placed skylights and a series of mirrors that needed to be changed throughout the day to reflect to the lower levels. She entered a room on the third floor, which held two small trundle beds, each with a trunk for belongings. The other bed had a large lump covered with a red quilt. My keen eyes picked up the candle that was recently extinguished.

Freya pointed to nearest empty bed, and a trunk that was missing a lock.

"Store your belongings here, then we will see about getting you set with a job. What are your talents?"

I wanted to say 'everyday curses and alchemy,' but it would've revealed too much about my past. "I can cook. Clean. Mend."

Freya had moved to the bed and swatted the large lump.

A squeal of surprise came from the quilt and a young girl sat straight up in bed. A book slid out from under the cover and thumped on the floor.

"Laziness will not be rewarded, Gail. Stop reading and get Rhea here some work clothes."

Gail was a skinny, freckled girl with the most intense green eyes and auburn hair.

"If you weren't my niece, I'd have you whipped," Freya chided.

"Yes, Auntie." Gail flung the blanket off her lap and quickly smoothed out her hair.

"Don't call me Auntie," Freya snapped.

The door slammed as Freya left and Gail gave a little jump in surprise. She turned, giving me an impish smile.

I picked up the book from the floor handing it back, but not before taking a gander at the title. I smirked, as it was a book of love poems. Gail snatched the book out of my hands and tucked it under her pillow.

"That's private."

"Sorry," I said.

She cocked her head, looked me up and down. "Well, it's a good thing you came because we could use all the help we can get right now." She turned, beckoning me to follow her out the door.

"Freya said you were short staffed."

"We are, but that's because the servants keep disappearing." We headed down the steps, turning into a hallway.

"Where'd they go?"

Gail shrugged like it was no big deal. "It's hard work, working in the palace." She pushed open a door that led into a laundry room. The scent of lye burned my nose. Women worked tirelessly washing clothes in stone basins large enough to bathe ten people. Large copper pipes ran across the ceiling, supplying hot water from the furnace room we had just visited. We skirted the women washing the clothes and made our way toward the back, where the clothes were drying on long wooden racks near open windows.

"Did they run off?" I asked.

A second shrug followed as Gail went to a long wooden table filled with paper and ink and rapped her knuckles on it. A shrew of a woman with glasses blinked blindly at Gail, then turned her graying eyes on me.

"Hey Mabs, we need a set of sleep clothes, work clothes and two sets of undergarments."

Heat rose to my cheeks, but in the heat of the laundry room, it went unnoticed.

Mabs backed into a closet and returned with stacks of black clothes and one red dress. The red was depressing. Holding it up, it was very similar to what Gail was wearing. A high neck dress with buttons along the collar.

"Sign here." Mab's voice was very low and gruff for someone her size. "The clothes will come out of your first month's pay."

"A month? I don't plan on being here that long." The blank stare I received from Mabs was enough to tell me my pleas were falling on deaf ears.

"Not my problem," Mabs said before muttering under her breath.

"Fine," I sighed, grabbing them from the table.

Gail watched the exchange but wisely said nothing as I looked at the receipt for the work clothes I signed for. "I feel like I was just robbed," I muttered sadly. The cost of the clothes was exorbitant.

"That's the way it is here in Kiln. Everything costs money, and if you don't have money, you're lower than dirt."

"That's not just Kiln," I murmured. "That's everywhere."

"No, nothing is like it is here. Come on, let's get you dressed."

CHAPTER NINE

I hated the clothes with every fiber of my being. The high collar dress buttoned up my neck and felt like hands choking my throat every time I took a breath. The sleeves were short, and the high waist skirt flared out to give movement for my legs. The trim was heavy with hand-stitched gold threading, and I understood it to be the reasoning behind the complex price for the dress.

I had plaited my honey brown hair into two braids and then wrapped them into a figure eight at the base of my neck. When I stood next to the other maids, I couldn't help but compare it to a bow.

We passed through the kitchen, and each took a piece of fruit and a hot pocket of croissant bread filled with minced meat. We ate as we walked, and I greedily licked every drop off my fingers. Even though I'd already eaten breakfast, my stomach was making up for lost meals.

As we walked the halls, I couldn't help but feel like an interloper and I kept playing with the seam of my skirt.

"Stop fidgeting." Gail's soft-spoken warning made any comfort I felt disappear.

I stood straight, my back stiff as we headed to our first task of the morning.

"What was that?" I asked.

"Quiet," she shushed.

"Is it another earthquake?" I asked again.

Her silence was my answer.

The throne room doors slammed open, and a tall man dressed in a black velvet doublet trimmed with gold and wearing a banded crown stormed out, turning toward the servants. Gail stepped back, her posture fearful, eyes downcast. Behind the king were two black knights. One was a giant. The armor almost couldn't contain his broad shoulders. His dark, unreflective helmet resembled a lion's head. A faceplate with lion teeth frozen in a roar covered his mouth, leaving only slits for his eyes. On his back, he carried a gold broadsword. The second black-armored knight was almost as tall, but slender. His helmet was that of a hawk, the plates of armor resembling feathers. At his hip hung a gold rapier.

Being new, I didn't retreat with the other servants, but stood perplexed, right in the path of the oncoming king and the two bodyguards.

King Goddrick of Kiln. He stormed up to me and halted, scowling at me for not having moved. But now I was frozen, not out of fear, but awe as I took in the lines of his face, the angry tic in his jaw that stressed the tanned cheeks up into his murky eyes. His hair was so dark it looked black in the daylight. And all the fire was directed at me—an inconvenience that blocked his way.

"Your Maj—" I curtseyed. I saw a glint of gold as a blade was drawn and I looked up as the large, armored giant stood in front of me. With the sword at my neck, he was glaring at me, daring me to finish what I was saying. I could feel the hum, the vibrancy of magic, and I reached up to touch the blade.

Instead, a heavy boot kicked me in the shoulder. I fell backward and stared up at the ceiling as two blades crossed my neck, the thicker sword and the rapier.

The two knights turned toward the king, awaiting his order, when a rumble started low in the ground. The candles in the candelabra rattled, and I looked up fearfully toward the glass ceiling. A cry of distress sounded from Gail. Dust fell from the buttresses falling like glittering snow. The swords withdrew from my neck as the men turned to protect the king. Shields were raised over his head and no one paid attention to the poor servant girl.

Gail darted forward, grabbed my elbow, and roughly helped me to my feet so we could escape around the corner during the commotion. As the earth continued to shake, more shouting followed, and a painting fell off the wall. Gail didn't release me or slow her pace until we had done enough twists and turns that I was lost.

We stopped somewhere near the kitchen.

"What were you thinking? No one addresses the king without an invitation," she gasped, clutching her side.

"Why's that bad?"

Gail frowned. "It's just a rule. One that can't be broken for fear of death. The king's blades would have silenced you for good if not for the quake." She spun on her heel and snapped at me. "Don't get in their way and you'll be fine."

"Who are they exactly?" I asked.

Gail called out to a passing servant boy. "Hey Mouse, can you explain this to her while I die from the stitch in my side?" Gail groaned and clutched her abdomen.

"Yes, Miss." The servant, a willowy boy with saucer-like eyes and a mop of red hair, cleared his throat and recited from memory. "The king's power comes from his three blades. His right hand is strength, strong to take down many enemies. In his left is wisdom, whose strikes are quick and sure. And then there's his silent blade called death. You never see death's strike until it's too late."

"Nice speech," I said, still just as confused.

Gail having regained her breath, rolled her eyes at me. "You met his right and left blade. I don't know if you could survive a meeting with the silent blade."

"Is he the one with the dragon helm?"

Gail's face paled, and she nodded. "He's terrifying."

"I have actually crossed him and survived . . . twice." I held up two fingers.

"I wouldn't count on being lucky a third time."

Gail taught me a lesson in humility by assigning me grunt work.

I spent the rest of the day on my knees scrubbing floors, watching the coming and goings of the soldiers, trying to learn their routines. My back ached and my palms were sore from holding the wirehaired brush and scrubbing the tiles.

Molneer was right. No one paid attention to a maid scrubbing the floor. Higher-ranking officials would speak openly, and I listened in as they deemed me beneath their notice.

"The king must work harder to appease the mountain," an advisor named Jarvis murmured to his confidant. His jacket bore a gold star. "Or there may not be a kingdom left."

His friend slowed and tugged on his sleeves. "The king is doing everything he can."

"Is he? I feel like he isn't trying hard enough. The earthquakes are becoming more frequent. They're almost daily. The towns are terrified, the mountain could explode any minute, and the dwarves have all but disappeared to the outer guilds. You know what that means?"

"No, we know nothing. The dwarves that settled here are not from the same guild that was destroyed a century ago. We can't blame them." Able shook his head. He was dressed in similar clothes to Jarvis, but his gold pin was a diamond shape.

I had to assume the symbols had meaning or ranks.

"Or they have left us because they know they can't save the kingdom. It will not be enough. I can feel it in my bones. This will be the end of Kiln and King Goddrick's reign," Jarvis said disparagingly.

Able frowned. "Stop it. Don't let any of the blades hear you talk like that, or you'll end up with a knife through your gut. It is not safe to cross the king during these trying times."

A trumpet pealed, and the men looked toward the nearest window and hurried off. I sat up and watched them leave. I wanted to follow and find out what was going on.

"What are you doing here?" Freya said, interrupting my thoughts. "Didn't you hear the trumpet? The king has called all of us to the courtyard for an announcement."

Freya took my bucket and frowned at my red knees before ushering me out with the rest of the palace staff to the courtyard.

As soon as we stepped outside, the sunlight blinded

me, and I had to cover my eyes to keep them from hurting. When my vision slowly adjusted, I saw that we were assembled according to our stations. All the palace staff in red were at the back of the courtyard and to the side. The troops were lined up in formation, facing the palace and the balcony. In the middle of the courtyard were an assemblage of fifty men and women.

The sun was directly overhead, and I could turn to look over the ramparts down the snow-covered mountain.

To the south side of the courtyard was the main gate and coming through it was row after row of soldiers. The soldiers in the middle of the courtyard parted ways and opened their ranks to their brethren.

At the head of the army, a knight in black armor drew my attention. It was the dragon blade. So he had survived the avalanche. He motioned with his hand and an enclosed carriage drove up. A servant boy ran and opened the transport door. A young familiar woman stepped out, her lavender hair a mess, her eyes filled with rage.

"Velora," I breathed out. The blade had captured Velora.

My jaw hurt from grinding my teeth together, and I knew I hated the dragon with every fiber of my being. During the whole exchange, I couldn't pull my eyes away from the man in black and I'd missed King Goddrick's entrance.

"Ah, my sharpest blade. You've returned with another bounty," the king called down to his man.

Under the rays of the sun, the armor shimmered, and that's when I noticed the plates upon the armor. The hammer marks and the way it was forged made it look like dragon scales. In the light of day, the horns of the helmet and the cut of the eyes in the helm made it very identifiable as an exotic dragon.

The third blade slipped off his horse and kneeled before the king.

The king wrung his hands together greedily before addressing those gathered before him. "Here ye, all citizens of Kiln. You have been summoned here by my order, for your kingdom needs you. You're here because there's a rumor that you have a certain magical talent or bloodline. Many of you came because of my summons and the chance to be handsomely rewarded. While many refused my commands, a greater physical action was needed to convince you of your duty and for that I regret."

A growing sense of unease swept up from the gathered guests, as a few called out in discontent. "I'm merely a healer, nothing more. Why am I here?"

"I was about to be married," a woman cried out. "I missed my wedding night."

"Silence," the king roared in anger. "More should have been demanded for disobeying a direct order from your king, but I am magnanimous in my rule. You all shall be compensated for as long as you use your talent and magic for the good of the kingdom. If you do so, you will be handsomely rewarded."

"What kind of reward?" A man with an eye patch and furred hat yelled up. I could tell he came for the money.

"We've all felt the mountain's temper over the last few years. We have done extensive studies of the prophecies and believe we have the solution to bring our kingdom prosperity and peace. A century ago, a dwarf stole all our kingdom's treasures and buried it beneath the mountain. I want that treasure back."

"I've been searching the tunnels for years," a man covered in coal dust called out. "And I've barely found any gold, much less a hoard."

"Which is why I've brought you together. I believe that to appease the mountain, we need gold. Lots and lots of gold. And I don't intend to scavenge the mountain anymore. I believe we can create gold. When our coffers are rightfully full again, the mountain will be appeased."

The women huddled together, looking confused.

The king was rubbing a ring on his finger as he spoke. "There has been an account of a woman who turned a tin cup into gold in the town of Verdan. I'm hoping that one or more of you can do the same."

A woman with dark black hair stepped forward. She curtseyed and then called up, "Your Majesty, it seems someone is spinning tales. For I know of no such woman in all of Verdan with that kind of power. Now a healer, or a hedge witch we have plenty."

"Silence!" The king's glare was cold, and the woman shuffled quickly back to her place in the crowd. "My blade has confirmed this talent, and do any of you doubt the sharpness of my blade?"

The air was filled with suspense as the blade stood next to the king's side.

The king smiled. "Fear not, I suspect that there may be more than one among you with this so-called power. So I've put together all of my resources at your disposal to fill my coffers with gold. If you so choose, you can leave right now and return to your poor desolate homes and village. The gate is open. No one is stopping you." The king pointed to the open entrance. "Or you take your chances and try your hand and walk away with more riches and more power than you've ever imagined. Choose now!"

He waited.

As expected, no one immediately left. Velora, who stuck out from the crowd with her unique colored hair, didn't budge. Did she not understand what was happening? Or did she?

The miner and a husky man with the eye patch both stayed. They watched the crowd, and I knew that they probably didn't have a lick of magic at their disposal. A woman with a toffee-colored braid took three steps toward the gate and paused.

"Go on," I breathed, encouraging her to leave. She looked at the gate and the snow-covered road beyond. I could imagine her debating returning to her family empty-handed. Her head swung back around to look up at the castle and all that it offered. She bit her lip in indecisiveness.

She spoke up loudly. "At home, I have four younger brothers and we struggle to survive the winters from lack of food. But I hunger for something more . . . something grander. It's my chance to choose. Even if I'm not the strongest at magic, I can't let this opportunity pass me by." The woman turned and came back to stand among the candidates. Her confession made a few of those that were heading for the gate pause.

No. Leave. Now's your chance.

One by one, those that *had* left turned around to join the others waiting in the courtyard. Not a single person exited the gate, and I sighed in frustration.

"Excellent," the king smiled. A smile that made me shudder. "Come, enjoy a banquet we have prepared in your honor. Soon there will be the final selection of those who continue on."

"Selection? Do you mean we can't all stay?" the man with the eye patch raised his hand. "I thought you said you would supply us with unlimited resources." He fidgeted with his pocket, and I noticed how oversized his clothes were. A thief, bent on pocketing those resources for himself.

"I know that many are here under false pretenses. Those will be weeded out soon."

I caught a sly look between a few of the women and the men.

As more instructions were given, I couldn't help but glare at the king and the dragon blade. As the men and women were ushered inside by the guards. I rushed forth to try to follow them and speak with Velora, but Freya grabbed my elbow.

"No, you have other work to do."

"More scrubbing floors?" I sighed.

Freya smirked. "Do you see all these guests? Someone is going to have to prepare food and feed them. Gail!" Freya called over my shoulder.

"Yes, Auntie?" Gail came up behind me.

"*Don't* call me Auntie. You'll be needed in the kitchen for the rest of the day," Freya ordered.

Gail groaned and flopped her arms to her side dramatically.

The kitchen is not where I wanted to be. I preferred to be out in the halls where I could spy and learn more about these women. Hiding my disappointment, I followed her into the castle and down a winding staircase that brought us to a lower level and into the hustle and bustle of a full working kitchen.

As soon as I stepped into it, the humidity was intense. More pipes ran up the walls, bringing hot water to the sinks. The kitchen was five times bigger than the manor house and it surprised me to see a fire salamander living in the coals of each of the fireplaces and ovens. When I walked past the first one, black eyes blinked at me and the salamander got up, circled, and then got into a better position to sleep.

The kitchen servants' outfits were different from mine and Gail's. Theirs had no sleeves, and they either had cotton pants that hit above the knee or a skirt. Both men and women alike wore white sashes around their head and hair to keep the sweat from pouring into their eyes.

I looked at their outfits longingly but didn't have much time as the head kitchen chef pushed me toward a basin of hot water and soap for washing the pots and pans. Inwardly, I groaned at the thought of more scrubbing. But again, the sweltering kitchen was a wealth of information.

For some of the staff, knew the histories behind a few of the people in the courtyard. As I scrubbed, I listened to the tales of these men and women. Annette was a seeker, her talent was finding things that were lost, and was called upon more than once to find lost children during a snowstorm. Brenna was a healer; it was said she could sew you up and you couldn't feel the stitches. Shannon was the animal whisperer, for she could hear their thoughts.

All natural born talents. As I picked up a cup to scrub it, I heard a high ringing, and I dropped it back into the water.

What was that?

Searching the sink, I continued to run my hands over every cup until I found it again. Lifting the silver cup out of the water, I studied it as the suds ran down the sides and onto my arm.

The cup *sang*. A perfect note that only I seemed to hear. Moments passed, and I realized it wasn't the cup, but the ore it was created out of that was ringing—and it wasn't alone. I reached under the collar of my dress for the charm on my necklace. I pulled the stone up and put them together. They sang in harmony.

My lucky charm was made from the same material as the cup. I abandoned the dishes and searched the kitchen for another like it, but it was the only one. And it seemed like I was the only one who could hear the ore sing.

"Stop daydreaming. Come on," Gail pulled me away from the suds and over to a cupboard. She took off her kitchen apron and grabbed a strip of red silk which she tied around her face, leaving only her eyes visible. "Your turn."

"What are we doing?" I asked, tying a silk on, and copying her. She handed me a pair of silk slippers, which I put on as she tucked my work boots into a cubby.

Gail headed up another set of stairs that ended behind the main dining hall. "I told you, we're short on help. We have to serve as well. Just remember to never, ever look anyone in the eyes. Don't speak. Grab that tray and let's go."

She pointed to a chute that had been raised from the kitchen below, filled with food. I picked up a golden cloche and followed Gail as she paused outside the doors. "Soft, elegant, and whatever you do, don't make a fool of yourself."

"But I'm none of those things," I hissed, staring in awe

at the banquet room that was a glittering candlelit cave. The ceiling was sixty feet high with golden chandeliers suspended from stalactites in the ceiling. Two long banquet tables ran the length of the cave, with more candelabras placed every few feet. Their flames flickered, casting a warm glow over the red tablecloths and the crowd that had gathered here for the test. On the far end of the cave was the head table on a raised dais with six chairs across for the king and his honored guests.

"Ready?" Gail whispered. "Follow me."

As soon as Gail stepped into the banquet room, her demeanor changed. Her footsteps became light, her body swayed as she moved like a dancer. My mouth dropped open as one of the other servants walked just as softly as her. When they placed the cloche down in front of a female guest, they removed the lid with a flourish, revealing the appetizing food.

I tried to mimic Gail. I thought graceful thoughts as I placed my cloche down in front of the man with the eye patch. Sure enough, I saw him slipping the silverware into his vest pocket. I was just about to raise the lid when I noticed the woman seated across from the thief.

Velora.

She looked bored as she stared around the room, rapping her fingernails along the table. Seeing her so suddenly made me falter, and the cloche clattered loudly against the thief's plate. All eyes fell on me, and I quickly glanced over at Gail, whose face paled. She swept her gaze to the head table. The king didn't notice, for he was in a heated discussion with Advisor Jarvis and Counselor Able. From the sounds that filtered down the hall, they were not in agreement with the king's decision to fill his coffers. They thought his focus should be on the earthquakes.

The king rubbed his hands together, and he shot them a dark look. I shuddered.

Gail waved for me to follow her back into the hall and I did, thankful that the king didn't notice my blunder.

"What's wrong with you?" she hissed.

"Sorry, it just slipped out of my hand."

My mouth went dry as I thought of Marco and Kash. I couldn't see either of them willingly letting Velora leave the manor to come to the palace. Did that mean that they were injured . . . or worse? I quickly turned and grabbed another tray and headed back into the room.

"What are you doing? You're going to screw up again."

"I can do it," I snapped and made a beeline right to Velora's side of the table. She was still disinterested in her surroundings, and when I set the cloche down in front of her, I whispered, "Velora . . .it's me."

She turned to look at me. Her eyes squinted as she tried to make out who I was behind the red veil.

"I don't know you."

"Shh," I whispered. "It's me Rhea."

"Who?"

"Maeve's sister?" I waited for the recognition, then realized I had only met her for a few minutes, likely not leaving a lasting impression.

Velora looked at me blankly, but I was running out of time. I made a sweeping gesture and lifted the cloche, revealing pork and vegetables.

Velora frowned.

"How did you get here?" I asked.

"A man in black armor came. They had swords and lots of horses."

Immediately, I knew who she was talking about. The bladesman.

"Marco fought them. But he lost, and now I'm here. They hurt him." She looked up at me and I saw her eyes fill with unshed tears. "He was bleeding. There was so much blood."

"What about"—my stomach knotted as I prepared to say his name—"Kash?"

Her shoulders fell and so did the tears. "Kash is . . . gone."

The floor moved under me. I grasped the table to keep from fainting, startling the woman next to me. Kash was dead.

I felt a hand grab my elbow and tried to pull me from the room.

Kash was gone. My heart was breaking, and I could feel the grief well up in me and overflow. The ground beneath my feet rattled, the gold goblets on the table shook, and the girls screamed. This time I screamed with them, but it wasn't one of fear. It was one of anguish.

Once I was away from the room, Gail released my arm and I fell to the floor and cried, rocking myself until the waves of grief lessened and when it did, the mountain stopped rumbling.

CHAPTER TEN

Kash was dead.

From the very first time I saw him—as he pinned me down in the sitting room after I tried to hit him with a book—I was attracted to him. I tried to fight it. It was a young love. Stupid to grieve over. Mother would be ashamed, but there was something about Kash. His humor and wit, and confidence easily tore through my defenses. And now I was angry. Angry at the man in black armor for killing Kash. Angry at the king for his stupid summons. And I was no closer to figuring out the problem in Kiln.

I lay in bed staring at the stone ceiling, knowing that was how my heart felt. Stone cold and numb. Gail slept in the bed next to mine. Her soft snores filled the room, and I tried to block them out. After my emotional meltdown and the palace stopped shaking, the dinner was cut short, and they sent us to our room.

Pulling the pillow over my head, I drowned out her noise, but it couldn't drown out the hollow sour feeling in my stomach.

It wasn't fair. I sat up and stared at the locked door, frustrated that Freya had followed all the servants to their rooms and then locked them in for the night. *Who does that? Why would they need to do that?*

I slipped out of my bed, my hair cascading down my back, being careful not to make any noise as I slipped my feet into my shoes. I arranged my pillow and spare clothes to look like my sleeping body and covered it with the quilt. I didn't want Gail to raise the alarm or get upset if she awoke in the middle of the night to find an empty bed and a locked door.

Lochen.

The door clicked and whispered open. Since I knew everyone else was locked in theirs, I wasn't worried about making noise as I headed down the stairs.

As I passed a marble column, I saw a light coming toward me from another hallway. I ducked behind a pillar and held my breath as three palace guards came around the corner, escorting the thief with the eye patch.

"I did nothing wrong," the man said and struggled against his guards, his pockets bulging with stolen goods. He freed one arm, and a gold dish fell out of his jacket and clattered along the floor.

"Stealing is a crime, punishable by jail," the captain of the guard stated, his voice void of feeling.

Freya stepped out of the hall and cut the captain and his guards off on their way to the cells. "Captain Adams, I have a suggestion for an alternate punishment for him."

"What punishment is that, Madam Freya?" the captain asked.

"I have it on good authority that Molneer is looking for more help in the mines."

The captain's stony face cracked a smile. "Is that so?

Already? I thought that they had sent help down just yesterday."

"And that help didn't work out so well," she responded, lowering her voice. "In fact, none of the workers are lasting very long, and he is requesting more daily."

"Wait, hard labor? No, I'll give it back. Throw me in a cell. I don't want to go to the mines. No one ever returns," the thief begged. He even pulled back the fake eyepatch to reveal two healthy, normal eyes. "I'll even give up the ruse, the fake begging too."

"There's nothing to worry about," Captain Adams said. "You can serve your time in the mine."

The thief dragged his feet along the ground, kicking and screaming as the captain and his guard took him toward the furnace room that lead underground. "N-no!" the thief cried.

I felt a moment of sadness, but I knew better than to interfere in business that didn't deal with me.

Freya watched them go, and a slight smile pulled on her lips.

When Freya left and the hall was silent, I slipped out of my hiding spot and pondered over what I'd witnessed. I didn't know that Molneer was working the mines. I'd been so lost in my thoughts that I got turned around and had missed the stairs toward the servants' tower.

"Why is a servant sneaking around in the middle of the night?" A deep voice said from the shadows. "Did you forget the rules?"

I spun, my heart having jumped into my throat. I searched the dark hallway as a tall shape moved away from the wall and stood in front of the window. The light cast by the moon illuminated the striking face of the stranger. He ran his hands through his long brown hair, and his green eyes narrowed.

My mouth went dry. "Rules?"

"No one may roam the halls of the palace after dark."

"You're roaming the halls?" I pointed out.

He grinned. "But then again, those rules don't apply to me."

I raised my chin toward the light. "Why are we not allowed to be out at night?" I asked softly.

The man studied my face. "Because it's not safe. It's said that if you go out after dark, be prepared to have your heart stolen."

Finally, an answer why all the servants were locked in their rooms. "Is it an onwae?" I asked.

This surprised the man, for he barked out a laugh. "No, it's not an onwae."

Thoroughly invested, I tapped my finger to my lips and thought out loud. "Well, it could be a werewolf."

He leaned his shoulder against the wall and watched me with amusement as I pondered the predicament out loud. "Definitely not a werewolf, but avoid the light," he added.

"Vampire," I stated, feeling assured of my guess.

A surprised snort came from the man. "Those aren't usually in our realm. All right. I admit. It's me, I'm the stealer of hearts and I do it with my charm. But I am a bit out of practice. My name's Damon." He offered me his hand, and I shook it. Taking in the massive muscles that ran up his arms. I looked like a child compared to him.

"And you are?" Damon pressed.

My heart ached, and I felt tears well in my eyes. His

confident teasing reminded me of Kash's. I couldn't speak for fear of crying.

"Is something the matter?" Damon's smile fell, and he became the epitome of politeness. "Was it something I said? I'm sorry, I don't get to converse with many women. It's my fault that I've made you uncomfortable."

I stepped away from the handsome stranger, giving him a wide berth as I headed toward the servants' quarters. "Excuse me, I must go." I turned back and as soon as I rounded the corner, I ran.

"I'm sorry, you must let me make it up to you."

I had already slipped from the room and was rushing toward the servants' hall. I took the stairs two at a time and stopped on my floor, grabbing the door and pulling, forgetting that it was locked.

"Lochen!" I unlocked the door without thinking and entered a room that was unfamiliar and already occupied.

Two girls slept in a room that was laid out like mine and Gail's. The closest redheaded girl was tossing and turning, while the brunette had her leg hanging out over the edge of the bed.

Behind me, I could hear heavy footsteps as someone was coming up the stairs.

"What are you doing here? How did you get in?" The redheaded girl woke up and was sitting up in bed staring at me in confusion.

I tried to motion to her to keep quiet, but she heard the sounds on the stairs as soon as I did.

"What is that?" she said loudly.

"Hush!"

I moved to her side and brushed my finger across her forehead. *"Somnus."*

Her eyes fluttered, and she fell back onto her pillow in a deep sleep. With a quick spell, I resealed the lock, just as someone tried the handle.

"It's locked."

"Course it is. They're all locked from the outside. Only the matron has the key."

"Why would the matron lock the girls inside at night?" Damon's deep voice carried through the door.

"Maybe to save them from seeing your ugly mug," the higher voice teased, before dropping in tone. "But really, Damon. You know why. It's keeping everyone safe."

"Everyone?" Damon said, incredulously.

"No," he sighed regretfully. "Just us. Are you sure she was a servant?"

"I don't know Spencer. Something was wrong. She looked like she was hurting."

"Uh oh, there you go, trying to save the damsel in distress again. You can't save everyone, Damon. We're not like others. We're not good."

"No, but we can try."

I waited until their heavy footsteps faded away.

With a sigh, I slipped out and took the stairs to the next floor up and found the correct door to my room.

CHAPTER ELEVEN

The next morning, I couldn't control the yawns that plagued me as I struggled to get dressed.

"Are you okay?" Gail added after my tenth yawn.

"I'm okay," I murmured through another. "I didn't get much sleep last night."

"It's always hard to sleep the first week at the palace," Gail answered. "And now with these extra people here for the summons, it's going to be more work."

I nodded but could feel my eyes wanting to close. I dared not share with her my night escapades, knowing she would disapprove of my snooping around. We headed down the stairs and paused near an open door. There seemed to be a commotion inside the room where I had sought refuge last night.

Gail had stopped and whispered with a few of the other servant girls, and she came back to me, a look of worry on her face.

"What's the matter?" I asked.

"Morgan is gone." She kept her head down and beckoned for me to follow. "Sara said she woke up and her bed was empty."

As we walked past the room, I looked in to see the girl I had spelled to sleep was the one missing. Her roommate was still sitting on her bed, her face full of confusion.

My heart raced, and I felt faint as I tried to recall my steps last night after I left. I was in such a hurry to make it to my own room. I didn't relock her door. *Was this my fault? Had I removed the only lock that kept the girls safe at night.* Not only that, but I spelled her to sleep, making her the perfect compliant victim.

"What do they think happened?" I asked, feeling sick to my stomach with guilt.

"They don't know." Gail picked up her pace, and I followed her down the hall to a wing I was unfamiliar with. "But it happens. Maybe she met someone? Better not to question why people leave. It only causes trouble."

"Maybe it was Damon," I muttered.

"A demon?" she gasped, mishearing me. "Where did you hear such nonsense?"

We went through the kitchen to grab our portioned-out breakfast pastry before heading to our morning assignments.

"What do *you* think happened to Morgan?" I took a bite of my pastry and chewed.

Gail was getting frustrated with my questions. "Look, new girl, stop asking so many annoying questions. Morgan ran away. End of story. You've only been here one day, and I doubt you'll be here two weeks tops." Gail handed me a feather duster and stormed into a room.

I went to follow her, but she pointed to the other side. "Stay over there. I want to think in peace."

We were in a beautiful round library whose shelves

were made of stone and chiseled out of the earth itself. Where one would expect it to be rugged, the shelves were smooth like glass. Lanterns hung from stalactites that contained a soft, glowing moss. Some lanterns were on pulleys that could be raised or lowered depending on how much light the reader wanted. In the center of the room was a large round table filled with more candles and stacked high with books. One could walk in circles among the many rows. It reminded me of a nautilus shell.

As I turned, my foot brushed a book on the floor. I bent down, picked up the book, dusting off the cover as a loud rattle came from behind. I turned to see a bladesman rush toward me, the rapier slid from his sheath and raised to strike me. I dropped the book on the table and retreated safely to the other side, keeping the table between us.

The bladesman's head twitched, and I could feel the darkness pouring out of his gaze. The rapier in his hand was steady, the tip following me like the needle of a compass as I moved around the table.

"The book is there," I breathed out. "I just picked it up from the floor."

The bladesman took a step toward me, the metal gleaming in the light.

Unreadable. That was the word that came to mind as I tried to read the face of the man behind the hawk mask. The helm hid his face and all emotions, but there was something else obscuring his eyes, like a black cloud.

I couldn't fathom what I had done to merit being sliced and diced.

Across the room, Gail's face was pale as the moon. She clung to a bookshelf for support and her lips quivered in terror.

"I was going to return it to the shelf, that's all," I said calmly.

Gail shook her head so hard I could almost hear her teeth rattle in her jaw.

I reached for the book again, and the blade sliced across the table fast. A sting followed. I jumped as a bright red line marred the top of my hand. His skill with the sword so fast, I didn't have time to react, and now a smear of blood dropped onto the book.

"How dare you!" I fumed. "Look what you did." With no regard to my bleeding hand, I grabbed my apron and carefully used a corner to wipe off the book, making sure not to let the blood mar any of the pages or leather cover.

It was learning of Kash's death that broke my solid fear of these men. I had nothing else to lose. While I still feared them, I hated them more. The whole time the bladesman never spoke, but he watched me silently. Judging me.

When I had cleaned up the spot on the book, I returned it to the table and pushed it across toward him. "There. Almost like new again. But next time, be careful. You could have damaged the book instead of me."

I raised my chin and glared in challenge at the hawk bladesman. I was playing a dangerous game. It was said that the left-hand valued wisdom, so I was betting he valued the books and I had dared to tread in his domain.

My hand still stung as blood slowly dripped onto the white marble floor. I didn't dare move to clean it, for I feared he would attack me if I so much as breathed wrong.

The hawk stepped forward, grabbed the book, and tucked it against his black breastplate before spinning on his heels and leaving. I stayed frozen until the last clank of his footsteps faded away, and then I collapsed to my knees, breathing hard.

Gail unstuck herself from her hiding place and came to chastise me.

"Rhea, what did I tell you," Gail hissed.

"What did I do?"

"You openly challenged one of the king's blades. If you value your life, you'll never be alone with one of them again." Gail grimaced. "I can't believe you survived that encounter. They can't be reasoned with."

"Why not?"

"Because that's how they were created."

"Created? Who created them?"

Gail's lips pinched together, and she shook her head. "I've said too much. Come. We're expected to help with lunch."

As we stepped into the hall, a row of servant girls were heading back toward the kitchen. I fell in line at the end of the row, my head down. I was focused on my wound that still stung.

Lunch followed a similar routine as last night's dinner, except that we were both assigned to dishes. We moved on to changing the bedding in the guests' rooms and bringing it down to the laundress. After a few hours, were back in the kitchen to help with the dinner.

When it came time for dinner, I begged Gail to let me try serving again. Anything to get out of that humid kitchen. She reluctantly agreed. I changed into the slippers and wore the veil. Lifting an empty tray, I practiced walking silently, my feet touching the floor with only my toes.

The dumbwaiter came up the chute with the first set of trays. I reached for the first, and Gail stiffened beside me.

"Oh stars," Gail whispered.

"What's wrong?"

"The king isn't here, but the blades are. Which means we have to serve the king's blades."

My gaze swept up the hall toward the high table. The king's chair was empty, but the seats immediately on either side were filled with the three blades.

"Do they ever take off the helmets?" I asked.

"Never," Gail said. "And they don't even eat, so serving them is just for show, which makes them even more creepy. Follow me." As I trailed Gail up to the head table, another servant approached from the right. Gail laid her tray in front of the lion. The servant on the right placed a tray in front of the hawk, which left the dragon for me.

I couldn't do it. My hands shook with anger as I came up behind and stared at the back of the helm, and the black scales winked at me.

Then I saw it.

A familiar gold knife tucked into his belt. Kash's knife. The bladesman killed Kash and then had the gall to wear his weapon.

My anger rose and so did the tray in my hands as it lifted high above my head. I bit my lip as I prepared to swing it down with all my might.

Gail gasped as she saw what I was doing. I closed my eyes and swung downward . . . and connected with nothing. The dragon blade had sensed my attack. He pushed himself backward, his chair sliding across the stone. The tray missed his head by inches. In a blink of an eye, I lay on my back, pinned to the table, a blade once again pressed against my throat.

Tears filled my eyes as I cursed at him.

"I hate you!" I screamed. "You deserve to die."

Just then, a piercing whistle rang out across the dining room. My head felt like it was going to explode. I winced as the room spun. I was going to be sick. Where did that noise come from?

Out of the corner of my eye, I saw the king standing farther down the head table, across the dining room full of people eating happily, with a silver flute pressed to his lips. Only a handful reacted. A man fell forward onto his plate of food in a faint. Three women grabbed their ears and tried to leave the room. Another woman cried out and fell from her chair.

"Make it stop!" I cried out, no longer caring as the piercing noise was going to be my undoing. My body spasmed and lights flickered in my vision and the whistle ceased. When my head stopped spinning, I brushed my hand across my nose and saw blood. That cursed whistle almost killed me and a few of the other people in the room.

King Goddrick noticed me splayed across the table and he wandered over to look at me. "She's one of them? Well, I'll be. I expected to weed out a few of the liars and gold diggers, but never expected one of the servants to be gifted as well." He turned to point across at the man and five women who were affected by the silver flute that he was now tucking into the pocket of his vest.

"You know what to do. Gather them up."

The three bladesman stared at the king and then cast silent looks to each other before acting. Two leapt over the high table, their boots landing on the floor with a thud.

They went directly to the women that had passed out. Then the dragon grabbed me by the front of my dress and hauled me from the table. I grasped his wrists to keep from choking as I stumbled after the bladesman out of the hall.

"Let go!" I screamed, clawing at his armor guarded wrist. He slowed, kicked open a door and flung me into the room. I fell, scraping my knees, imagining a dank cell. I had fought so far; I wasn't ready to give up yet. I scrambled back to my feet and lunged at him again, reaching for the knife at his hip. The blade sidestepped my attack easily. He grasped me around my waist and lifted me up. With a mighty toss, he flung me onto a soft mattress, and I bounced.

"What the?" I looked up to see him retreating, slamming the door with a thud. I saw for the first time my prison and I gasped at the opulent room. Everything was gold or painted gold. The sconce's, candelabras, the bed frame, tables, and if it wasn't gold, it was black. The wallpaper, quilt and even the curtains. I would have thought the room to be dismal except the exorbitant amount of gold made it feel warm.

"Stars above—" I moved to the balcony that overlooked the kingdom. The doors opened, and I stepped out onto the terrace. My heart raced as I looked over the ledge. It was a straight drop, hundreds of feet off the mountain. I couldn't breathe. I had to press my back against the doors and inch myself inside where I was safe from falling. Never had I seen the world from that height, and I wasn't in a rush to step onto the balcony a second time. One earthquake and I was sure it would collapse and fall off the mountain.

As if reading my thoughts, the ground trembled, and I

dove back into the room, far from the balcony and the walls, waiting until the tremors stopped. There was something unnatural about the quakes, but I wasn't sure what.

I couldn't stay here. As soon as I touched the door handle, I cried out as pain shot up my arm. They warded it against escape.

The king was keeping us imprisoned with magical wards. I paced, chewed on my lip, bounced on the balls of my feet, and contemplated all the things I was going to do to the blade that locked me in here.

Slice, dice, and use his head for target practice.

I wasn't kept waiting long before the door opened and King Goddrick himself came in, escorted by the hawk bladesman.

"I'm surprised to see that one of my servants has a talent for magic. I thought to have already vetted them," the king asked. The way he phrased the question really wasn't a question, but more of a statement.

I stood and dusted off my dress to address the king. "I am a new addition to your staff," I said, leaving off any honorifics, wondering if the king noticed the slight.

His eyes narrowed, and there was a slight tic in his jaw. He noticed.

"I welcome you to the palace as my guest."

"Hard to believe, considering my current situation. The door is warded."

He smirked. "So you're strong enough for the wards to affect you. That is good to know. But do you blame me? You did physically attack one of my bodyguards. You're lucky that they did not kill you on the spot."

"They're monsters," I fumed. "They killed my friends

and abducted a friend of mine." My heart ached when I thought of Kash and Marco.

"All at *my* orders." The king's eyes glittered dangerously. "So do you say the same about me since *my* guards were obeying *my* orders."

"If the shoe fits," I snapped. This was a dangerous game I was playing, but I no longer cared to play by the rules. Now I was setting my own.

"I'm sorry you feel that way," he said, but I could hear the lack of empathy in his voice. "But none of that matters. What matters is that you have magic talent. And I have reason to believe you are the girl from Verdan. The one who turned tin to gold."

I glared at the king, refusing to answer.

"I see I was correct in my assumption. That makes you extremely valuable to me."

"What about the others you summoned to the castle? Will you let them go?"

"Yes, most are already on their way home." He waved his hand in annoyance. "The silverstar flute helped me narrow down the candidates and I've selected a few to remain here to continue on the trials."

As he spoke, I couldn't help but feel like I was speaking with a serpent that was waiting to strike.

"What is it you want?" I asked.

He raised his hand as if it were the simplest of tasks. "I want the legendary Stiltskin hoard of gold, but everyone that has gone looking for it has never returned."

"That treasure is cursed. Grimkeep said so."

The king's eyes darkened. "No, the dwarves only said it was cursed to keep from returning what was rightfully ours. That gold belonged to this kingdom long ago. Rumple took it, and I want it back."

"Maybe it doesn't want to be found," I said uncomfortably. I couldn't help but think of the *thing*, the void that was also deep in the mountain. I was terrified of searching for the gold. What if I encountered it again? Could I survive? "Maybe it's safer not to disturb that which slumbers."

The king grabbed my chin and dug his fingers painfully into my skin. "Interesting choice of words, my child. Is there something you're not telling me?"

"No," I gritted out between clenched teeth.

He released my chin. "I don't believe you. But it won't matter as long as you keep me happy, and if I can't have the hoard, then I will be appeased by you filling my coffers with more gold than that wretched dwarf stole."

"And what if I choose not to?" I said.

"Everyone has a price." The king smirked.

"There's no amount of money you can offer me to help you," I snapped.

"Why do you assume I'm going to offer you gold? I offer you *life*. Your life in exchange for working for me."

I shook my head.

"Then let's make it simple. I'll let your friend with the lavender hair continue to keep her pretty little head on her shoulders, if you just work for me."

My quick inhale gave me away. "H-how?" I stuttered.

"Nothing goes on in this palace without me knowing. And if that isn't incentive enough, I'll add the servant girl, Gail's life, to the mix. But . . . if you run away or try to warn your friends, then my blades will hunt all of you down." He snapped his fingers, and the hawk drew his rapier and was at my neck before I blinked.

As the king continued with threats, I couldn't help but stare into the eyes of the bladesman. The hawk's head twitched, and not only that, but the blade in his hand did as well. An oddity that it would shake so much in the hands of a well-known swordsman.

"What choice do I have?" I said, knowing mother would be frustrated that I let myself get blackmailed.

The king's lips pulled back into a cruel smile. "None, whatsoever."

CHAPTER TWELVE

After the king left, I followed behind him, racing for the door as it closed. I grasped the gold handle, and it burned in my fingers. It was still warded.

"I will not be a prisoner." I fumed and paced the room, searching for a way out.

The balcony was the obvious choice, but I had a fear of heights. I didn't think I could handle climbing down. And I didn't have my satchel with my charms or the spindle.

I cursed under my breath and spent the next few candle marks looking over the warded door for a mistake. The spell was masterful and connected to a key. As night fell, my headache returned with the frustrated grinding of my teeth. I was a sorceress. I couldn't let a locked door get the better of me.

I sat on the bed, my knees pulled to my chest as the freezing wind came in through the open balcony doors. If I closed them, I knew I would feel imprisoned. It was that biting wind on my skin that reminded me that freedom wasn't far off. I stared into the burning fire and noticed the little creature running around in the embers.

Another fire salamander. Kneeling by the fire, I could

see this one wasn't fully black like the one I had seen in Molneer's home. This one was unique, with orange and gold scales.

"What's your name?" I asked, not expecting an answer.

The salamander came out of the fireplace and ran around the floor, leaving a trail of fire and ash in his wake before going back to his warm bed in the coals.

I wouldn't have believed it if I hadn't seen the ash letters. To the untrained eye, it would have looked like scribbles. I'm not even sure any of my sisters would have been able to decipher the name.

"Sol."

The salamander stomped all four of his scaled feet in excitement, scattering the coals. But seeing Sol helped me remember a spell that used a fireplace, and I grinned. I could escape . . . for a short while.

The sun had set while I worked out the spell from memory, and I had to guess at the time of night. When it appeared the palace had settled down, I knew it was time.

"Sol, keep my fire burning brightly, okay?"

The salamander spun around in answer.

Moving back to the fireplace, I pulled out a charred piece of wood and used the burnt end like chalk. With practiced ease, I drew out a spell circle in front of the fireplace, painstakingly drawing out each sigil. A smile of accomplishment fell across my face. I hadn't made a single mistake. After all, I had taught Eden how to do this. It was a travelling spell which would allow me to leave this room for as long as the fire burned bright. When it died out, I would be pulled back to this same location.

Taking a deep breath, I crossed the ash line. The

ground began to glow; the fire turned white. Sparks flew out of the fireplace and fell around me like rain. Blinding pain rushed through every limb of my body as I was surrounded by a fiery vortex and pulled into the spell.

I stepped out of a burning fireplace into the royal library. This time it was bathed in darkness, only illuminated by the glowing moss lanterns. I actually preferred it this way. I wanted to find information on the cursed treasure and the thing beneath the mountain.

I just had to find the information I needed before the spell snapped me back to my prison.

Making my way to the center table, I noticed a new stack of books, which included the familiar volume that the bladesman had sliced my hand for touching.

Well, the bladesman wasn't here. Greedily, I ran my fingers over the leather, feeling the delicate painted gold inlay. I couldn't help myself, and I took a deep breath, inhaling the scent of the paper and glue. The scent of wisdom, the scent of home. Cracking open the book, I scanned the page and saw the runes written within.

Ter Dell, the great dwarven city, was founded by the first king of Ragnar, King Einsamall, in the year of twelve hundred and three.

Where had I heard the name Ter Dell before?

Ragnar-as in Ragnar Mountains.

Was this book referring to the lost dwarven city?

A clearing of a throat alerted me I wasn't alone. "Do you mind?"

I looked up, and sitting behind a tower of books was a young man with sandy blonde hair and blue eyes. His features looked vaguely familiar, but I wasn't sure where I knew him from.

"Sorry." I placed the book back on the stack. "I didn't mean to disturb you. I wanted to read this book."

The young man leaned forward and pointed to the book in my hand. "That book. You can read that book?"

I frowned at his surprise. "Yes."

"These runes here?"

"I just said that, yes."

The man leaned back, running his hands through his blond hair in surprise. He was wearing a loose-fitting white shirt, green doublet, and black pants. On the collar of his vest was a gold pin.

He jumped up, knocking over another pile of books, and I stepped back in surprise. He grabbed the book out of my hands, flipped to a certain page and pointed to a footnote. "What does that say?"

"Move your finger and I'll tell you."

The young man moved his finger, and I leaned close to read the fine ink. It was penned by hand, added years later and not by the original author. "It says greed will be his downfall."

"Are you sure?" he asked.

"Positive."

"Absolutely fascinating." He cracked a grin, and my heart fluttered in remorse. It again reminded me of Kash's.

My mood mellowed, and I became somber and retreated. The man sensed my change.

"Wait a minute, don't go." He reached for another book among his stacks. "I've got more questions."

"I'm sorry. I shouldn't have disturbed you," I hedged uneasily. "I'll come back at a different time."

"I didn't dismiss you," the young man said, his voice suddenly filled with authority.

"Spencer!" another man bellowed as he stormed into the library. "You lazy bum."

I used the distraction to step back into the shadows as I recognized the new speaker that stormed into the room. It was the man from last night.

"Let me guess, Damon?" Spencer said irritably. "Your dirty laundry attracted mice."

"Why, you ungrateful . . ." Damon growled and lunged for Spencer.

The two scuffled playfully before Spencer held up a book to block the good-natured blows. "Damon, you won't believe what I found. A girl that can read—"

"Oh, that's great," Damon said sarcastically. "Someone who can read."

"—the language of Eld," Spencer finished.

Damon stilled. "Who?"

"She was just here." Spencer looked toward where I was previously standing, having slipped into the shadows to watch the two men interact.

"What are you waiting for? Find her!" Damon said.

Both of them split up and took to either side of the library and were working their way toward me. There wasn't a way for me to escape, and I couldn't help but notice the silent way they moved, as if hunting their prey.

Damon was the closest to me, and I knew they would find me, when suddenly, little bits of ash flickered off my dress. I knew the fire was dying out, causing the spell to return me sooner than I expected. As much as I hated to leave, and I'd enjoyed this bit of game, I'd also found some interesting information.

"Hey!" Damon spotted me just as a swirl of ash flickered around me.

I gave him a wave goodbye and disappeared.

When I appeared in my room, it was freezing. The salamander had long ago abandoned my fireplace, probably summoned to another fire, or had tired of keeping my coals burning. For salamanders were fickle creatures, unless tamed. If one had the pleasure of taming a salamander, they would forever be their familiar.

But the room was not as I left it. The balcony doors that I had left open were shut. Did the wind blow them shut? No, for it was not only shut, but the claw hook latch was in place.

Spinning, I searched the corners of the darkened room for intruders, but found none. I was alone. But someone had come into my room and now knew I could freely leave despite the locked door. The question became, who was it and would they give up my secret?

Sleep evaded me. I spent the rest of the night into early morning, sitting cross-legged on the bed facing the door, waiting for the intruder to come back.

Paranoia had me fumbling, and I made an obstacle course of furniture between the door and me. Having dragged the side table, two chairs, and a trunk in front of the door. This way, if I fell asleep, I would be notified of their entrance.

I came alert as the door unlocked and I heard the thunk as the door hit the table.

"What the—I can't. It's blocked," Gail's voice came from the other side of the mountain of furniture.

Slipping off the bed, I moved to remove the stuffed chair from off the table when a crash followed. Someone slammed into the door and caused the wall of furniture to collapse inward. The vase shattered, the side table cracked, and the chair fell forward as the immovable force of the dragon blade crashed through my protective barrier. A pillow fell toward him, and he attacked it with a vengeance, slicing it midair multiple times, and then kicked it to the ground.

The hated bladesman stood inside, his chest heaving as he surveyed his carnage. Then the dark helm came up and stared at me accusingly. As if he couldn't believe he cut down a pillow.

Had the dreaded blade rushed inside to save me?

"Good job defeating the bloody pillow. That was a close one. You almost died." I clapped my hands slowly, dragging out his bizarre mistake, loving that it was the dragon blade I had humiliated.

His body language portrayed his confusion as he gazed at all the down feathers that were raining around us. Frustration followed as he spun on his heel and headed outside the door. He motioned with his hand for Gail to enter.

Gail stood outside the door, her body trembling in fear as he passed. Then she ducked her head and slipped inside, her eyes going wide as she saw the destroyed furniture.

"What did you do?" Gail's voice was high-pitched.

"I didn't do anything. It was the blade. He was the one killing the furniture."

"You barricaded the door?" She stepped further in and skirted around the chair stuffing that was spread across the rug like clouds.

"Wouldn't you, if you knew the blades were on the other side?"

"But that's why Freya locks us all inside our rooms. For protection from them."

"And you couldn't have said that two nights ago?"

She shrugged. "I thought it was obvious. That's why I warned you to stay away from them."

I didn't want to frighten Gail further by telling her that locked doors didn't stop me, or whoever had entered my room. In this case, ignorance was bliss.

Gail set out clean clothes she'd brought with her, laying them out on the bed for me. They weren't my clothes, nor a servant's dress.

"What is this?" I asked, running my hand across the white silk wrap gown.

"It's a dress," Gail said. It seemed now that the blade was on the other side of a wall, her normal snarky attitude was slowly coming back.

"Yes, I see that."

"Don't think you're anything special."

I pinched my lips to hold back my laugh. Maybe her snarkiness was her way of dealing with the things she couldn't control.

"It's adjustable." Gail showed me how it had a gold clasp and buckles to adjust it to fit various shapes and sizes of women. She also brought leather sandals that wrapped around my legs up my calves.

The braids had come undone, and I was about to wrap them back into a bow when Gail stopped me. "You don't have to wear them in the servants' knot since you're not a servant. But then again," she gave me a smug smile, "you never were one to begin with. Was it just a ruse to spy on the king to gain his favor?" She didn't even try to hide the bitterness in her voice.

I undid the braids and ran my fingers through the wavy hair left in its wake. "No, you can gladly take my place."

Her face paled, and she shook her head. "It's your neck on the line. Not mine." She turned and motioned for me to follow her out. "But you won't last long. None of them will."

I pondered her words as I stepped into the hall and heard the subtle clank of footsteps following close behind me. I spun on my heel, expecting to see the dragon bladesman from earlier, but he was gone. Scared off in embarrassment, I hoped. My new guard was the lion blade. The lion stopped inches from my face. I felt like he wasn't as scary as most made him out to be. It was the dark armor and their silent aura that followed them wherever they went.

I stared into the dark helm, right where the bladesman's eyes would be, and that's when I noticed something disturbing. The reason that most of the staff probably feared these bladesman—the reason they didn't speak—they weren't human. Where the eyes should have been was nothing but dark shadows that moved and flowed like a watery mist.

"What are you doing?" I snapped.

Gail gasped. "You shouldn't address them. It's forbidden to speak to any of the king's blades."

"That's a dumb rule. Don't you think so?" I turned to address the bladesman. The helm nodded.

"Can you speak?"

He shook his head, and I felt a genuine sadness come from him. Careful, Rhea, I told myself. You remember this thing isn't good. Don't humanize him. But as he stood there, I noticed the dropped shoulders, and it reminded me of a dog we once owned with the droopiest ears and forlorn eyes. He conveyed so much without speaking. And I felt like I wanted to reassure the bladesman.

"Well, that's okay. I like the strong and silent type."

The blade stilled, and then I heard the slightest jingle. I looked up in surprise as the armor was shaking. The black chain mail rattled against the armor as he laughed.

"Is he *laughing*?" Gail said, her eyes wide.

"Yes," I said in disbelief. "He is."

Gail's face pinched. "Can you make it stop? It's creepy."

Immediately, the rattling ceased, and I watched as the blade straightened. His muscles tensed again, as if her insult snapped him out of whatever reverie he was in.

I sighed and shook my head. It was as if I had lost traction. I was getting closer to figuring out what these enchanted creatures were. If I could figure out what magic created them, I could destroy them. I would work for the king, and all the while plotting on how to annihilate his hands of power.

Gail ushered me into a beautiful parlor room with tall windows that covered one wall with deep red curtains. The parlor also contained a long-stuffed couch and many paintings, but none of them were portraits. They were all landscapes of the kingdom of Kiln. The walls were painted floral motifs, and the sconces were tulip shaped. There was a definite femininity in the design of the room. Was this because of King Goddrick's late wife? Again, the lack of portraits of the royal family only added to the mystery of the king and his heirs.

Around the table were six women and one man. All were wearing similar styles of wrap dresses or wrapped pants. The only two people I recognized were Carlotta, in red, and Velora, looking morose as ever in purple, which only accented the vibrant lavender hues of her hair.

"What's going on?" I asked Gail.

"How should I know?" Gail replied. "I only do what I'm told."

It was becoming quite obvious that Gail disliked me.

When I came in, all eyes settled on me and I briefly met each of them: Carlotta, the woman in red; Shannon, a petite brunette; Annette, the seeker; Brenna, a blonde-haired healer; and the lone man in a fancy felt hat was a milliner named Benton. He was the one who passed out on the table.

The human guard that escorted me moved to the window while the hawk, who was already with the other six, took over duty standing by the door.

The company looked to Velora and waited for her to greet everyone. Velora wrinkled her lip in disgust.

"That's Velora," I added for the upset mermaid.

"We know," Carlotta whispered. "She attacked a servant after that horrible event last night."

"What happened to us last night? Do any of you know?" Brenna asked. "I've never had that happen before."

"There was a high-pitched ringing noise, and we were the only ones who reacted to it," Benton said. "I passed out. Then I woke up in a beautiful room and they brought us here."

"It was a whistle made from silverstar." I rubbed my hands up and down my arms as I tried to shake off the memory of that horrible sound. "It's said that only those that are magically inclined can hear it whistle. It is one of the first tests they do when seeing if you are gifted," I explained.

I thought back to when we were young, and the stories mother told of the fae tricks. They would play the silverstar flute near the human lands and coax gifted children into their fairy circles. And they would disappear. "This was nothing like the gentle silverstar flute that the elves have. This one was twisted, meant more to inflict damage the stronger you are."

A few of the women looked uncomfortable. Shannon pointed to Velora. "She wouldn't stop screaming. She must be really powerful."

Brenna fidgeted with the hem of her sleeve. "I'm not trained, but I've always had a knack for healing people and easing their pain."

Benton pulled at the cravat at his throat. "I'm a maker. I can manipulate materials into different shapes."

Annette cleared her throat. "I'm a see—"

The king's entrance interrupted what Annette was about to say. The tension in the room rose and everyone sat up in their chairs as the last blade, the dragon, came in behind him.

"What happened to the others?" Carlotta spoke up.

"I have sent them home." The king shot her an irritated look. He didn't like being interrupted. "I will not need them. You, on the other hand . . . my decree still stands."

As he lectured us, the ground shook. The paintings rattled on the walls, the empty chairs slowly moved across the floor, and anything not weighted or heavy fell off the shelves. Velora frowned and looked at the floor as if it disturbed her. Two of the women screamed and pointed. I looked up as a stalactite broke loose from the ceiling and pierced the great wooden table mere inches from where I was sitting. My mouth went dry.

Two of the bladesman stood over the king protectively. I grabbed the edge of the table and stared at the three-foot piece of rock that impaled the wood. A silent warning from the mountain or something else?

When the rumbling stopped, the king cleared his throat. "I want you to create gold. One of you has already accomplished this task but is unwilling to share their knowledge with the rest of you."

Tension filled the room as the king deliberately wove discord and distrust among us.

"But how?" Annette asked fearfully.

"Find a way. My library, storerooms, kitchens, work-shops are at your disposal. I expect results." King Goddrick walked over to Velora, and his golden ring-covered hand rested gently on the back of her chair. "It would be such a shame to lose one of you so soon." Even though the king addressed the group, his eyes met mine, and I understood the silent warning. He didn't expect them to do anything. They were just hostages in pretty packages.

He had brought us all together, hoping to show me how much control he had over them . . . and me.

"I hope you'll do everything in your power to appease me," he spoke, looking directly at me.

I nodded, my fisted hands buried in the white silk skirt.

"Wonderful. Shall we begin?" The king clapped his hands and the three bladesman came and stood by his side.

I couldn't help but notice that the dragon blade's helm turned ever so slightly to watch me from across the room.

"Very well," I said, slapping the table and gesturing to

the giant rock in front of me. "Well, it can't get any worse. Let's go make some money."

Shannon's mouth twitched at my joke. The king's face darkened, and I wasn't sure, but I swore the lion blade started shaking again, and it wasn't from the tremors.

CHAPTER THIRTEEN

"What? No!" I snapped when Freya came and explained the king's wishes to me. "I do *not* want to be followed around by one of these haunted, hollow things." I pointed toward the three blades that were lined up outside the parlor room.

"It's not up to you. The king has ordered that a blade is to be with you at all times, ensuring that you are secured in your room."

"What? I'm still going to be locked in my room at night?" I scoffed. "What about the others?"

"It's for your protection. And they are being guarded as well."

"My protection?" I grumbled. "Or to make sure I don't leave."

Freya's cheeks turned red. "The king thinks highly of your skills and has ordered one of his blades to always be by your side."

Or a blade will be pierced in my side, I thought wryly.

"I can't imagine any of them being thrilled to babysit me."

"They don't have feelings," Freya said.

I didn't believe that to be true.

Inside the parlor, Carlotta and Annette had their heads together and whispered conspiratorially. Carlotta's eyes narrowed, and she pointed to me. Annette called over Shannon, and the whispers continued, followed by frowns and suspicious glances. The people within that parlor banded together. I was the outsider, and I knew the king did his job of sowing seeds of distrust. I could feel their jealousy and suspicions directed toward me. I couldn't have them looking over my shoulder, watching my every move as I tried to find a weakness in the blades. I didn't want a spy.

"Okay, fine." I sighed and looked cautiously at the room full of competitors. "I'll need a private workroom. Away from the others and prying eyes. Where I can be alone with my thoughts and tests."

Freya pondered for a moment. "There's an old section of the palace that might do."

"That will work. Can you make sure it's furnished with these things?" I grabbed a quill and scratched out a list of items, including quartz, flasks, vials, clay crucibles, burners, everything I might need to turn tin to gold. I added my satchel that had been stored in my trunk in Gail's room.

Freya read over my list. "It will be done." She looked at the blades. "Will one of you take her to the Gilded Hall?"

The dragon was the first to move away from the door, stepping by my side.

"No, anyone but you," I said heatedly. "How about you?" I pointed to the lion blade. "You, so far, are the only one who hasn't tried to murder me." The lion moved to come to my side, and the dragon turned on the other blades. I said nothing. No words passed between them, but I got the impression that the dragon was the leader. The lion retreated.

When the dragon returned to my side, I could almost feel him gloating. He stood tall, his shoulders back, and that helmet creaked as he turned to stare at me. I could almost hear him say, *Now what?*

I ground my teeth as I stared at the golden knife at his belt. He may think this was a game, but it was a game I was going to win.

"Fine, show me the way," I said sourly.

The dragon blade began walking with sure steps. I followed in behind him, staring at the black helm, imagining a giant target painted on the back of it. With every creak of his armor, I imagined taking a giant mallet and striking it like a gong.

As we passed through the halls and the natural light flickered across his armor, I couldn't help but stare at the workmanship it took to create the pattern within. The faint linework of gold in the scales. I'd first thought it was outlined and painted with gold, but now I wasn't so sure. I wanted to get a closer look at the blade's armor because I had a feeling if I could, then I might be able to put together the basic spell. It could lead me to figuring out how they worked. My brain turned its earlier frustration aside, and I formulated unique experiments on spells that I could use to determine their exact makeup.

The bladesman turned and held open a great wooden door. Grudgingly, I stepped into the Gilded Hall and gasped. It was like a giant birdcage made of gold. Windows surrounded the circular room and great iron pillars ran up the sides for support, culminating together in a knot in the ceiling. Two long wooden tables ran the length of the hall and at the far end was a massive stone fireplace.

"What is this place?" I asked in awe. "Why has no one used it?"

The dragon gestured toward a dusty green banner on the wall and the giant golden axe. I looked closer at the table, and that's when I noticed the height and the width of each of the chairs. The symbolic knots that were prevalent in the decor. Where King Goddrick's rooms were extravagant to the extreme, this hall was based on form and function.

"This is where the dwarven guilds used to meet," I guessed. "When there were more dwarves in Ragnar."

Another nod.

"This is perfect." It felt right to use the dwarven hall as my workspace.

I spent half the day setting up my tools. The blades left me in relative peace as I assembled what I needed.

I had never tried to create gold from nothing. Philosophers and scholars had spent years trying to use alchemy to create it. None of them were sorcerers. There were seven metals of alchemy, and I was familiar with all of them: gold, silver, mercury, copper, lead, iron, and tin. Gold was the most interesting to me, as it was unaffected by water, air, alkalis, and acids. I knew that transfiguration of metals needed mercury and sulfur. Maybe, if I had everything I needed, I could combine alchemy with my magic and create gold from nothing. But it would take time. That was something I wasn't sure the king was going to give us.

I had to buy time. I could use the spindle's magic and possibly create gold, but it was against our code to use our magic for selfish gain, and it would slowly destroy the spindle in the process.

I could create a transfiguration charm and change a singular item. Maybe that would appease the king and give me more time to figure out the blades and the thing deep in the mountain.

It was almost like being back in my workroom at home. I created a spell circle, and instead of the sigils, I used the alchemy symbols.

"Here goes nothing." I placed my copper coin in the center and watched as the spell circle lit up. It fizzled out, sparked. It was a dud. Smoke came from the coin, and I backed away. It was better to not touch it.

I grinned at my failure. It was all part of the process and why I loved potions and alchemy. You couldn't rush greatness.

"I need more metals."

I received odd looks from the palace staff as I walked around, picking up everything that was metal, then closing my eyes to figure out the makeup. Tin, copper, lead, silver. My actions drew in a crowd, and soon Annette was following me around doing the same, then Shannon joined us.

"I have no clue where to start," Shannon whispered conspiratorially to me. "How do I make gold?"

"You can't make something from nothing," I whispered. "You need to have a starting point, and then manipulate the matter and change its physical properties. Which is almost impossible."

"But can it be done?" she whispered.

I shrugged my shoulders. "Maybe if we had a year, but I don't think he's going to give us that long."

Shannon grabbed my elbow, her blue eyes filled with wonder. "It was you. You're the one who made gold in Verdan. You know too much. You started this whole mess," she hissed.

I pulled my elbow out of her grasp. "This mess? You came to the castle. You had the chance to leave on your own, but you stayed. You have no one to blame but yourself for being in *this mess*."

"You can help me. I have four brothers. I need to get the reward."

I shook my head. "Listen to me. You can't create gold. No one can."

Shannon's lip trembled. "You lie. You're just saying that because you're selfish." She grabbed her skirt and ran off.

Annette was watching our exchange with narrowed eyes. I ignored her and touched a gold candlestick. My knees went weak, and I stumbled, smacking my hip into the table. It wasn't just gold. It was cursed.

I took the candlestick with me and headed back to the Gilded Hall. The candle stick wasn't the only item I pilfered.

Maeve would have been proud of my thievery, as I also snuck in—well, I didn't sneak, more like walking in—and demanded the silver cup that sang from the kitchen. With a blade on my heel, the kitchen maid practically threw it at my head in her hurry to get us out of her domain.

I had all the metals I needed, and I preceded to run experiments on them. Testing their density, using chemicals to identify their makeup. Taking notes on both.

Food appeared at intervals throughout the day, and I

didn't even notice it. I was so focused on my work. When I tried to leave, the dragon blade stepped in front of me.

"Not now. I would like to go to the library," I grumbled.

He shook his head.

"I need more information than what is here."

Again, I was met with a giant black wall as he denied my request. I grabbed my satchel and put it over my head, letting it cross over my body. The dragon blade grabbed my elbow and led me back to my room. As we passed the halls, I saw the sun was setting and knew my free time was over.

"How am I supposed to work if I keep getting locked in every night?" I fumed.

Freya met us by the door to my room and I noticed her key was in hand. She must have already locked the others in.

"Freya, I need to keep working. I feel like I could get further along to solving the problem if I only had more—."

Freya shook her head. "Hurry, it's almost time. These are the rules, and you must obey them."

"But you don't," I challenged as I stepped into the room.

"I'm the only one that is guaranteed safety," she said.

The dragon blade watched the exchange, and his dark helm turned toward me. "Don't lock me in," I cried out. "Please."

He took a step forward as if to stop her, and then he stiffened as though he were in pain. The moon rose in the sky, casting a light in the hall. As it touched him, he recoiled.

"Freya," I called out, pointing to the knight. "What's wrong with him?"

She looked at the blade and her eyes went wide. "Nothing's wrong with him." She slammed my door shut, and I heard the key turn in the lock. The wards lit up and activated. When I touched the handle, my palm burned again.

I sucked in my breath and shook my hand to ease the pain. My fireplace wasn't lit, and Sol the Salamander hadn't returned. But the castle was naturally warm, and it seemed a fire was merely a luxury here, not a necessity. It looked like I really was going to be trapped in my room for the rest of the night.

Nightclothes were laid out for me, and I was grateful for the change in the routine. When I crawled into bed, I noticed a book was on my nightstand. One that wasn't there the night before. Picking it up, I grinned when I recognized it. The one written in Eld.

I stayed up as long as I could to read it by candlelight.

CHAPTER FOURTEEN

The balcony door slammed open, and I jumped up in bed, my heart pounding as I scanned my room, grabbing the book to my chest. The door slammed again, and I saw the wind was blowing it open and closed. Tiptoeing across the room, I slowly closed the door and spied a reflection in the glass. I spun, swinging the book with all of my might at the intruder.

A hand grasped mine, and with a tug, they pulled me forward and then flipped me easily onto the bed. My back bounced on the mattress, and I looked up as the shadow loomed over me.

"Why do you always try to hit me over the head with a book?" the shadow said.

The tome fell from my fingers, and I sat up, my hands covering my mouth to prevent my scream of excitement. "*Kash?*"

He struck a match and held it up. I caught sight of his grinning face, the scar on his chin visible as he lit the bedside candle.

"Who else would scale the side of a mountain to get to you?"

I cried out and flung my arms around him in a hug. He

smelled so good. Like fresh winter air and pine. He buried his head in my neck, and I felt the barest of kisses on my shoulder.

"I thought you were dead?" I cried out, pulling away, not afraid to show my tears of joy.

Kash wiped away a stray tear. "And I thought you were going to stay back at the manor, safe and sound. Not end up in the very place I didn't want you to go."

"I don't listen very well."

"No, you don't." He sighed.

"What about Marco? Velora said they hurt him."

Kash's expression turned stony. "He's fine."

"What do you mean, 'he's fine'? What happened?"

"He was injured in the fight as the king's men came to take Velora. He escaped into the mountains."

"But what about you? How did you escape? How did you find me?" I asked.

"Rhea." Kash's voice was filled with emotion, and he sat on the bed, his thigh brushing against mine. "It doesn't matter. It's in the past. I told you I would find you." He tucked a strand of hair behind my ear and leaned forward to kiss me.

I met his lips and let the tears fall. I was so glad he was alive that he was here. Everything would be all right if Kash was with me.

He pulled back, pressing his lips to my cheeks, kissing my tears away, then pulled me into his arms. We fell back onto the bed and Kash tucked me into his side, wrapping his arms around my waist.

"I've missed you so much, Rhea. I came here looking for you last night, but you were gone."

"If I would have known you were alive, I would have

never left the room. I'd wait forever for you." I reached up and kissed the bottom of his chin.

"I told you, I'm hard to kill. I'm just glad you're here now." Kash sighed and threaded his foot between mine. "I wish I could hold on to you like this forever."

"Why don't you?" I whispered.

Kash's chin rested on the top of my head as I leaned against his powerful chest and listened to the soft beating of his heart.

"Because soon the sun will come up," he said quietly.

"Then hold me until then," I murmured.

And he did. I slept curled against Kash's side and wasn't plagued by a single nightmare. I awoke to him kissing the top of my head and rubbing my back.

The sun wasn't even up yet.

"What's wrong?" I stretched, reluctant to pull away from him.

"It's time for me to go," he whispered. When Kash sat up, his thigh brushed my leg, and I noticed the golden knife on his belt.

I froze. "Why do you have that?" I said in a clipped voice.

Kash tensed. "Rhea, I need to explain."

I jumped up and moved away from him, putting plenty of distance between us. "Please, tell me there are two identical knives, Kash." I swallowed, feeling the betrayal separate us. "Tell me the horrible dragon blade has the same knife." Angry tears stung my eyes.

Kash didn't move any closer to me, instead he moved closer to the open balcony and into the morning light. He lifted his head toward the sun. "No, there's not. There's only one."

As the sun crested the mountain and the rays rained over him, he unsheathed the golden knife and his body was immediately surrounded by a black, misty cloud.

"Kash," I called his name.

"Rhea, I can't guarantee I will stay in control, but I wanted to explain to you last night. I should have. But I was too selfish. I knew you would reject me. Now it's too late. I have to show you."

Kash screamed in pain as his clothes shifted. Black scales appeared out of his skin and wrapped around his body, hardening into black armor.

I shook my head. "It can't be." I was in denial, but I knew all the same.

Kash stepped forward, but there was something wrong. He was fighting the mist that was encasing his head. He didn't seem to submit to the curse. He collapsed to his knees, clutching the dragon helm, and I raced forth to help.

"Don't touch me. He's too strong," he cried out as the mist covered his face, smothering his voice. The cries died out and his golden eyes disappeared. I saw the hint of red eyes staring back at me as the dreaded dragon blade was now in my room.

"Kash?"

The dragon blade was kneeling before me, his hand on his knife, and head bowed low. As I stepped forth, he swung out, the blade nicking me, drawing blood.

"Ouch!" I cried and fell back onto the floor.

Slowly, his body trembling, the dragon blade got to his feet. But I wasn't sure how much of Kash was in control and how much was that darkness that was usurping him.

Kash held up the knife and looked at the blood dripping from the blade, and I quickly remembered what Mouse said about the three blades. The lion valued strength, the hawk—wisdom, and the dragon—death.

The way the blade looked at the blood on the knife gave me chills. This wasn't Kash. This was something darker, and I had a feeling I knew who it was.

The dragon turned toward me. I got to my knees and reached for the magic for the ley lines deep in the mountain. If it was a fight he wanted, it was a fight I was going to win.

Before I could gather magic, my door unlocked, and I looked up just as the lion blade rushed into my room. His sword drawn, he met Kash head on and they fought. Kash was fast. He dodged, rolled, and came up behind his brethren.

What was going on? Why were the blades fighting each other? Then everything clicked. The similarities between their smiles. The same mannerisms and laughter. If Kash had a different persona as a blade, then the lion and hawk had human counterparts as well. Damon and Spencer. Based on his physical characteristics, Damon was the lion.

Kash came up to his back, facing the balcony, and Damon put his armored head down and rushed him. He grabbed Kash around the waist, locking his arms behind his back, and propelled him backward toward the balcony railing.

"Damon, no!" I cried out as he drove Kash off the edge. They both tumbled over and dropped like rocks.

"No!" I screamed and raced toward the ledge

Someone grabbed me around the waist and lifted me off the ground. My feet met the air as I fought to be set back down. I clawed at the black armor with feathers etched on it, and I knew it was Spencer holding me. "Put me down. Let me go!"

"Relax," Freya's calm voice came from behind me. "A fall like that won't kill them. Though it may knock some sense into the boys." Freya came around to face me.

My heart raced with uncertainty, and I wasn't sure if I could believe her.

"You can put her down, Spencer. It's obvious she knows who you are and figured it out. Although, I don't see how it's possible."

My feet suddenly found purchase on the stone floor as Spencer released me. I pushed Freya aside and ran to look over the railing, but I was met with only a valley full of mist.

"They'll be fine. That cursed armor protects them. The walk back up the mountain will do them some good. Cool off their tempers a bit."

"You knew?" I turned to look at her in disbelief.

"Of course, I knew. I'm the one that protects their secret."

"H-how," I stuttered. "Why?" I collapsed on the nearest chair.

"Blame King Goddrick. It was his lust for the Stiltskin hoard that did this to them. By day they are known as the King's blades, by night they can walk the halls as their normal selves. It's why we have strict rules about who is allowed out at night. A few of our key staff and our knight guards."

"Who are they?" I asked. "What happened to them?"

"They are the king's three sons, and it is those cursed

blades they carry that does this to them. But how or why, I do not know."

"Then why don't they get rid of the blades?"

"They've tried. Tossed them off the mountain, buried them, burned them. They are indestructible. They slowly go mad unless the blade is touching them at all times. It is their bane and saving grace in one." Freya turned, her eyes filling with emotion.

"What does everyone think happened to the three princes?" I asked.

She crossed her arms and sighed. "Spencer is studying abroad somewhere. Damon is on a sailing expedition to open the kingdom's trade routes, and Kash is apprenticing with the Goldiron guild."

"A little lie to cover up a big lie," I said.

Freya shook her head and placed her arm on Spencer's helmed head. The blade bowed, and she seemed to stroke the back of it as though she could comfort them. "It is easier to accept a prince sailing the seas looking for adventure than the demon standing in front of them."

Spencer looked at Freya and I saw the black shadow over his eyes lessen, and for a moment, I glimpsed his blue eyes. In an act of empathy, I reached out and touched his armor, then let my magic caress it as I tried to get a sense of the material.

He jerked away like he was attacked, and the shadow covered his blue eyes. I saw a flash of red staring back at me. He shuddered and then stood up, his hand reaching for the rapier at his side, and he stalked toward me.

"Get back," Freya warned and stood in front of me, blocking me from Spencer's sight, but he wasn't going to back down.

"Spencer!" Freya commanded. "You must not harm the chosen ones."

The hawk helm tilted to the side and studied me, then moved around Freya and came toward me.

"It's my magic," I said.

"They are ordered to hunt magic users down, but I don't understand. You're already at the castle. They've completed their orders." Freya cut off Spencer again, raising her arms upward to protect me.

The darkness behind Spencer's helm was familiar, and I could feel the hunger reach for me. I knew who was behind the curse.

Just then Gail, Velora, and Brenna entered my room and saw the commotion.

I moved out toward the balcony, and Spencer came after me. I gripped the edge, clawing the railing for dear life.

"Are you sure they can survive a fall?" I asked, seeking confirmation as I watched Velora picked up a giant decorative vase and tiptoe toward us.

"Yes, nothing can kill them," Freya cried out as Spencer knocked her aside. She fell into the glass door, shattering the pane.

I glanced at the poor woman, seeing the bloody cut on her forehead.

"You know," I called out at to him. "I kinda liked you. I thought we could be friends because of our shared love of books, but you're being a jerk." Spencer pulled back. The hand on his sword was shaking. "You just injured the only woman who cares about you like a son."

The shadows faded for a second and I heard his

audible cry, but then he was back to being controlled by the mists.

The rapier raised to strike me. "Don't say I didn't warn you." I made a motion with my hand and jumped to the side as a screaming purple-haired mermaid drove toward Spencer's back. Lifting the stone vase above her head, Velora swung it with all her strength and knocked him over the ledge. I watched his armor smash against a boulder on its way down and I cringed. He slammed against the side of a mountain and continued to fall.

Velora looked over the side and spat. "That's for Marco!"

"Thank you, Velora," I said. "And I have news. Marco is alive."

Velora's face beamed. "I knew it." She set the planter down on the ground. I realized by its sheer size it had to weigh more than a hundred pounds, and she easily swung it like it was nothing. I wouldn't underestimate her again.

"Aunt Freya!" Gail rushed to her when she saw her aunt collapsed on the floor. "What did you do?" she hissed at me.

"I didn't do this," I said with a sigh. "It was Spe—I mean one of the blades."

"Oh no," Gail wailed. "She's dead, isn't she?"

Velora rolled her eyes at the young woman.

Kneeling next to Freya, Brenna brushed her finger across Freya's neck and felt the slow, steady beating of her heart. "She's not dead," she scolded. Brenna pressed her hand across Freya's bleeding forehead and healed the cut on her head.

Gail gasped when she saw the cut close-up. "You healed her."

Brenna nodded and then released a long, drawn-out yawn. Healing Freya must having exhausted her. "I'm sorry, I need to rest." Brenna barely made it to the bed before she slipped into a deep sleep.

Moments later, Freya groaned, and her eyes fluttered open. She looked at her niece. "Gail, what are you doing here?"

"I was escorting these two to breakfast when Velora heard the commotion and came running to help. Are you okay?"

Gail helped her aunt to her feet and as she did, we heard a loud clanking and thundering. Gail trembled, and this time it was both Velora and I who stepped in front of the woman as the two blades, Kash and Damon, came barreling back through the doors.

Secretly, I was relieved to see they were okay, but I was nervous because I wasn't sure who was greeting me.

"Hold it right there, or we'll make sure to bring the mountain down on top of you when you get tossed over the balcony. Let's see you dig your way out of that," I threatened, holding out my hand. Both blades came to a sudden stop.

"You can do that?" Gail whispered.

"Now's not the time to question me," I singsonged to the Gail.

"Kash?" I asked, stepping forth to peer into the dragon helm. The blade trembled, and his head bobbed in the slightest.

Gail frowned. "Who are you talking to?"

Freya ignored her niece. "They seem to be back to their 'normal' for now. There is something about you that is making them unstable. I've never seen them lose control so much."

"I'm not sure how to take that," I mumbled.

Freya gave me a side glance. "Neither do I."

I looked between the two men standing before me, both intimidating killing machines, but I knew deep down they were men worth saving. And to do that, I knew I would have to break the curse on the king's blades.

CHAPTER FIFTEEN

I headed to the Gilded Hall with Damon on my heels. I wanted to avoid Kash. So far, Damon was the only one who hadn't turned all murdery on me . . . yet. It didn't mean I was going to let down my guard because I knew it was something else that was pushing the blades to act unnaturally. The very something I knew I was supposed to find and stop. But how? I was so distracted in my thoughts, I didn't see the shadow that slipped out of the ground until it was too late.

It grabbed my ankles, and before I could scream, I was pulled into the earth.

Sudden fear and survival instinct had me holding my breath. But the earth moved around me, creating a bubble of protection. Using mage sight, I could see the ebb and flow as earth magic circled, keeping me in a protective bubble as I slid through the ground. It reminded me of sliding down the hill on my homemade sled as a child. My fear melted away as we pushed up from the ground and ended up on my knees. The room was dark, steamy, and smelled of iron. The strike of a match sounded and its glow illuminated the face of a familiar dwarf.

"Grimkeep!" I cried out when I saw his bruised and battered face. "What happened?"

The flame moved through the darkness and found its home on the wick. Soon the room was brightened by the lantern. Room was an overstatement. We were in the small forge area off the Gilded Hall. Graced by the light, I could see that Grimkeep was covered with bruises and his arm bandaged.

"Had a run-in with goblins. Don't worry, they look much worse. And by worse, I mean dead." He grinned.

"Tell me about what's going on. You said you were going to meet me at the manor. You never came."

The dwarf's ears burned red, and he raised his shoulders. "I meant to come. I did, but I made a discovery. I never expected you to end up at the palace. Molneer told me where to find you. I take it your disguise as a servant didn't pan out."

"Turns out, I'm not very good at following orders."

Grimkeep chuckled. "That'd be your mother in you. But Rhea, look." He beamed, reaching into a sack lying on the floor and pulled out a piece of melted ore mixed with gold.

"What is that?" I asked.

"Beats me. It's the one artifact I found that is from the hoard that is not cursed or tainted, and the goblins wanted it bad."

"How odd . . ." I reached for the piece and as soon as I touched it, I could feel the hum of magic and a flicker of an image followed. My eyes widened, and I met Grimkeep's smile.

"Knew you would like it," he said.

"Grimkeep, it has a memory," I said excitedly.

"You can tell that?"

"I can, and with luck, I may be able to recreate what it once was before it was melted. I can't wait to experiment on it and see what secrets it holds."

Grimkeep frowned. "Be careful with it. It may be the key to finding out what's wrong with our kingdom."

"I will."

"What do we do now?" Grimkeep rubbed the back of his head. "Are you in danger? I can hide you in the tunnels."

I reflected on the blades and the thought of leaving them depressed me. More importantly, if I were going to find answers, I couldn't leave them or the materials I had access to. "I need more time. I must stay and figure out how to break the curse. But until then, I'll take this artifact and see what I can make of it."

"Take care, Rheanon." Grimkeep gave me a wave and slipped back through the earth. I waited until all signs of his magic had faded before I stepped out of the workroom and into the Gilded Hall. The three blades had swords drawn, and each of them were pointing their golden weapons at each other. Or more importantly, it looked like Kash had Damon pinned with the dagger pressed against his neck. Spencer's rapier was touching Kash's neck, and Damon had his own sword drawn, but it was trapped beneath Kash's boot.

"What's going on?" I yelled, surprising them. All three helms turned toward me, and Spencer's seemed to turn farther than the others, like a bird. I shuddered.

Kash backed away from his brother, letting him off the table, but not removing his knife. Kash pointed to me, and then back to Damon, and I interpreted his frustration. Apparently, my disappearance had spurred the attack.

"I'm fine," I groaned. "See." I gave a little twirl. "But now I really need to get to work."

Kash loomed over me, but I pressed my hands against his breastplate, pushing him back in anger. That's when I felt a thrum within the dark armor. A tremor of magic that reacted to my anger, and I felt a physical slap of power. When I gazed into Kash's helm, the swirling clouds that covered his eyes seemed to come alive in answer to my ire. A challenge.

"I may not know what you are, but I will . . . soon," I promised.

The magic stirred again and Kash trembled, his hand raising to his heart.

I hated knowing that they were cursed; that something dark was merging with them, controlling them like a parasite.

I turned to my worktable and noticed that someone had rifled through and stolen my alchemy notes. They weren't the easiest to decipher; lots of sigils and runes, and I didn't think any of the other people here knew how to read them.

But it wasn't until I saw the missing stone that I became truly worried. Someone stole my transfiguration charm. I looked around the room, searching under the table.

"It's definitely gone," I muttered. I went back to look at the pages of my notes where I had written out different alchemy recipes for glamouring marble. I didn't see any harm. Except that it put me further behind in my own studies.

But what could I do?

Nothing.

I needed to keep focusing on my experiments. At least I still had the glamour charm.

"Damon," I called, and the blade came. I motioned to the table, and he sat. I held my breath as I pressed my palm over his bracer, feeling the current of magic that ran through the armor. It wasn't cold like steel usually felt. It was warm to the touch. I gently trailed my fingers up his arm, light as a feather.

"Can you feel that?"

He nodded.

"It's a part of you," I whispered in awe. If I hadn't seen the transformation, the scales of armor erupting from Kash's skin, I wouldn't have believed it.

But now I was asking so much more. Of the three, Damon seemed to be the least threatening. His helm was the clearest, and for the moment, he was the one I trusted. "You are the blade named strength. I'm going to try to take the smallest scraping of your armor using a chisel and hammer. Do you think you have enough strength to keep still?"

Damon dipped his head.

Unwrapping the chisel set, I laid out the tools before me. I started to have second thoughts about what I was about to do. I needed to get a piece of his armor, but if it was attached to him physically—if he could feel every touch—I was pretty much asking permission to skin him . . . and hopefully he wouldn't kill me in the process. This wasn't just any armor; this was cursed armor with a protective magic.

I picked up the chisel and hammer and moved around

so I was at his back. "Your back has the least amount of nerve receptors. It may hurt for a moment, but as soon as I'm done, I will do my best to heal you."

Damon turned his head. He grabbed the wooden table and braced himself. Being this close to him, I could see the finely etched lines of fur that ran alongside the Lion helm. It gave him a shaggy mane that matched Damon's own long locks. I wondered if the cursed armor chose the forms based on the blade's physical appearance, or if it were something more concrete.

Kash and Spencer each grabbed one of Damon's arms and held it down.

"Oh stars, please let this work."

I placed the chisel at an angle along the back of his breastplate, just below the pauldron. Lifting the hammer, I hit the chisel with a solid hard smack. Damon jerked in pain, but the chisel skidded, not even pulling a metal sliver.

My heart raced as I realized I would have to do it again. Kash and Spencer looked at me and gave me another nod of encouragement. My hands trembled as I prepared to strike again, this time using more strength. Having spent many years bent over an anvil, I wasn't a stranger to the might needed to hammer out metal.

"Please forgive me, Damon," I said as I swung it a second time, using all my strength.

I felt the chisel dig in, and Damon tried to stand up. Kash and Spencer held him in place, and he struggled. I needed another solid hit. Without losing a beat, I swung a third time and felt the metal peel back the barest of a scraping that fluttered to the floor.

"Done!" I cried, tossing the tools. I picked up the black

shaving with tweezers and dropped it in a glass tube, sealing it with a cork.

Damon was raging—flailing—and Kash and Spencer struggled to contain the fierce lion. I took a risk and pressed my hands to his back as I reached for the ley line. Using my mind, I tried to direct the magic within the armor, imagining the skin underneath knitting back together.

Damon settled down at my touch. His head dropped forward onto the table as I healed him and then soothed his pain.

"It's okay. It's all over," I whispered and rubbed his back. A sudden cry was ripped from my throat as I felt the armor latch onto my hand, my fingers sinking into his back like mud. The armor had tasted my magic, and it wanted my power, the same desire as the dark void in the mountain.

Like an infant at a teat, I could feel the armor suck on my hand, and I felt weak as it drained me.

"No!" I cried, fighting to pull my hand away. Damon had passed out on the table and Spencer was pushing down on his back while Kash was gripping my wrist, trying to pull. But neither was helping to release me. I panicked as I remembered what happened last time. I hadn't escaped. It was a burst of light and magic that had released me from the magic eater's grasp.

"Help!" I cried out again.

The artifact Grimkeep gave me glowed from where it sat on the table, and a burst of light shot out of it, striking the armor by my wrist. The darkness recoiled. My hand was freed.

I collapsed on the ground in pain. Tears welled up in my eyes. My right hand was bright red and blistered—then healed. Cupping my arm, I grimaced in pain and looked at the hand that would probably end up scarred.

But I could handle pain. Pain would heal and lessen over time. If Damon had to withstand it, I could as well. The important part was the black shimmer that came from the glass tube.

I lifted the vial to the light and watched as the black sliver would morph between gold, metal, and then a black mist.

"What are you?" I said as it moved back to smoke and then reacted to my voice, flinging itself against the glass. "And what are *you*?" I turned to address the golden rock on the table.

Whatever it was, it was like no magic I'd ever seen or even read about.

CHAPTER SIXTEEN

By evening, I was no closer to finding out what kind of curse was upon the blades, or how to remove it. All I knew was that the armor was sentient and connected to the darkness I sensed within the kingdom. Which meant if I could defeat it, I had an opportunity to break the curse.

Dinner was a minor affair in the parlor room. The stalactite had been removed, and the table repaired. A new copper statue of a woman had been added near the window as a conversation piece.

Annette and Benton were commenting on the sculpture's lifelike features and the way she was looking into her cupped palms with hope. I didn't care for the aura coming off the figure, so I found myself on the far side of the room.

Brenna saw my injured hand and used her magic to heal the worst of the blisters. Instead of my hand being on fire, it felt like a tolerable throbbing. The poor girl fell asleep standing up afterwards, and Annette and I helped her to a sofa to sleep.

"Where's Carlotta?" Shannon asked.

"I don't know," Annette said. "She wasn't at breakfast or lunch, but then again, neither were you." She pointed to me. "Where have you been hiding?"

With all eyes focused my way, I felt myself shrink under the pressure of having to lie. I wasn't good at lying.

A cough came from the doorway, and the king entered, his cape swishing behind him. "I have sad news. It seems that Carlotta has failed in her alchemy attempt."

"What happened?" Benton rubbed his chin and looked at me, his brown eyes narrowed.

"She succeeded—in turning herself into copper." The king pointed to the statue.

Shannon screamed. Annette's hands flew to her mouth, and she looked like she was going to be sick. I couldn't tear my eyes away from Carlotta's serene, hopeful expression encased in the burnished metal.

My stomach dropped and a sour taste filled my mouth. Carlotta had stolen my notes and charm from my work-table and turned herself to metal.

This was my fault.

While everyone else moved farther away, I drew close to the statue. With shaking hands, I touched the charm in her palms. The copper was warm beneath my fingers, but there wasn't a soul. She was gone. There was nothing I could do.

It was her selfish desire for wealth that led her to this state. It isn't my fault. But I still blamed myself.

Trembling, I backed away from the statue, my hand reaching into my pouch and feeling for the other charms, making sure the rest were safe and accounted for. When I removed my hand, a golden thread from the spindle caught on my finger and slipped out of the satchel.

Velora noticed the gold thread and curiously began to pull.

Like a child with a toy, Velora yanked until the spindle

slipped out of my bag and onto the floor. She picked up the gold wrapped firethorn spindle, grinning.

"What is this?" King Goddrick reached for the spindle and fingered the thread. "Did you do this?" He turned to Velora whose eyes narrowed at being cornered.

"Yes," Velora raised her chin high, rising to the challenge.

"How?" he asked.

Velora's eyes strayed to mine for a split second and I shook my head, trying to convince her to back down. In a panic, she gazed at the table full of fruit and desserts and saw plump red strawberries.

"I made it out of straw—"

I could see her still-new human mind trying to process the words for things that she had seen in our world. Butter became butt, strawberries were straw. How was she going to lie about creating golden thread if she didn't even know the word for strawberries?

"Can you do it again?" The king was almost drooling with pleasure at the thought of gaining more gold.

"Of course, *if* I feel like it." Velora flipped her hair over her shoulder and sat down in the king's presence, turning her attention back to her food.

Audible gasps followed. The rest of the occupants stood in silence and awaited the king's famous retaliation for the dishonor he was shown.

Instead of calling down the blades that stood behind him, the king kneeled next to Velora, his voice becoming sweet as honey. "And what can I do to help assist you in creating this miraculous feat?"

Velora's eyes glittered, and she pursed her lips, reveling in the power she had attained. A woman's trick. One that she knew how to use, for even mermaids understood the power of a woman's charm.

King Goddrick placed the spindle in her hands and closed her fingers over it. "I'd even offer you a marriage contract."

She cringed and shook her head. "Lots of raw fish and I will make your gold."

"Excellent. I will see to your wishes, but I too have demands, and I want it by morning."

Velora's eyes fluttered the slightest as he called her bluff. "Your wish, I command."

The king left and the tension in the air dissipated. Annette and Shannon jumped up from their chairs and rushed to Velora's side.

"Is it true? Can you spin gold?" Shannon asked.

"Can you show me?" Annette begged.

Velora basked in her newfound fame, and I groaned. Did she not know what the king would do if she failed? I pushed my plate away, hissing as I forgot about my freshly healed but still sore hand.

Soon after the king left, servers with trays of freshwater mussels appeared. Velora squealed in excitement at the fresh food. She greedily picked up each mussel and slurped the meat from the shell before tossing it to the floor. I'd never seen the girl this happy before. The buffet of seafood continued as another servant brought in crawfish and trout. Velora devoured each tray without sharing a single bite. It mattered not, as no one was interested in fish that were still moving.

After the parade of food, a parade of dresses followed. Gail and Freya brought in trunks of silk dresses, golden armbands, and elegant hair combs.

The awes stopped and I could feel the jealousy rise among the women. Unable to hide their feelings, it marred their beautiful faces. Shannon's cheeks had turned splotchy, Annette was pulling at her golden curls with a vengeance as if she were envisioning weaving her own hair around a spindle.

Benton worked furiously, focusing on a gold-colored napkin. His hands shimmered, and the napkin shifted and changed into a swan, but it didn't solidify or become gold. He sighed and shoved the cloth away angrily. His maker abilities only worked on changing the current physical shape of an object.

Brenna encouraged Benton, her hand resting on his arm, and his cheeks reddened.

Freya interrupted our dinner, and one by one escorted us back to our rooms. For the most part we were in the same wing of the castle. Velora was now escorted to the floor above mine, and I could only imagine what was waiting for her there.

After Freya locked the others in their rooms, we headed toward mine. "You don't have to lock me in," I whispered, walking next to her.

"It's the rules," Freya said.

"But what good are keeping the rules if I already know the secret about the blades."

"That isn't the only secret in this palace. There are many that are not safe for you to discover." She slowed when we came to my door.

"If you lock me in, I guarantee Velora will fail her test. The king will arrive tomorrow to find an empty room. And then what will happen?"

"He will punish her severely." Freya's hands trembled.

I clasped her wrinkled hands between mine and pleaded. "And that will be on you, for I could have stopped it. I can help." I stepped into my room and turned to look at her, pleading with her to not lock me in.

"But if you get discovered, it is I who will pay the price and be punished." Freya's bottom lip trembled. She pushed the door closed. I heard the key insert itself into the lock, but not the click that followed afterward.

Her footsteps faded away, and I tested the handle and felt the door swing inward. Quickly, I closed it again and thanked the stars that Freya had come to her senses.

Judging by the setting sun, I knew it would be awhile before everyone had all retired and it would be safe for me to make my way about the castle. I laid on the bed to take a quick nap knowing that tonight would be a long night of experiments. And now, because of a lie, I had to help a girl create gold.

My hand still throbbed painfully during my sleep, causing my mind to mirror the pulsing pain. In my dream, I was walking down a dimly lit tunnel. The ground was void of prints, and there were no markings on the wall to discern where I was headed. All I knew was the sound of a beating heart surrounded me.

"Come to me. Free me," the voice beckoned. "Release me and I will give you all that you desire. I'll grant your every wish."

"What I wish is for you to be gone," I answered, letting my voice carry. In the very realistic dream, I could feel the temperature rising. My clothes were sticking to my skin, my damp hair clinging to my face.

A rumble deep in the mountain followed. "Foolish

child, you cannot banish me. For I am, and I will always be."

Then, as if I were walking backward, my dream flowed in reverse, the throbbing sped up, and I awoke back in my bed. My heart beat in my chest as though I had run a thousand paces. My palms were sweating, and the hair on the back of my neck was wet.

It was just a dream . . . I think.

As I sat up in bed and held my still healing hand, I couldn't help but wonder if I was connected to the thing in the mountain. That by feeding on my power twice, it had linked with me.

The moonlight poured through the glass balcony doors, lighting my room, leaving very few shadows for intruders to hide behind. I'd slept longer than I wanted to, and now had a very long list of projects to finish in a few hours.

I opened my unlocked door and almost walked into a powerful chest.

Strong hands caught me around the waist as I stumbled into Kash's arms.

"I knew you would fall for me." Kash's golden eyes met mine. Even though he was teasing, I could read the shame he was hiding behind a false smile. His dark curly hair was slightly wet, and he was wearing black pants and a crisp emerald green shirt.

Kash's hands tightened around my waist, and his head dipped as he hugged me, pressing his face into my shoulder. When Kash pulled away, his face was anxious. "I'm sorry. I had no right." He ran his hands through his wet hair. "Not after yesterday. Not after I tried to hurt you."

"You're right," I said, my voice cold. "You shouldn't be

anywhere near me. You betrayed me." Seeing Kash in the flesh and not embodied by a cursed suit of armor made all the pent-up feelings I had held back over the last day come tumbling out. I brushed him off and headed up the nearest set of stairs to get to Velora's room.

"Rhea, wait, hear me out," Kash called out after me. I stopped on the steps and glared at him.

He followed me, his face conveying his pain. "I have powerful feelings for you, and the curse knows that. It uses them against me. It uses them to control me."

"You came to my home. You lied to me, deceived me, toyed with my heart, and then lead your troops to my door," I snapped. "That was your plan all along. You are the king's silent blade, after all. I never knew just how deeply you cut until your betrayal."

At my harsh words, he straightened like a soldier and took the brunt of my anger. "Rhea, it's the curse. It wasn't me."

"How do I know that? I only knew you during the night when the curse was dormant. It was those lies that sting the most because I don't know what is real."

My heart was hurting. I was angry. Angry at being duped. Angry that I didn't see what he was doing. Angry because I wasn't smart enough to catch it.

"Rheanon. I want you to know that I never intended to hurt you."

"What was your plan?" I asked. "Seduce me, make me fall for you with your soft kisses so I could then walk with you like a lovesick puppy right into the king's clutches?"

Kash was trembling, his hands balled into white-knuckled fists. "That day in Verdan, you ignited a hunting instinct in the blade he had never seen the likes of before.

He was going mad with desire, and the fact you outsmarted him only made it more infuriating. He refused to stop hunting you, and because of that my conscious awoke. When the blade was sheathed and I came to, my horse was gone, and I was alone. I really did stumble on the manor by accident. And just my luck, I found you."

"Why didn't you capture me that night, or alert the soldiers where I was?"

"Because *I* don't obey the orders of the king, only the blades are under compulsion to do so. I did everything I could to protect you. It's easiest on our physical mind to sleep during the day while the curse takes over, and then live our true lives at night. The same for the curse. It's like you said, dormant at night and has no idea what we think or are doing. But sometimes during the day, if we fight it, we can see and hear what's going on, and we have some control over our bodies. But there's only so much our mind can take before breaking. So we more often than not give in to it."

I thought about Kash's confession, considering the blades' struggles to stay sane against a stronger entity. *Could I have the same strength to resist, or would I slowly withdraw like they did?*

Kash continued his plea. "Every morning, I would run far into the mountains before I unsheathed the blade and let the curse take over. Then, when night fell, I would return to you. That day of the avalanche, you crossed his path. I suppressed him enough to try and save you. When you fell, and the avalanche took you, I wanted to die."

"But I didn't," I whispered.

"And I was ever so grateful. I thought you were dead, and I retreated into the recesses of my mind. I didn't want to live anymore. Then I felt the blade's desire kick in, alerting me to your presence. I began to hope. And it *was* you. Then as soon as night fell, I forced the blade to be sheathed."

I continued up the stairs, and we kept our voices hushed. Even though we knew the castle was asleep, there was always the chance of running into King Goddrick.

"It's interesting how you talk about sheathing and releasing the blade regarding the curse. How connected is it to your weapon?" I asked, running my hand up the wooden bannister. When we reached the next floor, we stopped in an alcove under a window.

Kash held out the cursed knife. I refused to touch it. "It's fine. You've held it before at the manor."

"I know. It didn't feel cursed. It felt normal."

"That's because you never held the blade during the day." He continued to hold it out, and I hesitantly picked it up. Once again, it felt normal. Just thinking about it made my skin crawl.

"Can't you keep it sheathed permanently?" I asked, handing it back to him.

"If we don't unsheathe it willingly, the transformation becomes extremely painful. You saw what it does to our bodies." Kash tied the sheath back onto his belt. "It's the choice of pain between getting stabbed hard once or being burned alive."

"How long?" I asked. "How long have you been cursed?"

"Three years."

"And how long has the mountain been trembling?"

Kash blinked as he thought back. "It's only recently started. Do you think it has something to do with it?"

"I don't know."

Just then, a tremor started low in the mountain. The chandeliers swung, and the ground shifted beneath our feet. My eyes were immediately drawn to the cavernous ceiling, and I watched in terror as it crumbled, and a large outcropping of rock fell.

I froze, unable to move.

Kash rushed at me, his chest hitting mine as he pressed me against the side of the wall, sheltering me from the mini collapse. The mountain continued to rumble, and my mind was brought back to the avalanche and being trapped beneath hundreds of pounds of snow and ice.

My body trembled. Kash's breath was warm. My cheek pressed against his chest, and I could hear the beating of his heart. I felt safe and protected. When the mountain settled, he pulled me away from the wall and leaned down to look into my eyes.

"Are you okay?"

I nodded numbly.

"It's like the mountain was listening to us," Kash breathed out. He took my hand and led me around the large rocks that were littered in the halls. I wondered how much of the palace was damaged. How many more earthquakes could it survive?

Footsteps came running up behind us, and Spencer appeared. His sandy brown hair was a mess, his worried blue eyes met mine. "You're okay?"

"I'm okay." I leaned to look over his shoulder as Damon took the steps a little slower, his green eyes filled with pain.

"Damon, are you okay?" I noticed his shirt was unlaced. "Let me see your back," I demanded.

"Trying to get me to strip now?" he teased lightly.

"Stop it, I need to know if it left any permanent marks."

Damon turned and lifted the white shirt over his well-muscled shoulders. There was nothing other than the faintest white scar. I ran my finger over it, feeling the raised white skin. "Does it hurt?"

"Not really. Only the memory is painful." He turned, pulling his shirt back down before tucking it into his pants.

"You remember?" I asked.

"That's because the curse has less control over me. I find I can retain more of my own consciousness than my brothers." We continued walking toward Velora's room and stopped outside her door.

"Why is that, I wonder?"

"I've often questioned the same thing, and I think it has to do with a certain trigger."

"A trigger. What kind?" I asked.

"I believe it is our desires," Damon explained. He was about to go into more detail when we heard a scream from inside Velora's room.

The men looked at each other. Without hesitation, Damon tucked his shoulder and slammed it into the door, trying to break it down.

"Wait!" Spencer pushed Damon back. He gripped the handle and opened it. "It's unlocked."

"Freya," I breathed out, realizing she left the door unlocked for me.

We rushed into Velora's room to see it in utter and complete chaos.

CHAPTER SEVENTEEN

"Make it stop!" Velora screamed, her face was puffy, and her eyes were red. She rubbed at her eyes and stepped over a straw bale. She sneezed loudly, sending more of the loose straw into the air.

When Velora saw me, she grabbed my hands. "Please, make my nose stop exploding!" As she begged, she turned to the side and another set of sneezing fits followed. "Oh," Velora groaned and collapsed on the floor in a pile of the straw.

"I think you're allergic to straw." I covered my mouth with my hand to hide my amusement. "I didn't know mermaids could have allergies."

"Achoo!" Velora sneezed and clawed at her arms, her skin covered with red welts. "It won't stop itching. It's worse than when I got tail rot as a child."

Along with the bigger, nicer room, the king had also filled every available space with straw. In the corner sat a spinning wheel. Her own mouth had caused this problem.

"You were the one who said you could turn it to gold," I chastised.

"I lied. I was hungry. I get grouchy when I'm hungry. Can you blame me?" She pouted, and I found it irritating how beautiful she looked while pouting, even with a puffy face and red eyes. Some women have all the luck.

"No," I sighed, looking at the mess. "I don't blame you, but this is going to take all night and I don't have a charm for this. Well, not anymore," I muttered, thinking of Carlotta.

Spencer stepped close. "Just tell us what you need us to do?"

"I need you and Kash to gather every available reel of yarn that you can find in the palace and bring it here."

My golden spindle had been left in the room on Velora's night table. I grabbed it and felt the hum of magic. I knew by using it I was slowly going to drain it, but I had little choice. I needed to help her.

Picking up my golden spindle, I pulled out a long strand. I made a few knots in the thread. I ran it through my fingers and began a complicated finger weaving technique. The repetition brought back a memory of sitting in our drafty tower with my six sisters as we practiced knitting, cross-stitching, and mother chastising us about the links in our chains. She deemed it practice for creating the perfect sleeping spell. As long as I tied in the right knots and placed the right sigils in the floor around the spinning wheel, it would work . . . I hoped.

Everything that passed through the spinning wheel and touched the golden thread should turn to gold. I had no hopes of actually twisting the dry straw into thread. That was a farce. We were going to burn the straw and instead feed spools and spools of regular yarn through spinning wheel. I tied the thread and locked it in place along the spokes.

"Now we have to get rid of the straw." I pointed to the fireplace.

Velora frowned at me, but I stamped my foot. "Now, Velora!" She crawled across the floor, the straw stuck in her hair. With angry fistfuls, she tossed it into the fire, and it was immediately gobbled up by a golden salamander who hopped out of the cinders to snatch it midair. The little creature was happy and hungry.

"Sol!" I recognized his coloring, and the fire elemental came out of the fire. "Do you think you could help me?" I begged. "Do you see all of this straw? It can be yours. I just need all of it eaten or burned by morning."

Sol stamped his feet in excitement, turned in a circle, and disappeared in a poof of smoke. Moments later, the room was filled with hundreds of salamanders as they greedily ran along the room, burning up the straw and consuming the ashes left behind.

Velora jumped up in excitement like a little child and wanted to keep trying to pet the flaming lizards. "They look like guppies that are on fire!" She bent down to pet the nearest salamander.

"I wouldn't do that if I were you," Damon warned, and lifted his foot as an orange salamander began to burn up the straw, almost catching his boot on fire. "They don't like to be grabbed in surprise."

"She's a water creature herself," I said. "Fire and water aren't necessarily compatible."

"Ouch! You flaming piece of driftwood," Velora cried out, grabbing her burned fingers. In retaliation, she flicked her hand and a spray of water streamed at the salamander, who easily dodged. "Take that. You ugly fire guppy!"

Over the next candle mark, the salamanders burned up

all the straw and ate the ash, leaving no evidence of the straw behind, although Velora managed to leave large puddles of water in her wake. Kash and Spencer returned, and I sat Velora down in front of the spinning wheel.

"Now, you have to do the rest." I showed her how to attach the thread and weave it through the wheel, demonstrating how the foot pedal would draw the thread through. As it touched the spindle's enchanted thread, it turned to gold and refilled the reel.

"When it's done, feed through another." I pointed to the boxes of reels lined up on the floor.

"Do I have to?" she sighed.

"If you want to keep your big room, your fresh seafood, and dresses . . . then yes."

"If you don't, it's back to cooked meat for you." Kash gave the wheel a casual spin and Velora covered her mouth at the thought.

"No, I'll do it." Her fingers grabbed the thread, and she pumped the foot pedal, her deft fingers flying as she fed the thread through at an inhuman speed.

"Well, I don't think it will take her long at all." Spencer whistled in surprise as Velora zipped through a reel and quickly threaded a second.

"No. I think we are safe to leave her and go to our next task," I said, covering my mouth with a yawn. I tucked the almost empty spindle into my satchel, the magic almost depleted.

We headed back to the Gilded Hall and sat around our worktable. Even though we had all been here hours before, it was different because they were no longer in their cursed form. There wasn't an awkward tension, and I didn't have to worry about getting stabbed in the back.

I handed Damon the flask with the sliver of armor I'd peeled from his back.

"It looks . . . alive," Damon shuddered as he peered into the corked flask and tapped it. It shifted from black metal to mist, then back.

"My thoughts as well," I murmured.

Spencer was looking through my notes. Kash sat on the table, his legs swinging freely as he winked at me, unashamed of showing his feelings. My cheeks grew warm, and I cleared my throat, nodding toward the books. I handed one to each of them.

"We've read these?" Spencer said, sighing. "I've gone over them extensively. There isn't anything about cursed armor."

"We're not looking for a way to break a curse. We're looking for a record of an ancient entity," I explained. They had laid out each of their weapons on the table, and I kept them all sheathed. Using my gift, I touched each one and tried to determine what they were made of.

I would have expected the blades to be made of layers of sweet iron or high carbon steel—but I found none of those metals in these weapons.

The knife with its curved handle in the shape of a dragon's head, the rapier with its double head and engraved hawk motif, and the broadsword were all made of a metal that I didn't recognize. It was the same as my charm. But unlike my charm, it didn't sing.

It terrified me to dig further into the weapons for fear of waking the darkness. As I continued to take notes and test it with my magic, I would catch glimpses of the previous owners of the weapons.

When I touched Damon's blade, I saw visions of a

young general being honored after winning a war. I felt his pride and responsibility. The blade, a prize given to him by a king. Spencer's rapier was older, once belonging to a scholar by the name of Aster, a student of the books. He was given the weapon to study, not for the purpose of battle. When I touched Kash's blade, I sensed it belonged to someone much older, a king of the past.

My only source of information was the history book where I could compare the descriptions of the late King Einsamall, the first dwarf king of Ragnar.

But none of the history books spoke of what happened to the weapons or how they reappeared hundreds of years later. How did King Goddrick find them, and what would possess him to bestow them and the curse upon his sons?

I looked up from my scroll to see Kash with his head down on his arms, his black hair hiding his eyes.

Damon was no longer reading but prodding the sliver of metal in the glass again for fun. Each time he poked it, it shifted back to mist before settling back into a black sliver.

"Stop that," Spencer chided as he looked up from one of the three books he had spread out before him. "You're making it angry."

"It's from the skin of my back. I can do what I want with it." Damon leaned away and put his boot on the table.

Spencer's lip curled up in disgust. "Just don't go and name it, all right?"

Damon's green eyes twinkled mischievously. "Too late, I named it Scabby."

Spencer groaned and tossed a book at Damon's head. Damon ducked, and the book smacked into Kash, who woke up, prepared for an attack. He jumped so high he fell backwards in his chair and it broke.

"I thought you were supposed to be the alert one." I walked over to Kash as he looked up at me from the ground.

"I'm sorry. I haven't slept much lately. Fighting a curse is exhausting, but for you, it's worth it." His lips pulled back into a cheeky grin. I felt that familiar rush, and my breath caught.

"I still got it," he said smoothly.

"Got what?" I purposely exhaled and held out my hand to help him up. Kash didn't need it as he sprung forward, causing me to retreat and back into the table with a bump.

"Careful," Damon warned, holding up the flask. "You spooked Scabby."

"Its name is not Scabby," Spencer argued.

"When you get your own piece of back flesh, you can name it whatever you want. Until then, stop making fun of Scabby," Damon said, taunting his brother.

Kash ignored both of them as he continued to stalk me. I leaned back, and he placed his arms on either side of me, drawing close. His golden eyes searched mine, ignoring his brothers bickering. He turned his head and whispered into my ear, "I can still take your breath away."

I reached behind me and pulled the sheathed knife and poked him in the stomach.

Kash let out a grunt of pain and he retreated. "It seems I can do the same to you," I gleefully whispered back.

"Touché." Kash laughed, clutching his midsection.

"Hey, Rhea." Spencer waved me over to his side of the table. He had put the book down and was staring at the artifact Grimkeep had given me. It was sitting on the worktable, and we had been using it as a paperweight since I hadn't had time to study it closer.

"Yeah?"

"Did you see this?" He pointed to a crevice that had slipped my notice.

Spencer handed it to me, and I peered into the spot that had melted and folded over on itself.

"Bring me a light."

Damon held up a candle, and as the flames flickered over the ore, we saw a rune and then a second one. Not just any runes. Eld runes.

"The forgotten language," Spencer said in awe.

"Not only that," I said in excitement, "this ore has a memory. I may be able to reconstruct it into its original form."

"Then what are we waiting for?" Spencer asked. "Let's get forging."

"Not tonight." Kash's voice carried the command across the chamber. "Tonight is over."

"Come on!" Spencer was practically bouncing with enthusiasm. "We've just discovered a significant find."

"No, we can't expect Rhea to work miracles on very little sleep. Not only that, but we also need to rest. We are mentally stronger to help her during the day if we do."

Damon nodded. "We can be more aware if we're rested."

I hated that Kash was right, but as soon as he mentioned sleep, I could feel my eyelids drooping. The silent yawns I had been holding back all night slipped out.

We headed back to my room and Kash slowed to drop me off. Damon kept walking.

Spencer hesitated. "Just one more question—"

"No, Spencer. I will not let us run her into the ground searching for a way to break the curse. We lived with it for a few years. What's a few more days?"

Spencer slumped his shoulders and continued down the hall. I didn't actually know where their rooms were. When Spencer was out of earshot, I turned to Kash.

"Except that I don't know if I have days." I had forgotten about my task and put these studies above the king's demands.

"Tomorrow." Kash placed a finger on my lips, silencing me. "We will start again tomorrow." He opened the door and waited for me to go inside.

I turned to look at him and saw the sadness he was hiding. The moonlight highlighted his eyes, making their gold color seem even more effervescent.

"But what guarantee do I have that it will be you when I wake up tomorrow? What if you try to kill me again?" I asked, clutching my injured hand.

Kash reached to brush his knuckles across my cheek. "Well, I give you permission to toss me off the balcony again and again. That seemed to knock some sense into me."

I let out a chuckle.

"There's my girl," Kash teased.

I held the door open for him, making a show that I wasn't locking it. "Can you stay with me till I fall asleep?"

He shook his head. "It's too dangerous. But one day, I swear you will wake up, and *I* will be by your side and not the blade."

"I don't know. I kind of like the strong and silent Kash."

"Oh, you wound me." He plunged a fake dagger into his heart and staggered. Then he stood up straight, his smile falling from his face. "Till tomorrow," he promised. He leaned, and I wanted him to kiss me like before, but he hadn't. I think he was waiting to earn back my trust.

"Till tomorrow."

I wanted to keep talking, I wanted to spend every minute of moonlight we had left by his side, but Kash closed the door, signaling that it was time for me to sleep. I headed to my bed, and sunk into the mattress, passing out before my head hit the pillow.

CHAPTER EIGHTEEN

"She did it!" Gail cried out as she opened the balcony doors to my room. Light streamed in and with it, a bitter wind. I shivered and crawled further under the blankets to escape the winter's icy fingers.

Gail saw my attempt at burrowing under the covers and she sighed. "I guess you don't care that another girl has outdone you?"

"Huh?" I mumbled into my pillow, still half asleep.

"That Velora girl has turned straw into gold! The entire palace is talking about it."

"Really?" I rolled over and looked at her groggily. "Good for her."

Gail grabbed the bedding and yanked, pulling it off my body. I cringed and curled up in a ball, tucking my feet under my dress.

"Why is your fire out? In fact, every room I've been to is like this. It's as if the salamanders were too busy to tend to the fires."

"Or they're too full," I added.

Gail frowned. "Now, that's silly. How could they get full? But never mind. Today is a day of celebrations. It's the first day of our Winter Festival. Fireworks, delicious food, reindeer races, and a carnival. It's the one night a year we don't sleep."

"But what about the curfew?"

"There's no curfew on Winter Festival because it's held at the Winter Village."

"Where?" I asked.

"Halfway down the mountain. Near the soldier garrison. As soon as the storm ended two days ago, they began putting up the festival tents and building the ice rink. I've heard that a Magical Menagerie has already arrived."

"Surely, the king doesn't mean for all of us to attend?"

"I do, in fact," King Goddrick said from the hall.

Gail curtseyed and quickly left the room, leaving me to address the feared king in wrinkled clothes. At least I had fallen asleep in my dress and wasn't in a nightdress.

The king stepped into the room wearing a golden crown upon his head, and a dark red jacket trimmed in speckled Avrin fur, lined with gold buttons. He was in full royal regalia, and he unconsciously rubbed a thick gold ring on his middle finger.

I slipped out of the bed and curtseyed. "Thank you, Your Majesty, for your benevolence."

"I am surprised that your friend succeeded. I half expected her to fail."

"You'd be surprised what a determined woman can do when cornered," I said.

"No doubt." The king moved to stand on the balcony and look out over the mountain into the valley. "Today, thousands of my people will gather to celebrate midwinter in the palace's shadow. The Winter Festival is not to be missed, and it's the greatest spectacle in the seven kingdoms. People travel far and wide to see the wealth my kingdom provides. I shall spare no expense. Velora has guaranteed us a fruitful winter."

He was boasting. What will he do when the golden spindle has dried up and can no longer turn items into gold? One problem at a time, I told myself.

King Goddrick confronted me, his eyes narrowing with suspicion. "There also seems to be a problem with my blades. I assign one to you, yet find that all three are frequently missing."

"The blades obey no one but yourself, King Goddrick. Maybe they are taking their guard duties seriously."

"Maybe," King Goddrick turned his gaze upon me, his eyes narrowing in distrust. "With all your experiments and potion brewing in the Gilded Hall, I thought maybe *you've* figured out their secret."

"I have." I licked my lips and steadied my breathing, looking the king dead in the eyes. "The blades aren't human but are rather an entity that can neither be harmed nor destroyed."

The king's face morphed into one of absolute smugness. He crossed his arms over his chest and smirked, taking pleasure because he believed he still held their true secret over me.

I played the red herring because I knew I was going to ask a particular question. "The gold in your palace. Where did it come from?"

King Goddrick's lips pinched together. "From my personal mines in my mountains." He rubbed the gold ring on his finger.

"What about your ring?" I asked.

"This is a family heirloom," he rushed out.

"During my experiments, I tested some of the gold items in your palace."

"A little presumptuous, don't you think?" Those hawk-like eyes narrowed even further.

"There are pieces here from the cursed hoard," I blurted out, staring right at his hand and the ring he was running his thumb under.

King Goddrick grinned knowingly. "And?"

"I just thought you would like to know, considering that it's had adverse effects on—"

King Goddrick cut me off. "Be careful how far you dig into my affairs. You may not like what you find." The king snapped his fingers and the dragon blade entered. His eyes especially clouded today, his armor rattling heavily as he marched in to hover over me. The king snapped a second time and Kash drew his knife, the blade arcing through the air to point at my neck.

I couldn't help but take a step back in fear, not knowing who was staring back at me.

The king laughed. "You were correct. They're my blades, and they obey me."

"Yes, Your Majesty." I bowed my head as far as I could without the blade nicking me.

"I'll leave this one with you." King Goddrick turned on his heel, his red cape billowing after him. As soon as he left, the knife in Kash's hand didn't lower. I still stood there trembling, unable to force myself to move. Unable to look into the dragon's helm for fear of who or what was looking back.

"Please, Kash," I whispered, trying to break through to his consciousness. "I know you're in there." His hand trembled, and the knife lowered. It was as if he was fighting to keep control. But Kash did finally retreat to the outer hall.

Gail sidestepped him before entering. "That one's trouble."

"No doubt," I said, rubbing my neck. I could almost feel the blade against my skin, and an echo of emotion still followed me.

"Come, you'll need clothes for the outdoor festivals. I'm so excited. I haven't ice skated in years."

As Gail laid out winter clothes, I was grateful for the thick wool dress with antler buttons and black fur-lined boots. She even provided cream woolen gloves with golden snowflakes sewn onto the cuffs.

Freya was waiting for me in the hall. I opened my mouth to thank her for leaving my room unlocked, but she shook her head, warning me from speaking. Looking up, I saw the others were also in the hall. Velora wore a vibrant green wool dress with silver accents. She was being showered with even more extravagant gifts than the rest of us. I didn't care, but it was obvious the same couldn't be said for Shannon and Annette. Their faces were dark with envy, their lips pinched in displeasure. Their hearts had been poisoned with jealousy. Benton stood next to Brenna, her arm threaded through his, her cheeks rosy already from blushing.

Benton leaned close and placed his hand on her scarf, and it lifted and folded into a perfect rose shape at her neck. She squealed in delight. It seemed this test had brought some of the people together.

This would definitely make today's events more interesting. Freya explained we would eat breakfast together and then head down the mountain for the first of the many events of the day.

But I never made it to breakfast as a streak of orange and gold blur crossed my path, running in circles, a trail of flames following close behind.

Sol had left the safety of his flames. Fire elementals were not meant to stray far for long periods from their flames, which meant something was wrong.

I hung back as everyone left, and he continued to spin in circles until I followed him toward the Gilded Hall.

I veered off and headed toward the workroom. I had left Grimkeep's artifact, and I had a sneaking-suspicion I shouldn't have. It was an important piece of history, and I'd foolishly left it unguarded. At the thought, I took off in a run, the clang of Kash's armor rattling behind me. As soon as I dashed through the open doors, I looked into the dark hall and sighed in relief.

There it was on the table, safe and sound. I had panicked over nothing.

Except Sol was still frantic. He raced up the table, and then back down, the flames along his back were slowly ebbing out. He needed to get back into a burning fire before he flickered out.

"Sol, there's nothing here. It's fine. Let's get you into the fire." I kneeled in front of the fireplace to get a fire going.

Sol let out a cry and raced toward me. He scrambled up the side of the brick and launched into the air, biting the long-clawed hand that snaked out of the chimney to tear at my face. Sol sunk his teeth into the goblin's hand and an inhuman scream let loose. The goblin dropped out of the chimney and into the ashes.

There was no mistaking the thin spindly arms, the oblong nose, sharp pointy fangs, and the smell of sulfur that accompanied these devilish creatures.

"Goblins!" I yelled.

I grabbed the fire poker that was hanging on a hook and flailed it, but more goblins were filling into the room. They were coming out of the fireplace, up from the hidden grates and wood chutes, like bees swarming out of a hive.

I was worried that Kash was still under the king's influence. Would he protect me or fall under the dark spell? Who would I face?

Kash's knife whipped out, and he backhanded a goblin that jumped onto the table, making a grab for the artifact. The goblin tumbled backward into another that had climbed on the table.

They were after Grimkeep's treasure.

Three goblins launched onto Kash's back, scratching, clawing, and one even tried to bite Kash's helm, but the armor protected him.

Sol collapsed in my lap, the warmth of his body quickly fading. His scales felt like ice.

I wasn't going to lose him.

"Fiergo," I cried, and a ball of fire exploded into the grate, sending a wave of flames upward into the chimney. I could hear the screams as the goblins clawed their way upward and away from the magical blaze.

I dropped Sol into the inferno and watched as he soaked up the magical flames. I didn't know elementals could change their size, but Sol grew, his body eating the fire and absorbing my magic until he was the size of a large Kern Hound. His eyes flashed with excitement as he raced out of the fire and began attacking all the goblins, snapping them between his teeth, tossing them over his shoulder into the wall, his tail whipping out and bowling them over.

A goblin grabbed Grimkeep's artifact and took off running toward the exit.

"Over there!" I yelled as I swung the fire poker at the nearest goblin, smacking him in the skull and sending him tumbling head over heels.

Kash picked up Sol and tossed the giant fire salamander across the room like a flaming arrow.

The goblin saw the halo of light around him and looked up to see a massive smiling fireball with black, beady eyes crash into him with an explosion that rocked the chandeliers. The two tumbled and rolled across the floor like a blazing tumbleweed, scattering arcs of light. The goblin dropped the artifact as he was preoccupied with swinging his spindly arms, trying to douse his clothes that were incinerating into ashes.

Sol grabbed the artifact between his teeth and was running back to me. With each step he took, I could see his size diminishing as the magic was consumed.

There were too many, and as we fought, more kept streaming in along the ceilings. Kash had gone berserk. I wasn't sure who or what was controlling him. I watched in awe as he lived up to the name of the silent blade. He twisted, turned, striking with his dagger before hitting two more targets. All of it a silent deadly dance as he continued to fight and incapacitate the goblins.

Sol made it to me, and I kneeled down to grab the treasure and I almost dropped it as it was infused with power. My power, and it was resonating back to me.

Shake and bake, an echo filtered through my mind.

"What?" I said in disbelief, as no one was speaking to me.

"Goblins hate earthquakes and fire," the voice explained.

"Oh, makes sense, I think."

I knew I must be going crazy, listening to a voice in my head, but I reached down to the floor, pushing through the stone for the ley line of power, and found the closest one. I only wanted to make the ground shake, focusing it in the room so I didn't take the entire mountain with me.

"Shake," I whispered. The ground trembled, and the goblins froze in fear. A few backtracked up the chimneys and across the ceiling.

With one hand on the ground, I reached the other out and touched Sol. His golden scales were hot like boiling water, yet he wasn't burning me. I found the ley line and gripped it, feeding power into Sol at the same time. The fire salamander grew again. This time I didn't stop, continuing to feed him magic. His feet stamped in excitement, his head elongated, and churning balls of fire seeped out of his nostrils.

"Now bake," I urged Sol, who turned and released a blast of fire at eye level of the goblins.

They screamed as the room continued to quake as my fiery salamander chased them down. He burped fire at a final goblin that was attempting a last-ditch effort to get to me.

Kash blocked his path. With the shaking room, the dangerous blade and a burping fire salamander were too much. The goblin backed away.

When the room was empty, I released hold of the ley line and the shaking stopped. Sol quickly returned to his normal size, and I collapsed to the ground, still cradling the artifact.

"Good riddance, stinking little mouth breathers."

I stared around the room, searching for the speaker before gazing down at the artifact. The runes inside the treasure glowed with magic before fading away, and an eerie silence followed.

CHAPTER NINETEEN

The goblin attack didn't go unnoticed, and I heard the coming footsteps of soldiers. Quickly, I shoved the treasure into the embers and called out to the salamander. "Sol, can you and your brethren hide this? I'll call for you when I need it."

The salamander replied with the last dregs of his fiery burps.

If the goblins really were afraid of fire, then I could think of no safer place than in the nest of the fire salamanders. Sol crawled into the fireplace and wrapped his body around the artifact, giving me a sly wink before disappearing into the flames.

The guards arrived and so did the hawk bladesman. They began the removal of the goblin bodies. Kash grabbed my arm, his grip painful as he hauled me from the room.

Spencer cut him off, and the two silently stared at each other. Kash's body trembled beneath the armor. Blood splattered across the front, and even his hand on my arm was coating my skin with the stinking goblin blood.

Spencer would not back down, his hand going to his rapier in challenge.

"I'll be fine," I snapped, fearing the darkness gathering

across his eyes. I had glimpsed gold, but it was quickly being replaced by black as Kash was weakening. Losing control. I placed my hand over my nose. "You smell."

The helm snapped toward me so fast, I could almost read how affronted he was at the possibility.

"It's the goblin blood." I pointed to the splatter on my skin and then gently pried his fingers off my upper arm.

I had just removed Kash's possessive grip when King Goddrick appeared. "What happened?" He looked over my shoulder at the mass of bodies that still littered the floor. "Why would the goblins come to my hall?"

"Goblins are attracted to treasure," I said, skirting the truth. "Maybe your newfound wealth has brought them to your doorstep."

Goddrick's eyes widened in fear. "I need more guards on my treasury. Seal every entrance, sewer, and water grate. Find out how they got in and barricade it. I will not have my wealth stolen by goblins." His eyes narrowed, and he looked at Kash covered in blood. "Once again, my deadliest blade has proven useful."

Kash shook, whether from pride or anger, I wasn't sure.

"Don't worry, they won't attack here again," the king boasted. "My blades will take care of them."

The rest of the morning flew in a haze as I was shuffled into a clean dress and then escorted outside to where an open sleigh was waiting. I wasn't in the mood to watch races or partake in the various celebrations. I was still wondering about the voice I'd heard in the Gilded Hall.

"I'm not going crazy," I said out loud.

"Oh, we're all a little crazy," Annette cooed as she slipped into the sleigh, sliding onto the bench seat across from me. "Otherwise, we wouldn't be out in the freezing cold."

"I hear you," Shannon said, shivering, pulling her green wool wrap jacket closer around her shoulders. "There'd better be some food or single men where we're going."

Velora seemed the most eager of the ladies and she pushed through to take the empty seat next to me and leaned over to whisper. "I will see Marco today."

"Really," I said. "How do you know?"

Velora rolled her eyes. "If what you say is true, that he survived the attack, then he will find me," she said confidently. Velora smoothed out her skirt and craned her neck to search the crowds.

"We haven't even left the palace grounds yet," I teased.

"It doesn't matter. He will come."

The driver cracked his whip, and the reindeer startled; we jolted forward, and I grasped the side for support. Being in an open sleigh made me nervous. What if we were caught in another avalanche? What if a snowstorm came? I was becoming negative about being outdoors because nothing ever seemed to go right for me.

As soon as the wind whipped against my cheeks, I pulled the fur-lined hood over my face and buried my hands under my thighs for warmth. We slowed when we came to a village of colorful red and blue tents. The staff had worked hard to create a winter wonderland. Red and blue flags lined the road, marking out the path for the walkways and what would be the reindeer's race this evening. A wooden stage had been constructed and already a band was playing music. As we passed, I glanced inside the tents to see private sitting areas with chairs and settees with blankets and furs for people to seek warmth and shelter from the wind. Merchants and vendors had already claimed the smaller tents, and I could smell cinnamon, and sugary treats, popped corn, and roasted nuts.

One tent stood out, as it was the largest of the bunch. I knew from the banners flying and the number of soldiers stationed outside that this was the king's personal tent. The hawk and lion blades were stationed at its entrance. As our sleigh passed, I couldn't help but notice that both Damon and Spencer's head followed our route.

Behind the tents was a well-established military outpost, and I knew we were near the guard tower that Herst had tried to describe to me. So many of these outbuildings were here year-round, including the stables, barracks, and a blacksmith forge.

My interest piqued when I saw Molneer in the back of the forge working with a smaller smelting furnace.

When we disembarked the sleigh, I wanted to head over to the forge, but knew I would have to wait to slip away from the rest of the group. But my presence didn't go unnoticed. A dark shadow immediately appeared on my right.

I didn't even need to look to know that Kash had joined me. I could almost feel the melancholy that hovered whenever Kash was nearby. A perpetual sadness. When the dragon blade appeared at my side, the ladies gave us a wide berth, which was fine because it gave me time to think.

As Velora was the honored guest, she was the one who was paraded around the festival, much to her chagrin. We were basically treated as her ladies-in-waiting. She looked like a petulant child who wanted to be anywhere other than here.

A royal page was our guide, and he led us on a tour of each of the vendors where we were given attention and showered with gifts. Sweet confections, sticky buns, jeweled combs, and more.

I was thankful that it was Velora and not me getting the scrutiny of the villagers. I watched her sitting on a chair on the platform, and I heard many comments about her beauty and whether she would be the next queen. Velora did not like that idea at all, and quickly shot them down. "I don't want to marry the king. I'm going to marry Marco."

I was about to make my escape to the forge when I was sidetracked by Shannon once again.

"Did Velora really spin straw into gold?" the woman asked me casually, while giving a side eye toward Velora. The mermaid was moving from group to group looking for Marco.

"Why are you asking me?" I said as I stared behind her at Molneer, who had caught my eye. The dwarf raised his hammer in a wave before placing a crucible back into the furnace. I knew he worked on smaller items that required finesse; adornments for shields, or inlays for swords, for the smelting furnace was used for jewelry making more so than weapons.

"She may have said something about you helping her. So I wanted to ask you if you'd help me spin straw into gold so that I can receive an honor like this?" Shannon waved at the winter festival.

"Believe me when I say she did the work."

"But you helped." Shannon's eyes narrowed.

"I didn't say that," I countered and moved away.

Shannon wasn't letting me off that easily. "You *will*

help me," she hissed, grabbing my wrist, her fingernails painfully digging into my skin.

I gasped and pulled my hand, but she wouldn't release it. Her strength was almost inhuman, her eyes dilated. Her gold bracelet brushed against my skin, and I felt odd. Like the ground was moving sideways, and my head was going to connect with it. I pushed her away roughly, and as soon as our contact broke, my head cleared.

Now, I was the one who grabbed her wrist. "Where did you get this?" I yelled angrily.

Shannon's eyes were wholly black. "I want to be her. It should be me that's honored, not her! *Me*."

"Take it off," I commanded. "Remove that bracelet at once."

Shannon shook her head, her hands grabbing fistfuls of her long hair as she collapsed to her knees. "It's not fair. It should be me. I'm the daughter of a Lord. I worked hard to rise to the king's notice, but he ignores me for her."

"It's the bracelet. It's making you go mad. You must remove it." I made a grab for her wrist, but in a wild fit, Shannon smacked my hand away, her nails like claws as they drew blood.

Turning toward Kash for help, the blade stood frozen, his gaze focused on the bracelet. When Shannon moved to attack me, Kash didn't lift a hand even though he was supposed to guard me.

The darkness that covered his eyes, hiding his true identity from the world, was swirling with excitement.

"Could it be?" I whispered and moved toward the blade, for it was obvious it wasn't Kash with me at the moment.

Shannon didn't like that I was retreating, and she

reached for me again. This time, I turned and attacked her. Grasping her bracelet on her wrist, I reached for the blade's armor and brushed across the metal and gasped.

Eyes were staring back at me. Red eyes surrounded by fire and smoke, and I knew they were connected. They were from the same source. I had meant to let go. As soon as I felt their origins, the stamp of the same dark magic in the bracelet was similar to the magic in his armor. They were the same. I was paralyzed as I became the conduit between the two. Magic was leeching from the bracelet, searching, trying to cross me to get to the dragon blade. And I understood.

The cursed treasure wanted to be found. It wanted to be reunited. It sought each other out.

The Stiltskin hoard.

My fingers wouldn't release their hold on the cursed armor and once again, I heard a deep dark laugh. "You're mine, Rhea."

My eyes fluttered as I could feel my heartbeat slowing, my lungs refusing to draw breath. A flash of wild magic came and knocked me over, and I swore I saw a purple banshee standing over me protectively.

CHAPTER TWENTY

I stood on the edge of a cliff next to a once majestic underground city that now lay in ruin. Great stone towers reduced to rubble littered the roads. Tall marble statues decimated, and all that remained were the pedestals. I was seeing Ter Dell, the dwarven city that was destroyed a hundred years ago.

Above me, a beautiful waterfall fell from the cavernous ceiling into giant water wheels that were straining with effort. I felt vibrations through the earth. I recognized that rhythm like my heartbeat. The water pumping through the wheels which powered the mines, and the mighty trip hammers as they crushed metal ore. It was the sound of the dwarven mine brought back to life.

But who was running it?

The answer lay not within the city, but outside it. For at the edge of the city was a narrow stone bridge over a deep abyss. There were no rails to guide my hand. Spires of boiling steam erupted on either side of the walkway. As I drew closer to the bridge, I could feel the heat on my skin. It burned and crackled.

My feet moved without my instruction, following the

inaudible invitation that I knew would be my doom. I tried to pull away, to resist, but my feet worked against me.

I couldn't keep going. It was too dangerous. I was lost in a vision, and if my mind couldn't separate from this actual dream, I knew I could die. Like falling asleep and never waking up.

"Wake up!" I yelled mentally. My feet approached the edge of the walkway, my skin was blistering, and my eyes were crusting and drying out.

"Wake up, Rhea, or die!" I screamed again.

Three feet left and I would walk onto the platform. Using every bit of determination I had left, I looked to my right, at the waterway below, and I whispered the command, *"Fall."* To escape dreams, it was easier for our brains to comprehend an action.

"You're falling, Rhea!"

My body went limp, and I felt my mind relax as I slid sideways and tumbled as water rushed over me.

"No!" I heard the dark voice scream, and I knew I had escaped his clutches once again.

Ice cold water hit my face and I gasped, sitting up. My hair fell in wet tendrils down my cheeks. Lifting the wet strands, I saw I was sitting on a fur-covered chaise lounge and a woman in boots stood in front of me. I was inside one of the tents, a brazier burning in the middle of the room producing waves of heat. Canvas covered the ground, and on top of it were many elaborate Sion rugs overlapping each other. Rugs that were now sopping wet.

"That should do it," Velora grunted, dropping a bucket onto the floor.

I pushed my hair out of my eyes and looked up into her smug face.

"I saved you." She held out two fingers. "Twice. Once from the shadow thing, and the second from burning."

"What?" I asked, confused as I tried to understand her stilted speech and process what had happened.

The empty bucket on the floor was the culprit for my soaking wet dress and the puddle I was now sitting in.

"The shadow?" I asked.

Velora shook her head. "When you touched the girl and the black knight." She held her hands apart. "A dark shadow swallowed you." Her hands came together and cupped into a circle. "I used my magic to separate you." She raised her chin and smiled at me. "The second time, when you were sleeping, your skin was burning hot to the touch. So I cooled you off." She pointed to the empty bucket.

I couldn't help but laugh, but then my laughter broke off into uncontrollable shivers.

Velora took a dry blanket and wrapped it around my shoulders in a motherly manner. Her lips pursed together, and she ran her hands up the sides of my shoulder, patting them, but it wasn't gentle. It felt like I was getting attacked.

"Marco does this for me when I'm cold," she said, and all of a sudden, it made sense. Velora was doing her best to help me feel better. And since mermaids were genuinely selfish creatures by nature, it was interesting to see her adjust to human emotions.

"Have you seen him yet?" I asked.

"No, but he'll come. You'll see," she said confidently.

The tent flap opened, and the dragon blade entered, his hand on his knife.

Velora jumped in front of me, her hands splayed into claws, and she hissed, ready to attack the blade that injured Marco and brought her here.

The dragon blade reached for his knife and Velora's fingernails grew longer. As the tent flap closed, I saw that night had fallen and with how much the dragon blade was trembling, his shift was nearby.

"It's okay, Velora," I cautioned her. Standing up, I moved to her side. "Watch."

The dragon took a step forward, and he held the blade above his head and unsheathed the knife. A powerful burst of magic shot outward like a smoke bomb, and I could see the armor evaporate from Kash's skin, wafting into the air before it condensed, and the mist sought shelter inside the blade just as he closed it, cutting off the magic. Kash stood before us, his face covered in sweat, his chest heaving, and he wobbled before falling to his knees. Kash's dark hair fell forward, and his arms trembled to hold him up from sliding to the floor.

I stepped around Velora and kneeled by Kash, placing my hand on his trembling back. Kash lifted his head, his golden eyes filled with pain and remorse. "I'm so sorry, Rhea. I didn't mean to. I tried to hold him back, but he wanted you. He took you there. I couldn't do anything about it. If he would have killed you, I don't know what I would have done." Kash groaned, covering his face with his palms, his grief evident.

"You did your best. You protected me during the goblin attack."

Kash's face drained of color, and he shook his head. "I

don't remember a goblin attack. That wasn't me." Kash backed away. "I need to go away again. It's not safe for me to be near you even now. I think it's using my feelings for you against me."

"Stop it," I snapped. "I survived. Just be thankful that the blade had another target—the goblins . . . which seemed to be a common enemy. I wonder why?"

"No one likes goblins." Velora wrinkled her nose.

"I need to find my brothers." Kash stumbled to his feet and headed out of the tent, but was intercepted by Damon and Spencer.

"Relax." Damon grabbed Kash's shoulder and pushed him toward an empty chair. "We're here, we've got it handled."

"I don't understand." Kash leaned forward, his hand on his knees. "Why now? Why is the king extending the curfew? Why let us have a night to roam free in public? We haven't been allowed this much freedom in years."

"It's a test," Spencer said, his keen eyes watching the tent flap. "I overheard him when he didn't know I was aware. He wants to see how loyal we are to him, and what our relationship with Rhea is. It seems we are not to return to the palace at all tonight."

"What?" Damon roared, and Spencer motioned for him to lower his voice. "What is he thinking?"

"He's up to something. And until we know what, we should still stand guard over Rhea," Spencer answered.

I raised my hand. "I don't need a guard. I can take care of myself."

"Yes, I suspect as much," Spencer grinned. "But as blades, we were under orders to guard you. I have a feeling the king is waiting to see if that order-under compulsion-flows through to the night. I think he's been wanting to test it for a while."

"Ah, I see," I said. It made sense. Everything about the last twenty-four hours had been strange.

"The king is still expecting a mountain of gold, Velora." Spencer pointed to the mermaid. "He's set up a special tent with the spinning wheel and stocked with bales and bales of straw."

"Straw?" I pressed my hands to my temples. "What am I going to do now that I don't have reels of yarn?"

Spencer shrugged. "We'll figure it out together. We'll find a way in which we can still help Velora produce gold. We've got until sunrise," Spencer said.

"Not all of that time. We're required to make a few appearances." Damon held up a scroll, and he looked uncomfortable.

"Appearances?" Kash seemed confused as well. "We don't *do* appearances. We are never allowed in the public eye. Haven't been for years."

"Well, why do I have this, then?" Damon handed Kash a schedule, and sure enough, on it was a timetable of the evening events. Dancing, fireworks, and announcing the winner of the reindeer races, which would cross the finish line in the middle of the night. Each of their names was written next to an event.

"We should check with Freya." Spencer got up and headed out of the tent. "Kash, are you coming?"

Damon handed Kash his cloak that had fallen to the floor. Kash immediately grabbed it and placed it around my shoulders.

"It's fine. I'll warm up by the fire." I stood to move by the bronze brazier, while I tried to think of what in the world we could do to produce gold.

"I failed to protect you once. I won't fail a second time," Kash said.

"I'm not sure why everyone always assumes I need protecting." I gazed into the embers in the brazier to see Sol lazing about on his back like a dog waiting for a belly scratch. I had somehow gained a new pet, or a familiar.

"It's just that you're so . . ." Damon started, holding his hand about the height of my head, but Kash shot him an ugly glare.

"Don't say it," Kash warned.

"Small," Damon finished.

With a smirk, I flicked my hand at the flames and the room erupted in a flash of light. A joyful glee came from within the brazier as Sol seemed ready to fight again.

Damon backed away and swatted the edge of his cloak that had caught fire. "I stand corrected."

"Never underestimate short women," Kash said. "Dangerous things come in small packages." I elbowed him in the side and his face lit up. "And books," Kash added. "Don't let her anywhere near books. Women and books can be hazardous for your health."

Damon's face scrunched up into a look of utter confusion as he tried to piece together Kash's warning. I was laughing hard. Kash grabbed Damon's shoulder and dragged his brother out of the tent.

When we had the space to ourselves, I couldn't help but feel sorry for Velora. She had gone to sit on the other side of the tent and pulled a blanket over her as if to sleep. She caught my eye and answered my unasked question.

"I'm tired. I slept very little last night, and I've been dragged all over this stupid festival. I will sleep here until Marco comes."

"You still have to spin another tent full of gold."

"No, I won't. Marco will arrive."

I sighed and brushed my hand over my dress, and it was almost dry. I stayed by the brazier, rotating slowly as I pondered the dream. Why was I seeing Ter Dell? Was that the key?

Velora sighed and rolled over. She dragged her hand across her eyes to block out the light, a gold bangle dangled from her wrist.

"Velora, where did you get that bracelet?" I asked.

"From the funny little man," she sighed. "He gave one to everyone."

Did she mean Molneer?

"Take it off," I commanded.

"No," she huffed, sitting up to glare at me. "It's mine."

"Velora, I think the bracelet is cursed." I crossed the tent and reached for her wrist. She hissed, her teeth became pointed, and her fingernails had become deadly claws again. Then she swiped at me.

"This isn't like you! I think the bracelet is doing something to you."

She hissed again, eyes dilating into slits, and I knew better than to take on an irritated mermaid.

"Fine, but Marco won't come if you're wearing the bracelet," I lied. "He will think you fancy someone else."

Her dilated eyes rounded out. Her face took on a serenity that I'm sure lured hundreds of sailors to their deaths. The jewelry went flying across the tent and hit the canvas wall.

I kneeled by the bracelet. I could tell that it was from the cursed gold without even touching it. My gifts were becoming stronger, or I was developing a sensitivity to the ores of this kingdom.

Pulling out a kerchief, I wrapped the bangle in it and tucked it into the slit in my dress and placed it next to my enchanted thread. I needed to find Molneer. I had *many* questions.

Heading out into the night, I was surprised to see that I had an additional guard. Dressed in black leather with a fur-lined helm, he followed a few steps behind me. Two more waited outside the tent. My guess was they were Velora's guards. I guessed the king couldn't rely on his blades to guard me all day and night.

I pushed the silent guard out of my mind, grateful that he kept a few paces behind me, and didn't seem intent on stopping my explorations of the festival. Immediately, I was taken with how different the festival felt at the late hour. Colorful torches decorated the night, and it wasn't magic, but science. Different chlorides or sulfates were added to the torches to create the vibrant colors.

Music filled the air, and dancers filled the streets. The moon was bright and full, giving a picturesque view of the mountain range, highlighting the castle farther up the mountain. Jugglers and jesters lined the path, beckoning would-be tourists into their alley of entertainment tents. A man with a mustache was amusing a crowd with a table of crystals in front of a wagon with beautiful wind chimes. I watched a fire breathing tightrope walker enrapture the crowd, and I stopped near a fortune teller's tent to watch. A man in white and black striped pants and a red vest with a curly mustache was calling people over to watch in wonder at their next performance.

An enormous green hand parted the canvas flap, grabbed my shoulder, and yanked me inside the tent.

CHAPTER TWENTY-ONE

"Rheanon." The voice was deep and filled with authority. "You've lost your way."

As my eyes adjusted to the dim lighting within the tent, I had to hold my breath as I took in the sight of an ogre preparing to sit on her colorful cushion. When she turned in the small space to address me, I took in her pale green face. She was adorned with makeup, and her lipstick accented the pointy teeth that shot up from her underbite. Golden hoops dangled from her pointed ears, and colored moss and beads were braided into her thick black hair.

"You're Ogress De Le Cour," I said, referring to my mother's friend. "For there can't be two ogre fortune tellers that travel with this circuit."

"You are correct. The Magical Menagerie has come to Kiln on your mother's request."

"She's checking up on me, isn't she?" I said, feeling irritated.

"With no magical contact coming and going through this kingdom, this is the best way. Besides, we were the ones who reported to Lorelai that there was something more dangerous going on here than we first feared."

"You've always been the eyes and ears for her."

"Entertainers make the best spies." Ogress grinned, revealing more of her twisted lower teeth.

I held back my shudder.

"Now, for my payment." Ogress held out her thick hand and waited. "I can't start without it."

My hands reached into my pocket and all I felt was the bracelet and my spindle. I pulled out the folded cloth. "I don't think you want what I have. It's cursed."

"Bah, I eat curses for breakfast," she huffed. "No really. Curses won't affect me. Hand it over. I want to see it in person."

I handed the cloth wrapped bracelet over. She carefully lifted the edges and closed one eye to peer at the bracelet. Then she brought it up to her nose and sniffed deeply, before wrinkling her face.

"I thought so. It smells like him."

"Who?" I asked.

"Greed," Ogress snarled. "I've come across his handiwork a few times in my life, but it's only to see the aftermath of his destruction."

"Who is Greed?" I asked.

"It is not a who . . . but a what. Greed is an entity that feeds off of human emotion; impossible to kill, and it grows stronger where human will is weak. It was Greed who destroyed the Ter Dell kingdom, and I can see that he has sunk his claws into the human kingdom of Kiln. It's worse than I feared."

"How is this bracelet connected to him?" I asked.

Ogress leaned forward and whispered. "Do you know my secret? Has your sister Eden shared it with you?"

I shook my head. "No, secrets aren't meant to be shared. Unless you're near Aura, then all hope is lost." I smiled faintly, referring to my sister who could read minds.

"Then let me explain. Your mother created this tent." She pointed to the colorful cloth. "Do you see the thin silver strands, the magic spells woven into the very fabric? Seeing spells, silencing spells, foresight, all of them augment my gift. It was in this very tent that I saw Eden's future, but for *this* question, I have to go to the past."

Ogress closed her eyes and clasped the bracelet between her palms.

"*It is* gold from the hoard of the great dwarf, Rumple Stiltskin, who gave his life to imprison Greed within the mountain, in a vault. Since then, the one known as Grim-keep knows the vault's location and is the protector of Greed's burial place. But Greed has been controlling the goblins. They've been digging out the gold, bit by bit. They were searching for something."

"What are the goblins doing with the gold?" I asked, my heart filled with turmoil. The memory of Shannon's gold bangle, the same one Velora wore, flashed through my mind.

"You already know the answer to that. And who is behind it?" Ogress said.

My mouth went dry as I came to terms with Molneer's betrayal.

"What about the blades? How can I remove the curse from the king's blades and free them?"

"That is not an answer I can see in the past or the future. You will have to ask Rumple Stiltskin himself."

"But how? You said so yourself that he is dead."

"Dead does not mean gone. Are you not a sorceress and an all-powerful alchemist?" she huffed angrily. "You already have the piece you need. Why else would Greed want it so bad that he would risk sending his minions to the palace? If you think it out, he knows he will never be free."

"The artifact that Grimkeep risked his life to bring me," I gushed out.

"There she is," Ogress laughed, slapping her knee. "Now, you know what to do?"

"I do now. I think I became overwhelmed and lost my way. I wanted to break the curse on the blades, and keep the king appeased to save my friends."

"Now, now," she chided. "We all need to be redirected from time to time. It's okay to ask for help. Destroy Greed, and you'll save everyone." Ogress took the bracelet, snapping it midpoint. She reached up and clipped it on her ear, adding to the golden collection.

"But how do I destroy Greed?" I asked.

"That I do not have an answer for." Ogress closed her eyes and sighed, her giant head cocking to the side. "But I can tell you that your mermaid friend is gone."

"Is she in trouble?"

"No, it's as she predicted. Marco has come and taken her away, so tomorrow morning will bring forth a furious King Goddrick."

I cursed under my breath, knowing that if Velora was gone, there went having to spin a tent full of gold, but what will he do in retaliation?

"Thank you for your wisdom, Ogress," I commended her. "It was very valuable."

"You're welcome, dear. Oh, and one more thing. Help is coming."

"Help?" I asked, but Ogress said nothing about who.

"You don't have to fight alone." She leaned to the side,

revealing a hidden back door to the tent, and beckoned for me to exit in secret.

After I thanked her a second time, I slipped out of the back door, avoiding my guard, and made my way back to where I had last seen Velora. Sure enough, the tent was empty, and the guards stationed outside were surprised to find it so. I walked around to the back of the tent where I had seen Velora sleeping on the couch. There was a giant rip in the canvas, and two sets of footprints leading away into the woods.

I grabbed a downed evergreen branch and wiped away their trail, hiding the evidence of Velora's escape. I tossed the branch into the woods before storming over to the smelting forge, only to find the forge still hot, but the dwarf long gone.

"Molneer," I grumbled in frustration. I examined his workspace and found the smallest flecks of gold dribbles, the crucible he used to melt the gold, and the molds for the bracelets and a stone stamp press for coins. Next to the smelting furnace was a bag that stunk terribly like rotten eggs, and I wrinkled my nose as I could smell the waft from goblins.

They'd been supplying Molneer with gold stolen from the Stiltskin hoard, and he'd been making trinkets with coins and circulating them around the festival. And how long had he been reintroducing the cursed treasure into society? Forcing Grimkeep to constantly hunt it down, not knowing that he was being betrayed by his own cousin.

Why was I such a fool? He'd used the ward on his mantle to sense magic, and instead of sensing gold for him to hunt after that avalanche, it sensed me. I was too trusting and let him talk me into going right to the palace.

He placed me under the king's nose. Did that mean that Freya was involved too?

Anger rolled through me. I had never wanted to hit something as much as I did right then.

"Rhea." Spencer raced up to me. "There you are. Come quick."

"Not now," I snapped bitterly, bypassing the smaller mallets and heading to the one used for hammering steel. I hefted the hammer and gave it a mighty swing, and it crashed into the table. It bounced off after cracking the wood. Again I continued to strike, destroying the crucible and all of his tools to make the cursed jewelry. "How long?" I growled.

Spencer watched as I released my anger out on the workspace. When I was done, I took the goblin sack and tossed it into the furnace, letting the flames cleanse the cloying odor that hung in the air.

When my angry tirade was over, Spencer came to my side. "The king knows Velora is gone. It's not good. He is calling all the chosen to the stage."

"She shouldn't go." Kash stepped out of the darkness, his chest heaving. "She should run."

"And you know if she did, what will happen come morning?" Spencer snarled. "Whose conscious will it be on when eve comes, and we find her dead? Even worse, when we don't remember which one of us killed her."

Kash's face was a stony mask. "I would never."

"You may say that now," Spencer put his hand on his rapier, his voice breaking with emotion, "but I know the odds are in favor of it being you or I to land the killing blow."

Kash's eyes met mine, and I knew what he was thinking. "Stop, there's no use worrying over what has yet to come. I have a plan. Or I will if we can survive the night. Are you with me?" Kash's voice lowered, and he stepped so close the toes of our boots were almost touching. "I'll always be with you," he whispered, "for as long as you let me." His eyes glittered with emotion, reflecting the fire in the forge. They looked like molten gold, and I inhaled.

Kash heard it, and his lips pulled back into a mischievous smile. He opened his mouth to comment.

"Don't even say it," I warned.

"What, that I'm breathtaking?"

"Shut it." Grabbing his sleeve, I dragged him after me as I followed Spencer to the main stage. As we passed the tents, I noticed that Ogress De La Cour's tent was already gone, as were the wagons and the tents belonging to the magical menagerie. As fast as they had come, they had departed. I had to assume glamour and magic aided in their escape. They'd either sensed the king's coming announcement, or Ogress had a premonition. Whatever it was, I knew they would be safe.

"Wait." Spencer turned on his heels and reached into his cloak. He broke apart a piece of wax and began rubbing it into little balls.

"What are you doing?" I asked, as he pushed the hair away from my ears and pushed the wax balls into them.

"Protection." He winked; his voice now muffled by the beeswax earplugs. "Just in case."

"Is he using the silverstar flute again?" I asked fearfully.

He shrugged. "Never try to find a reason behind a mad king's actions."

As we approached the main stage, I saw King

Goddrick in all his glory. They had brought out a golden throne whose backseat was at least seven feet tall, and he was now pacing in front of it. There was something off about his gait, and I feared he was unwell. Then I noticed what he was wearing. The king wore his golden crown, the filigree necklace at his throat, the ornate buckle, the chains on his cloak, even down to the buttons in his boots were all gold, and I knew without even stepping closer that Molneer had made them, and all of them were cursed.

"Where is she?" King Goddrick screamed into the night. "Where is the one with lavender hair? Why is she not coming when I summon?"

From the folds of his cloak, he pulled forth the silver whistle and blew hard.

I heard the cries and whimpers of Shannon, Annette, and the others as they reacted to the magic within the whistle. Annette clutched her ears; Shannon fell to her knees in the snow. Brenna collapsed into Benton's arms. I only heard the slightest hum because of the wax in my ears, but I feigned a painful reaction, wobbling and holding my head with one hand. With the other, I reached out to Spencer's hand and gave it the slightest squeeze of thanks, and he squeezed back reassuringly. His quick thinking saved me from blacking out.

"Why were my guards not with her?" The king turned and glared at the two men that had been standing outside Velora's tent. "My blades will deal with you in the morning," the king threatened, and the men slowly backed into the crowd. "Where's the other one?" Goddrick yelled, his hand covering his eyes as he searched.

"I'm here, Your Majesty." I stepped forward into the light so the king could see me.

He struggled to focus on me, his head swaying. His eyes back and forth. "Yes, yes. You are still here, and my blade is still sharp, I see."

Kash took a step closer to me, his hand slipping under my cloak, brushing my back while he pulled out his dagger and gently put it in front of me. It was aimed at my stomach, but his face was a stony mask of indifference.

"Don't fear me," he whispered between clenched teeth, his eyes never straying from the king.

"I don't," I said softly, focusing on playing my part . Kash ran his thumb in a circle along my spine, and I shivered at the intimate gesture. It was his way of trying to comfort me in a situation where he had to play the loyal assassin, but my flinch helped play into the drama, and the king's smile grew.

"I knew you were mine," he said, staring right at me, but I wasn't sure if it was directed at me or Kash.

"The rest of you." He turned to the four remaining chosen. "Failures, all of you."

"Your Majesty, what you ask is impossible." Benton stepped forth and tried to reason with the king.

"Silence!" King Goddrick screamed so loud, spit covered his chin. "You," he pointed to Kash, "will not leave her side. If there isn't a tent filled with gold by morning, I want her dead."

I felt my knees go weak, and they would have buckled if Kash hadn't grabbed my elbow and pulled me to his side. To the onlooker, it would have appeared as though he shook me like a giant rag doll.

Goddrick was no longer speaking to me. Instead, he had turned and was now talking to the air.

"Yes, yes. I know. Very troubling. But won't be long

now. You'll see. All will be well, and then we can both get what we want."

"King Goddrick," I called, but he was no longer attentive. He walked behind his chair and into a sectioned off area of the tent, pulling the sides down to give him privacy.

I tried to free myself from Kash's grip, but he wouldn't let me. Instead, he pulled me into the frosty air, and my tears froze on my face.

"Pull yourself together," Kash hissed. "It's not too late to run."

"What have I done?" I pulled the wax balls from my ears and the world suddenly became overly loud. A noisy ruckus drew our attention, and a man pushed a vendor in the chest. They quarreled loudly over the price of a sweet bun. The vendor grabbed his tray and hit him in the arm. Other discontented voices joined in a chorus of anger. One woman tried to steal the other's cursed bracelet. Screams followed, and one attacked the other, trying to rip her hair out.

"It's starting," I gasped. "I'm too late."

We passed another group of angry festival attenders, and Spencer stepped in to break the crowd up. A mug of ale flew at his head, and he ducked.

"Get Rhea out of here!" Spencer called out as he took a punch in the stomach.

My feet became like lead, heavy, and each step felt impossible. Kash scooped me up in his arms and carried me. As he did, I could see the barest flicker of red in his eyes. Greed was not as dormant as the princes believed.

Kash carried me into his tent, the one he shared with his brothers. It was set up like the others, with chaises, cots, and various blankets. He set me down on the nearest fur covered cot and kneeled in front of me.

"Don't blame yourself," he whispered.

I wiped the tears with my sleeve. "I should have done something sooner."

"Rhea, this has been going on longer than you even know. Long before you arrived that day in Verdan. Today is the culmination of a longstanding problem."

"Then why didn't you stop it?" I turned on him, letting Kash be the focus of my rage, which I knew was wrong.

"He's our father," Kash said, the word father with grief. "One does not simply disobey the king, especially when he holds our fate in the palm of his hands. We are nothing more than puppets that he controls. We were disobedient young men. Troublesome, and lackluster in our desire to serve the king or country. Spencer was more interested in his studies. Damon cared more about becoming a knight. I —" He broke off. "I had no desire for throne or kingdom. I preferred hunting and searching the Ragnar mountains for the lost kingdom of Ter Dell more than princely duties."

"When did it all stop?" I asked. "When was the last day you were yourselves?"

"It was the day that a dwarf with a black beard appeared on our doorstep. He swore he knew where Ter Dell and the lost treasure were. He proved it by providing my father with a ring."

"The gold ring he wears on his left hand?"

Kash nodded. "The dwarf gave my father three finely crafted blades and presented them to each of us. When we unsheathed them, our curse began, and it's continued every single day since. I don't remember the last time I saw the midday sun." He gazed into the brazier; his eyes unfocused. "Every day, I lose more of myself to the blade's wishes, and withdraw further into the recesses of my mind to escape the taint. Some days I struggle to awaken and put the blade side away."

Kash's right hand balled into a white-knuckled fist. "One day, I think I won't wake up." He raised his hand and uncurled his fingers. "And I'll cease to exist."

"I won't let that happen," I retorted. "I'll break this curse."

Kash shifted on the seat, his thigh brushing mine as he drew close. He pressed his forehead to mine, and whispered, "Ever since that first night where you attacked me with a book and tied me to a chair—"

"I believe we're both guilty of tying each other to chairs," I interrupted.

He smiled, pulling away, his eyes dilating, his breath warm on my lips. "True. And at the same time, you've tied my heart in knots. I've only known you for those hours we shared during the night, but let me tell you, each one of those minutes was precious to me because I was with you. You've awoken something within me. A yearning to fight back the darkness, to live each day for you. I dream of you during the day, and I wait anxiously to spend every moonlit moment with you." Kash's hand cupped the back of my neck, his thumb brushing my lips.

I was impatient. There was tension building between us, and if he didn't quench the fire, I would. I reached up and pulled him into me, pressing my lips to his. My initiation surprised him, and I grinned in triumph as I was the one to claim him as mine.

He pulled me onto his lap, his hands wrapping around my waist. "Rhea," he breathed out my name, his voice husky, "I have a confession. I want you to be mine."

A thrilling knot built in my stomach at his words, but Kash broke the kiss, quickly depositing me on the chair and moving across the room, creating too great a distance for my taste. It felt like he was worlds apart.

"Kash." I swallowed, trying to catch my breath and settle the frantic beating of my heart. "I want that too," I said courageously and stood, crossing the room to wrap my arms around his waist.

Kash shook his head and broke my grasp, and I felt my heart flutter with fear.

"No, you don't understand. That's the problem. Because *I* want you, the *blade* wants you. My desire for you is feeding the blade's power, and I can't control that monster during the day. I can feel his longing for you growing because of me."

"You said *want*—not love," I whispered as my heart slowly broke. "Greed feeds on human desire, and it's your desire for me that's feeding it." Now it was my turn to back away from Kash. "It's not real," I said in disbelief as my eyes stung.

"I don't know?" Kash looked at me, his eyes glassy with unshed tears. "I want it to be real, but I can't tell what is truth or lie anymore. What are my feelings and what are the blade's. How can I know the truth when I'm possessed by a curse of greed?"

"Then you'll have to believe me when I say that what I feel is real."

He nodded, his lips pulling into the slightest of smiles that didn't reach his eyes. "That will be enough for me, then." Kash grabbed a pack off the ground and stuffed items in it. Blankets, gloves, hats.

"What are you doing?" I asked.

"I want you to run. Leave right now, and never look back. If you can get away, farther than the blade can travel by day, then I will spend my nights putting as much distance between us as possible, just like before. I will fight for you until my last breath."

He pushed the pack into my arms and led me toward the tent flap.

"I won't run."

"Please," he begged. "I can't be responsible for your death, or for what the blade does to you."

"You won't be responsible for my death because I don't plan on dying," I argued.

As we stepped into the night, Kash brought me to the side of the tent in the shadows. In the distance, I could hear the first of the reindeer sleighs returning down the mountain path.

We stared into each other's eyes, and I wanted to rush toward him, throw my arms around Kash's strong midsection and promise him I would make everything okay. But I knew that for this next part of the journey, I would have to do it alone.

"Kash, I—"

He cut me off and picked me up, holding me in his arms as he kissed me. One final kiss of goodbye. I knew it. He knew it. I didn't want it to be a kiss of regret, but one of remembering. As sorceresses, we swore to never cast love spells, but maybe this one spell wouldn't be counted as such.

"*Mememto*," I whispered between kisses, tracing the

sigil for remembering on his back with my finger. My words rose into the air as I spelled him to remember me in this moment. I knew he wanted to forget, and I could very well be cursing him further. But I didn't want either of us to forget what we shared, no matter how short it was.

"I'm sorry." Kash pulled away first, dropping me back down in the snow. "I'm sorry for abandoning you, but it's the only way I can protect you."

I struggled to not let my ire seep through into my voice. "Kash—"

"Just go!" Kash begged. "I'll do what I can to distract the guards and my father." He gave me a final push, and in anger, I headed toward the woods, focusing on where I was walking and refusing to look back. I slowed as a sled pulled by reindeer raced in front of me.

I saw Spencer waiting in the shadows as Kash headed toward the king's tent. "So you're leaving?" he asked, pointing to the pack on my shoulder.

"You heard?"

"No, but I know Kash, and if I was in love with you, it's what I would want."

"He's not in love. It's the curse," I said bitterly.

"That's what we all say." Spencer sighed, pulling the cloak closer around him. "We've come to blame everything on the curse. It's easier than admitting our own faults."

"I struggle to find yours," I said.

Spencer laughed. "Then you are not looking in the right place, for I have plenty. The only one who is perfect is Damon. He strives to live by the knight's code. To not covet, to protect those less fortunate. His greatest desire is to be a protector of his people, which is why I believe the blade has the weakest grasp on him. The curse only amplifies what's there. And Damon is not greedy. If Kash didn't have feelings for you, then it couldn't be amplified."

"But he's a hunter, and I'm the prey that got away."

"Is that how you felt in the manor when it was just the two of you? When he returned each night to watch over you?"

"How do you know about the manor?"

Spencer rubbed his chin. "There're no secrets between us. We tell each other everything."

"What if it's not love, but something else?" I was scared to say the word lust.

"It's not," he said firmly.

"It could be."

"He's a prince. Before the curse, hundreds of beautiful women surrounded him. You're the only one who has ever captured his attention. If that's not love, then I don't know what is. He mourns your absence like I mourn books, like Damon mourns the loss of our father to this thing he has become."

Spencer's words of wisdom opened up my mind to a plan. "Thank you for your friendship."

Spencer let out a long breath. "Kash is a fool for telling you to go."

"Well, Kash will have to deal with it."

"Good luck, Rhea. Run far, run fast. And I'm sorry if I kill you come morning." His voice became gravelly with emotion.

I shuddered at his words but put on a brave face. "If I die, I pray that it's by your blade and not Kash's. I don't think his mind could survive it."

"He won't." Spencer trembled. "I don't think I could

either, but we can't refuse the king's orders." He reached out a hand, and I shook it, his grasp warm and strong.

He bobbed his head and headed out into the field of tents. As soon as I was alone, I ducked into the nearest tent and pulled out a glamour charm.

When I had been all dramatic, throwing things around in the forge area, I had found an item that Molneer had left behind. His tinderweed pipe. Quickly cupping the pipe, I closed my eyes and pictured the first day where I met Molneer and he'd offered me soup in his home. The low drawl of his voice, the scent of the pipe smoke, his thick, calloused hands from working the forge. The wiry texture of his black beard and the make of his clothes. Then when I opened my eyes, I blinked and looked down to see the thick ruddy vest, the long beard that reached my ankles, and I could almost smell the sweet scent clinging to my clothes, telling me I had cast a very strong glamour.

Now, would it be enough to fool the blades come morning?

CHAPTER TWENTY-TWO

The swing of the hammer in my hand was freeing. The rhythmic pounding was soothing as I let my anger and frustration ring out in the forge. And the best part, no one bothered me as I shaped the artifact of metal in front of me into an ingot. Sol was inside the forge's flames. After I'd summoned him and he brought me the artifact, he took it as his personal duty to keep the fire at a steady heat.

I had chiseled out the gold section of the artifact and it now lay in a crucible, waiting to be heated, while I worked on the section of steel that was hidden under the runes.

Using my tongs, I placed it back into the forge and watched the metal heat.

"Little hotter," I called, pitching my voice low to sound like Molneer.

Sol closed his eyes and the heat from within intensified as I judged the color of my metal. I pulled it out and laid it on the anvil, hammering in a familiar rhythm.

The artifact had an echo, a memory, and I would use magic and pull the memory to the surface to help me find its true form.

"What were you?" I whispered. "Show me." My

hammer came down, and the metal bounced against the artifact. I reached deep into the mountain for magic and fed it into the metal.

The barely visible runes still etched into the ingot glowed and I caught a glimpse in my mind. "There you are." I smiled as I drew out the shape with my hammer.

Pounding and heating, pounding and heating, back in the forge and out. If I listened, I could almost hear the metal speaking to me.

"Bigger."

"Hook needs to be more curved."

"Make sure it's balanced. Need to take heads off with one clean heft."

The one-sided conversation continued into the night, all the way until I took an eye drift, and I punched a hole through the steel. Then I quenched it in a barrel of oil, the steam raising up and singeing the hair on my arm not protected by the leather glove. The blade didn't crack. Then came the fitting of a handle. I had little to shave down because there were wooden handles already in the shop, many prepared for the weapon I was forging.

"Now the gold."

"Gold on a weapon is useless," I argued to myself. "It's too soft."

"Need the gold."

I saw the original in my mind and knew that I could never gold plate the axe to the same degree as the original blacksmith had.

But I did it anyway.

And without even knowing what I was doing, I chiseled out runes along the blade's edges. My hands moving of their own, matching the image in my mind, carving out a name of the owner.

Then came the grinding. Sitting at the stone wheel, I hummed under my breath as I sharpened the edge of the double-sided blade. When it was completed, I looked for a scroll or horsehair to test the blade's sharpness.

"Dwarf hair is the best for testing a blade's sharpness because our hair is strong and wiry, but that won't work since you're obviously not a dwarf."

I stared at the axe and blinked in surprise. Many times I would speak to myself as I forged, asking myself questions, arguing with myself, trying to push my magic and talents to new heights. But that wasn't what happened here. Someone was speaking to me.

"Hello?" I said softly into the air.

"Yeah?" the voice replied.

I stared at the great axe I'd made. "You're really talking."

"I've been talking for a century, but you're the only one who ever listened." The axe had spoken audibly, and it wasn't in my head.

The runes. I rubbed my hands over the runes and read the name I had engraved. "Who are you?" I asked, my hands shaking as I lifted the axe into the air. "Or I mean, who *were* you?" For there wasn't a doubt, I had not just used the echo to recreate the weapon, but I had—using magic—imprinted a memory into it.

The Book of Eld.

I gasped, remembering what I'd learned as I'd read it. I'd accidentally used dwarven magic when creating a dwarven weapon.

"You know who I am. Or can't you read? You put my

name right there on the blade," the axe huffed at me. "I'm Rumple Stiltskin."

"...impossible," I breathed out, staring at the weapon.

"Improbable, but not impossible. Nothing is impossible when you're me."

"If you are really Rumple Stiltskin, then how are you here?"

"You really are daft, aren't you? And here I thought you'd be a powerful sorceress, that you'd figure it out. Shut your mouth, company is coming, and you look crazy talking to nobody."

I promptly snapped my gaping mouth closed as a retinue of soldiers passed by the forge. Grabbing the nearest ingot of metal, I put it into the forge with tongs and prepared to heat treat it.

"Working through the night, Molneer? I thought you were done with your jewelry. What else you doing?" A soldier with the captain emblem on his collar asked.

Before I could turn and answer, Rumple called out for me. "Off you go. Dwarf business, and you're not a dwarf," he said gruffly, in an almost perfect likeness of Molneer.

I slammed my hand onto the handle of the axe in warning, hoping to silence it.

That seemed to make the captain laugh. "Same old Molneer, as secretive as ever."

I squeezed the handle, and the axe didn't have another comeback. The soldiers passed on by and I let out an anxious sigh. "What did you go and do that for?" I hissed. "You could have blown my cover."

"Girl, as soon as you would open your mouth, you'd have given yourself away. A real dwarf wouldn't sound like a mouse."

"I don't"—I coughed and lowered the tone of my voice —"sound like a mouse."

"S-u-r-e," Rumple dragged out. "Want some cheese?"

"You're not a nice dwarf," I snapped. "And my name's Rheanon, or Rhea—not girl." Pulling the ingot back out of the fire, I tossed it onto the anvil where I ignored it. I picked through the leather scrap piles and began to fashion a bandolier with a leather tie to carry the axe.

"Dwarves aren't nice. We don't have tea parties and offer scones and crumpets. We are dwellers of the earth, protectors of the mountain and Ter Dell," Rumple boasted loudly.

"Well, you've done a lousy job of it," I said. "Because Ter Dell is gone, or have you forgotten? And there are hardly any earth dwellers left to protect the mountain, except for Grimkeep, and he seems to have his hands full protecting what's left of the city from goblins."

Rumple fell silent.

"I'm sorry," I said, my voice sounding very mousy with remorse. I measured the leather across my shoulders and added a buckle from a wooden crate sitting on a shelf. I found an awl and punched holes into the leather to make it adjustable.

"I had forgotten." Rumple's voice was filled with sadness. "My home is no more."

I scooped up the axe and measured the ties to attach it to the molded leather holster. Slipping the axe into the bandolier, I used the leather ties to tighten the holster before sliding it onto my back. Immediately, I was impressed by how light the weapon was.

"You're extremely light," I said in awe.

"You take that back! Dwarves are not light. I weigh at least eighteen stone."

"Maybe you did as a dwarf," I said with a smirk. "But as a weapon, you are indeed light."

A sputtering came from behind my back. "Well, that's because I'm made of the silven ore from the mines of Ter Dell. Looks like steel, but ten times lighter. Dwarf secret."

"It's not a dwarf secret if you tell people," I said.

"You don't count. I'll dub you an honorary dwarf because of the fake beard."

"Gee, thanks."

"Want to know another secret?" Rumple asked.

"No," I answered as I snuck across the snowy field, heading to the tent that was set up for Velora to spin gold.

"Our beards have pockets!" he said smugly. "Hidden ones. You won't believe what we can pull out of them in times of trouble. I once hid a small throwing axe, a pint of ale, and a meat pie in mine. It was so grand and long. All the ladies wanted to run their hands through it."

"You're pulling my leg." I stopped and tried to imagine Grimkeep's beard with hidden pockets. Granted, their beards were long, ornate things with many runes and beads braided throughout. I wondered if that's what the braids were for, to help hide the pockets.

"No, one time I—"

"Shh," I whispered. "This is serious. I need you to be quiet."

"But you're the first person I've talked to in a century. I can't help it if I'm chatty."

"Are you sure we shouldn't schedule you a tea party? I'm sure I can bring the crumpets and you can chat to your heart's content," I whispered as I took in the two guards outside the tent. Why were there guards if it was empty?

Rumple immediately clammed up, which I took as a good sign.

Sneaking forward, I laid in the snow and lifted the flap to the tent to see a woman crying as she sat in front of the spinning wheel.

It was Shannon.

I sighed. The king would not let this go. He really wanted another tent full of gold, but we were running out of time.

The edges were looped and staked into ground, so I took the axe and made a slight cut and sliced upward before sneaking in.

"Who's there?" Shannon said, standing so fast she knocked over the stool.

"It's me, Shannon," I said, forgetting that I was still in a dwarf glamour. When Shannon saw the giant axe on my back, she backed away. "Stop, don't come any closer."

I froze, not wanting to frighten her more for fear she would alert the guards. But I didn't need fear of scaring her further because old Rumple couldn't keep his trap shut. "I'll help you, fair maiden. Why are you crying?"

"I have to turn all of this straw to gold by morning or the king will have my head." Her hands went to her mouth, and she cried.

"Why that big, hairy runt of a —" Rumple started, but I coughed loudly silencing part of his outburst. "Okay, deal. We'll turn this into gold, but what will you give us?" Rumple continued.

"What do you want?" Shannon asked.

This time, I walked over to the center pole of the tent and swung my back into it, knocking the axe into the post.

"Ow, son of a Terst Bjorn!" Rumple cussed in the language of Eld.

"I'm sorry, what did you say?" Shannon muttered. "You want my first-born son?"

"Yes!" Rumple cried ecstatically.

"No," I said trying to unbuckle the axe.

"Which is it?" Shannon sounded unsure. "If that is your wish, I will gladly give him to you if you save me from my plight."

I turned, giving her my back. "Rumple," I ground out between clenched teeth in a whisper. "If you so much as answer, I will drop you down the nearest volcano."

"Been there." He chuckled, before raising his voice. "You must name your first-born son after me."

Shannon seemed relieved. "Oh, is that all? I can definitely do that. What is your name?"

"One moment," I muttered and moved across the tent and dropped the axe onto the ground. I pressed my foot to the wooden bar and lifted it up in the air, threatening to break it. "You will stay silent for the rest of this task, or so help me, I will stomp you into the ground. You will disappear into another realm! Got it? No one wants to name their son Rumple Stiltskin."

The axe stayed silent, but I could almost feel the disappointment. I wanted to save Shannon, not worry about offending a hundred-year-old echo of a dead dwarf's pride.

Moving across the carpeted tent and skirting the piles of straw, I stopped in front of Shannon, and she smiled sweetly as I reached up to press my finger to her forehead. "*Somnus.*"

She fell forward, and I caught her, then leaned her on the chaise lounge.

"You know, Rumple is a good, strong name for a dwarf," he said cautiously, and I could tell I did indeed hurt his pride.

Digging into my pocket, I pulled out the thread and gauged at how much magic was left within. Since the last golden spell, a few more of my knots had come undone, which meant the spell was weakening. I wouldn't be able to do this a third time.

There wasn't an alternative. I didn't have any spools, nothing but the straw and I was out of time. So I needed to work fast. With deft fingers, I created a net. Pulling the string out until I had almost nothing left. Then, with a spell and a prayer, I tossed it over the straw, and it shimmered before turning into gold. As I did the second pile, I felt the thread weaken in my grasp. A corner of the net became brittle.

A candle mark later, I was done. All the straw was gold, and it was almost perfect timing because I could see the sky lightening. I tried to pick up the threaded net, and it fell apart, turning to dust in my fingers. I reached for the firethorn spindle and saw it was drained; the magic gone. It was nothing more than a simple spindle.

Footsteps crunched on the snow, I grabbed the axe and rushed out of the ripped back tent, running my finger up the cut, I spelled the seam closed, just as King Goddrick entered.

"Well, I'll be!" he crowed. "She did it, and she worked herself so hard making me gold she fell asleep."

"*Her*," Rumple grunted out. "It was *you* that did the deed."

"Hush," I whispered as I tried to listen to what the king was going to say next.

"What's that you say?" The king's voice could be heard clearly, but I didn't hear anyone else speak. I carefully laid back on the snow, the cold seeping through my clothes. I lifted the edge of the tent and peered inside.

The king was by himself. There was only Shannon, but she was asleep. He was talking to himself. "The people are greedy. They don't appreciate me. I must teach them all a lesson. I'll send them into the mines where the goblins will devour them, starting with the chosen. Then they won't be after my gold."

"Who is he talking to? Is he mad?" Rumple whispered, and I could feel his anger.

"Shh." I rolled my eyes at my chatty axe.

"Yes, yes. And the girl Rhea too." The king chuckled, and he kissed the ring on his hand and left the tent.

My stomach roiled with queasiness, and I looked up at the gray sky that was slowly turning light.

"Girl, what is he speaking of?" Rumple asked.

Screams filled the air, and I saw smoke coming from the tents on the far side of the festival. Fighting had broken out among various pockets of villagers, and even the troops. It was the madness caused by the cursed gold taking effect.

I could spend the rest of my life trying to find every piece of cursed gold and remove it from every person. Grimkeep had been doing it for years, but I had to find a different solution.

"Rhea, please," Rumple begged. "I've seen this madness before. It won't stop until everyone is dead."

This was the first time he said please. "What do we do?"

"We need to go into the mountain once again and confront the one who is responsible. I'd said another would take my place, but it seems that it will be me once again—and a scrawny girl. This time will be the last. Do you hear me, Greed?" Rumple yelled in challenge. His voice so loud it echoed into the morning. In the distance, birds scattered, and dogs howled. "I will defeat you!"

I gazed at the snow-capped peaks above–the Ragnar mountains. I knew what I'd have to do, but whether I could survive it and avoid the blades was another matter.

CHAPTER TWENTY-THREE

"You could have warned me you were going to announce our location to the world," I huffed as ran away from the tent. Rumple's bellow in outrage alerted the guards, and they were heading directly toward our location.

I pumped my arms, moving as fast as I could, and ducked behind a smaller tent to hide.

Soldiers ran toward the tent we'd vacated, and I breathed a sigh of relief that it wasn't the blades on our tail. I could easily outsmart and outrun a human, but not if my enchanted axe wanted to outright challenge his enemy.

"We have to go Ter Dell," Rumple growled. "We have to make sure that Greed isn't released."

"He has weakened the vault," I said and quickly relayed everything I knew about the cursed treasure, the goblins digging it out, Molneer crafting the gold and releasing it back into circulation, how Grimkeep was doing everything he could to protect the city while retrieving the cursed trinkets.

"I can't believe this Molneer would betray his own kind and work for Greed. He's no dwarf," Rumple raged. "When I get my hands on him, I'll challenge him to—"

"You don't have hands," I sighed.

"Fine, when you get your hands on him, hold him down, and I'll chop him to pieces. Then I'll flay his . . ."

As Rumple continued to describe in perfect detail all the pain he would inflict onto Molneer, movement across the snowy field caught my eye.

Freya came out of a tent. On her heels, Annette, Brenna, Benton, and Captain Adams. They stepped into an open sleigh and Freya sat across from them. Her expression was somber, her eyes cast downward, and I knew then that she was the one taking them to the mines, and they didn't know.

I stood up, dusted the snow off my pants, and strode across the field with a purpose.

"Shut your mouth," I whispered. "Don't speak at all."

As I came to the sleigh, I grabbed the side and stepped up into it, surprising Freya.

"Molneer? What are you doing? I don't need you to escort me. I know the way."

I gave her a glare and sat down next to her. When Freya saw the axe, she moved over, giving me more room on the bench.

Captain Adams snapped his whip, and the sleigh started forward. We drove through the streets, and the morning rays brought truth to the incidents that occurred the night before, many of which hadn't ended. Tents knocked down, vendor booths destroyed and vandalized. The soldiers were marching the streets trying to intimidate the people into behaving, but how could they succeed when half of the troops were the ones vandalizing the tents? Even the king's golden throne was destroyed and thrown into a fire when another riot had started by the stage.

Greed's influence had grown, planted like a small seed whose evil had slowly taken roots in the lives of the people. As Grimkeep said, they were all going mad and destroying everything—even each other.

But I couldn't stop the current course of destruction. I couldn't hold back the wave of evil. I needed to locate the root and cut it out, and I would find it in Ter Dell.

Just as we headed out, a great black form caught my eye. I saw one blade focusing on the closest fight that had broken out, his back to us.

"Please," I whispered under my breath, trying to scoot down, beneath the sides of the sleigh and out of sight. "Please, don't look this way."

In my periphery, I saw the blade turn. "Please, not the dragon. Not the dragon."

He turned, his profile backlit perfectly by the sun. It was the dragon blade.

I knew the minute he spotted our sleigh, for his head snapped toward us and his back stiffened.

Keeping my focus downward, I refused to make eye contact. I knew that if the blade looked at me, he would see through my glamour.

In the end, it wouldn't be our closeness that would give me away, but a familiar dwarf that passed in front of the blade between him and us.

Molneer.

The dragon blade stared at the dwarf that was walking past him, and then glanced up to me sitting next to Freya, and then back to the real Molneer.

The dragon took a few steps toward our sleigh as we

slowed to let a man pass in front of us as he dragged a sled full of crates.

Another forty feet and he would be upon us.

"C'mon," I grunted, my foot bouncing on the floor in nervousness.

When the path was clear, the captain didn't seem to be in any hurry to leave while he chatted with the sled driver.

Thirty feet.

I gripped the sides of the bench seat, and even Freya had noticed our oncoming blade and the force with which his gaze was upon us.

"I'm scared," Annette said, looking toward the blade.

"It's nothing to worry about," Freya said, but her own unease revealed the lie.

"HO!" Rumple yelled loudly, startling the reindeer and the captain. The sleigh took off at an abrupt pace up the mountain trail, leaving the blade far behind in the distance.

I leaned back in my seat and breathed out a sigh of relief as the blade became nothing more than a speck in the snow. But I heard it. A faint warning carried on the wind.

Mine.

I knew I hadn't really escaped.

We rode in silence up the mountain path. Freya would frequently give the captain directions to change his course.

She kept giving me a side glance, and I wondered if she suspected something was amiss.

"You're awfully quiet, Molneer," Freya finally said. "Is something wrong?"

I turned my head away to look at the passing evergreens.

"Just thinking of a way to convince you to be my first wife, my dear," Rumple answered gruffly.

I spun around to look at her.

Her lips were pinched together in irritation, but I caught the slight smile at the corner of her lips.

"Not your dear," she answered.

I leaned back and crossed my legs, drawing my hand over my mouth so she couldn't see that it wasn't me talking. I hoped she assumed my voice was just muffled, because even though Rumple had guessed the same sentiment, his voice wasn't the same as Molneer's.

"That's only because you haven't seen what I have to offer. Dwarves have hidden secret delights to please even the pickiest woman."

Annette snorted, and Brenna covered her mouth to hide her smile.

Freya blushed. "I don't think—" she started.

"I cook a mean meat pie," he purred. "No one can resist *my* meat pie."

I struggled to keep my shoulders from shaking as I resisted jumping out of the sleigh. But I had to tilt my head and raise my chin with a grin as I attempted to publicly woo the frigid Freya.

Molneer had been trying to seduce Freya for a long time. There was no way Rumple could pull off what Molneer could not do.

I stroked my beard, covering my mouth again.

"And I be deadly with a duster," Rumple's voice lowered seductively.

This time, I did laugh, and so did everyone in the sleigh. I bent over, hiding my head between my knees.

"Please stop," I whispered. "I can't keep a straight face anymore."

"But I've hardly brought out my best pickup lines. Women love the idea of domesticated dwarves," he whispered. "You've never seen me in an apron. My muscles bulging, my manly beard dragging across the floor."

"I can't." I hiccupped, trying to suppress my laughter. After what seemed like ages—but was really only a moment—I regained control of myself and reassessed my glamour.

Freya was no longer looking at Molneer with her usual derision, but with a hint of interest. Good gracious, did it really work?

Thankfully, the rest of the sleigh ride passed in silence until we came up to a mountainside. It was nothing but a sheer drop of rock and shale, and where it had collapsed under a landslide was now covered in snow. This wasn't a mine entrance.

Freya stepped out of the sleigh and ran her hands along the mountain. Brushing her fingers along the rocky stone, she found a spot where the glamour faded and gave way into a hidden entrance covered by a ward.

"How do you know the secret way?" Rumple cried out indignantly.

Freya spun, her eyes wide as she stared at me, realizing that the voice definitely didn't belong to Molneer.

"*Who?*"

I dropped the charm into the snow, removing the glamour. The world shifted as my disguise faded and I stood before her, a young woman with a giant axe strapped to her back.

"Rhea?"

"Not just Rhea, woman. Answer me! How do you know the secret way into our mountain?"

Freya looked around in fear, her hands trembling. "Who's talking?"

Brenna, Annette, and Benton huddled together in confusion. Captain Adams kept them from interfering, holding his sword in front of them.

I reached over my back and unstrapped the axe, the gold glittering in the sun. Rolling the handle in my palms, I shifted the blade to get a better grip.

"I'd like to introduce you to my friend." I smirked. "He talks, chops off heads, and is apparently great in the kitchen. You need to answer his question before he starts mouthing off again."

Freya backed away, clutching her skirt. "I was shown the way by Molneer."

"These aren't the king's mines. You've been sending people into Ter Dell," Rumple sneered. "Why?"

Freya's shoulders dropped. "Molneer said he needed help running the dwarven mines. It was too much to do by himself, and hardly anyone wanted to go. He said it was the only way."

"Freya," I said her name softly. "The Ter Dell mines are overrun with goblins. Did you know?"

Her face paled. "No, that can't be." She reached into her pocket and pulled out a handful of gold coins. "See everything that they've brought up?"

"Humans can't survive down in the mines," Rumple said. "Only goblins and dwarves. And there are very few dwarves left in these mountains. Or so I've been told."

"Then why has he been asking for help? I don't understand?" Freya brushed her thin hands across her brow. Her stance became wobbly.

Captain Adams had lowered his sword, his face filled with disgust as he realized the implication before Freya did.

"You know what goblins eat, don't you?" Rumple growled out.

Brenna fainted, and Benton caught her in his arms. Annette looked like she was going to be sick, putting her hand over her mouth as her shoulders shuddered.

Freya shook her head in denial. "That can't be true."

"How many?" I asked, my voice dry with horror.

"I don't know what you mean . . ." Freya said.

"You aren't short staffed. Molneer has been paying you to send people into the mines, all to line your pockets with cursed gold." I raised the axe to her throat. "So I will ask one more time. How many?"

Freya's lip trembled and heavy tears fell from her eyes. She looked to Captain Adams and nodded, implicating him as well. "We've sent hundreds of people into the mines. I sent my eldest son to pay off his debt. Oh, stars." Her hands flew to her mouth. "Does that mean he's de—" She couldn't finish her sentence as she wailed loudly and collapsed into the snow, the gold spilling from her fingers, disappearing into the white blanket.

I glanced at the dark tunnel and then turned to Freya. "No more. I shall be the last."

"What?" she asked in confusion, sniffling through her crying.

"No more shall enter this mountain, *ever*." I held out my hand and Freya knew what I demanded without any words.

She pulled a pouch of gold from her pocket and handed it to me. As soon as it touched my palm, I felt the thrum. A deep throbbing that felt familiar, and then I knew where I had heard the rhythm before. It was the sound of the mines of Ter Dell.

Captain Adams sensed that the tides had changed, and he grabbed Annette's elbow by surprise. Before I could even react, Annette captured his wrist, put him in a pressure lock, and tossed him over her shoulder into the snow.

"Don't even think about it," she hissed. "I've got five older brothers."

Benton took the sword from the captain's hand and pinned him to the ground. "Tie them both up, Brenna."

I felt Rumple's approval of their brave actions.

Once they had Freya and Captain Adams tied up in the sleigh, they approached me.

"What should we do?" Benton asked.

"Run. Go far from here. The blades may try to find you again. Don't return to Kiln until you've heard whether I've succeeded." I nodded toward Freya and Captain Adams. "Go to Verdan. The owners of Goat Head Inn will help you with supplies. Drop these two somewhere far away, and then run farther than anyone might travel in a day," I said.

"Are you sure you can do this?" Annette asked as I turned toward the entrance to the mountain.

"I don't know, but I have to try."

Annette placed her hand on my shoulder and closed her eyes. "If you get lost, I can find you." She smiled humbly.

I shouldered the axe on my back. "I have a guide. If I don't come back, it's because I'm dead."

The smile fell from her mouth, and her brows drew close in worry.

"I don't plan on dying."

I stood in the snow and watched as the three magic users climbed back into the sleigh. Annette sat in the driver's seat while Benton and Brenna guarded the traitors. With a snap of the whip, they were off, heading back down the mountain.

I suddenly felt very alone.

Can I do this?

Rumple spoke, reminding me I wasn't on my own.

"It's time to face the past," he said, his voice sounding tired as we trekked into the mountain.

I pulled a light charm out of my bag as we entered the dwarven mine.

"Are you lost?" I asked for the millionth time as I stubbed my toe.

"I don't get *lost*," Rumple grunted. "I may have forgotten. The tunnels don't look the same. There's been many cave-ins since I was here last."

"No doubt," I grumbled.

I crouched low on the uneven path as I crawled over boulders and ducked under a low hanging ceiling. My hand rested against a round stone as I tried to climb up a small ledge, only to see the faint outlines of a face in the stone. It was once a memorial, and when my eyes adjusted to the darkness within, I could see the remains of several monuments. Stone shields, swords, beautiful marble—all destroyed.

I gasped and held the charm up to see the ruins.

"Where are we?" I asked Rumple.

"This was once the Hall of Remembrance," he stated. "All of our greatest heroes had a place here where all the guilds could come and pay honor to our heritage."

I slowed, staring at the bust of a dwarf king, his beard long and intricately braided. In his hand was a long spear and knife.

"That was Ragnar the First," Rumple said as I continued, stepping carefully over the bust. Then I came to a pile of dust.

"That's what's left of Haeren. Our great dwarf queen."

It took a long time to crawl through, under, and over the collapsed statues and monuments. As I traveled, I heard more of the Ter Dell dwarves' history. Of their late King Ragnar the Fourth who died when the city collapsed.

"What happened all those years ago? The history books don't go into detail."

"Why should they? There are no more Ter Dell dwarves to tell the tale. You only have the human account of the fall."

"What of Grimkeep?"

Rumple sighed. "He would be my great nephew. My sister had settled in the valley of Merren with the dwarves of the plains. But why any dwarf would want to settle above the land and not below it is beyond me. Shouldn't even call themselves dwarves, but humans."

After the Hall of Remembrance, the cave opened, and there were divots along the wall. Reaching up, I dipped my fingers into a curve and felt liquid. I smelled my hand but didn't detect a scent.

"Lamp oil?" I guessed.

"Light it and watch," he suggested.

"*Fiergo*," I said, and a spark hit the trench and a flash of light followed. The oil caught fire and raced along the wall. Every few feet, another carved trench came out of the wall and the fire lit up. They were dwarf sconces made of stone, and when one lit, a hundred others down the tunnel lit as well, bathing us in a warm light.

I put away my charm and knocked back the remains of a spider web, the sticky wisps brushing against my hand as I entered another cavern. An oppression immediately overtook me, and I felt weighed down by an insurmountable feeling of utter hopelessness.

What's the point of going any further?

I'll never survive once I reach my destination.

I'll probably get lost and die of starvation.

Maybe it's better to give up now.

My feet turned heavy, like lead. I was soon dragging my boots along the dirt floor. My head was cloudy.

"What are you doing?" Rumple called out as I sat down upon the nearest outcropping of rock and placed my elbows on my knees.

"Sitting," I said.

"We don't have time for sitting. We need to be moving."

"Why bother?" I answered, my brain foggy.

"Because we have a job to do!"

"A job? I'm not getting paid. In fact, I think this whole thing is someone else's problem. It's not mine."

"What do you mean 'it's not your problem'? Greed is everyone's problem. It's a universal problem that won't end with Kiln. If Greed escapes, then it won't be just Ter Dell that is wiped from the map, but all the neighboring towns, and then kingdoms."

"Again, why is this my problem?" I rubbed my temples, trying to massage the nagging voice that had taken over my conscience. "My mother hates this kingdom. She left it. She never wanted to return. So then, why did she send me, and what am I supposed to do? Fight an invisible enemy? One that a whole city of dwarves couldn't stop?"

"What has gotten into you?" Rumple snapped.

"Why do you keep talking? Yap. Yap. Yap. You never shut up," I groaned and slid the bandolier off my shoulders, dropping the talking axe onto the ground.

"Wait, Rhea, where are you going?"

"I'm shedding some excess baggage . . . as in you."

I walked away, off the main path and down the steps of a darkened tunnel.

"Wait, you shouldn't do that. It's too dangerous to go on alone."

"I'm tired of carrying you. I'm tired of your constant nagging. You're not my mother."

"Darn right, if I were your mother, you wouldn't dare to drop me in the dirt. For I am Rumple Stiltskin, and I am—"

"Annoying!" I sighed dramatically.

"No, wait . . . come back . . . please?" Rumple's voice softened as he begged.

CHAPTER TWENTY-FOUR

I walked until the voice stopped and the pressure in my head lessened. There was still an overwhelming feeling of misery that weighed heavily on my shoulders. Like a pack of stones filled with absolute despair, and it was easier to retreat into the dark, into my mind, than to face the problems.

The depression grew, and I couldn't handle the emotions that were overpowering me, but I inherently knew that if I continued down this path, at the end I would be granted peace.

Light from the other tunnel had dwindled to nothing. Only the faintest glow remained from algae that grew along the wall in opulent colors of green and blue, bathing the cave in soft hues that reminded me of a watercolor painting. Rocks luminesced under the algae, making my fingernails glow. I slowed my descent down the stairs as it leveled out and I stepped into a room; the floor covered in white shale that crunched beneath my feet.

With each step, more crunching followed, and I knew not to look down. To not look closer at what I was stepping on, or my progress would stop and the feelings of unworthiness, sorrow, and depression would drown me. Even now, I struggled to breathe because everything was too much. I wanted it gone. Tears filled my eyes and my foot caught. I slipped, falling forward into a pile of shale. Except it wasn't. Suddenly, the pressure lifted as fear overcame the pain and I stared into the face of a white skull with a recognizable eye patch.

"No . . ."

Scrambling backwards, I swam through a sea of human bones.

Terror shot through my body. My blood pounded in my ears as I tried to race up the tunnel and away from the horror behind me. I fell forward and my foot caught behind me, my hand at a weird angle hanging above my head.

I pulled on my foot and wrist. I could feel them ensnared, trapped, unable to move—but no physical attachment was keeping me in place. Calming my fears, I took a deep breath, studying every little detail. I could hear the faintest clicking noise as something was drawing closer to me.

There! The slightest shimmer attached to my wrist, and another attached to my foot, and I could feel the emotion attached to the string. Using my mage sight, I closed my eyes and then saw them. Hundreds of miniscule strings all running up and out of the cave. I'd brushed across one of them, and it latched onto me. I touched the string, trying to break it, and heavy emotion overcame me once again. Feelings of unworthiness.

You can't escape this. You're not a hero.

You're nothing. No one.

The string wouldn't snap. I scraped it on a rock, trying

to sever the connection, but it had buried itself too deep in my skin.

I couldn't believe I had fallen into this pit. I had read about a creature like this in the Book of Eld. It was said that a goblin was cursed into the shape of a spider, and she lured victims into her web of lies and fed on their despair.

My heart continued to race as I took to biting the web attached to my wrist, but it wouldn't detach. Using magic didn't work, and fire just deflected off of it. The more I struggled, the faster the clicking noise came, and I knew there was a hideous creature on the other end, alerted by my struggling.

I froze, listening as I lay on the ground surrounded by bones, and I tried to think of how to escape a web of lies. My wits had always been my best weapon.

You won't be able to think your way out of this.

You're going to die here. Accept it. You know the truth.

My eyes snapped open, and I sat up, staring at the web and the way it sunk right into my wrist.

The truth.

"No, I won't," I said confidently, a smile forming along my lips.

It's much easier to give up. To go to sleep.

"I'm not tired," I said. The negative thoughts were never mine, but that of my enemy. Thoughts were fed to me. Lies by a great deceiver.

"I feel great." I stood up and held back the wince as the web yanked at my wrist. "I've never felt more confident that I will, in fact, kill you. Escape this pit, and defeat Greed."

The web trembled slightly, and its hold on me weakened. I started racing toward the exit.

Stop! It's not worth it. Give up.

I gasped in pain and glanced at the web connected to my wrist. It was thicker, injecting me every time *it* spoke. I could feel depression weighing me down, and the string would tighten and regain its strength.

"I won't give up." I took another step up the stairs. "I will succeed," I grunted and tugged against the web that was desperately trying to drag me back down into the pit of despair. "It won't be easy. But I am not alone." As I fought for each step, I continued to climb. At the top of the stairs, I could see light. I was almost back to where I'd started. If I could just get to Rumple.

Thousands have come to my pit out of loneliness, despair, hopelessness. None have ever escaped. What makes you think you will?

The clicking grew louder. The silver webs that were strung along the wall wriggled, and I knew the creature was coming up the tunnel behind me. I would not turn around. I would not.

"Because I do not listen to the lies of my enemy. You don't know me, or what I'm capable of." The webs loosened, and I ran up the steps. The threads now shook the stairs, vibrating as it chased after me.

"You're a scared little girl, and your blood will taste sweet on my tongue." The creature's voice no longer spoke to me through thoughts.

The thing had an actual mouth.

"Is that you, girl?" Rumple called as I achieved the last step. The axe was only a few feet away.

I reached for it and fell on my feet as the web around my foot was yanked backward. My fingers brushed the leather bandolier, and I held on as it flipped me over and towed me toward the tunnel.

"Tricky, Tricky," the creature said, and I felt my stomach roil at seeing the cursed monster staring back at me. It had the abdomen of a spider with eight black spindly legs, each with sharp and deadly spines shooting off like daggers. The torso and head were that of a goblin, its eyes white like death. The mouth was a deadly mixture of sharpened goblin teeth hidden under wickedly curved fangs.

I gripped the axe, and the goblin attacked, another stream of web attached to my other hand. Another injection of despair slowly crawled through my blood, and I felt a paralyzing chill wash over me. My grasp loosened on the handle and another tug pulled me closer to the spider. My head thumped along the stairs as it dragged me back down toward its mouth.

You've failed like all the others.

"I can defeat you," I whispered, feeling tears well in my eyes. "Because I am not alone. I have friends." Another tug and the axe almost slid from my grip.

"Arachnis, you coward!" Rumple roared, coming to my aid as he distracted the giant spider.

Arachnis froze, her head turning right and left as she searched the dark cavern for the owner of the voice.

"Who's there?"

Rumple's assured voice woke me, and I wrapped my fingers around the leather strap at the last moment. The spider's black, pulsing abdomen sat right above me. A whip of air flew past me as it shot out web in every direction, trying to snag the speaker. Then I understood the creature's need for luring its prey. It was blind.

"How do you know my name?" Arachnis cried out. It seemed the spider goblin no longer considered me a threat. I slipped the axe from the bandolier.

"I know your name, Arachnis, for we've met before."

"Rumple?" Arachnis changed her tactic and began to plead. "Then you should let me have this girl. She is of no use to you, and I am very hungry."

"I once pitied you because you were cursed, so I let you live. But it was a mistake I won't let happen again."

The spider trembled above me, and it attempted to retreat into the tunnel. It grasped my leg, and my bottom thudded down every step. I gasped as I hit my head on the way down.

"Release her!" Rumple roared.

"When she's dead," Arachnis cried out.

The axe glowed in my hands, and I felt my body move on its own. I swung outward and took out the spider's leg.

Arachnis screamed and dropped me. I rushed to my feet just as another sling of web came my way. It was as if another person had taken control of the axe in my hands. It moved toward me, and I dropped low, the web shooting over my head. I swung upward, and the axe sliced through the spider's abdomen. Warm blood splattered across my dress. I wanted to release the axe, but Rumple wasn't done, for the fight was far from over, and he was fighting this battle for me.

A leg swiped at me, and I went flying back into a wall. A stabbing pain ran up my calf as Arachnis stabbed me with a spine attached to her leg.

Heat burned through the muscle and I cried out, but I didn't let it stop me. Rumple didn't give me time to think as he swung, cutting clean through the spine. I did nothing more than hold on as Rumple attacked, parried, and with a final swing, sliced through Arachnis' neck, severing her head.

The spider goblin fell in a clump on the ground, its seven remaining legs twitching and spasming.

Finally, I felt the axe's magic release me and I dropped Rumple.

I rushed away to empty the contents of my stomach. When it was over, I sat on the floor next to an axe covered in stinking black goblin blood.

"You did good," Rumple tried to console me. "Was this your first fight?"

I nodded, unsure if I could speak without throwing up again.

"Well, I could tell . . . because you fight like a girl."

CHAPTER TWENTY-FIVE

"Fighting like a girl isn't a bad thing." Rumple tried to change his tone when I stormed off, leaving the spider goblin carcass behind me.

I couldn't get the sight of bones down in that pit out of my mind. The number of human remains I'd seen . . . how many of those skulls were servants? How many had unwillingly lost hope, walking aimlessly toward their death?

I was conflicted, feeling upset at killing that cursed creature. As I sat by a stagnant pool of water and washed its blood from my palms, I found my eyes welling up with pity at its predicament. It wasn't always like that . . . until it was cursed. Or was it?

Then my pity turned toward anger as I scrubbed my nail beds. That creature would never again snare someone in its web. I ran my fingers over my wrists, feeling the phantom strings she'd held me with. With her death, the lies that had bound me fell off, and I was free. But I could still feel that echo of doubt, the poison of her words in my soul.

Truth, I told myself. *Truth will set you free.*

Rumple had continued with his rant about my fighting

skills, and I ignored him as I dunked him into the pool of water to wash off the blood.

He came up sputtering. "You could have warned me!"

I frowned. "I didn't know you could breathe."

"Well . . ." A long pause followed. "I don't."

"Or feel, for that matter," I continued. "I don't even want to know how you see or where your eyes are. There's too much metaphysical stuff to wrap my head around."

"I have senses and emotions. Getting suddenly dunked felt like someone attacked my bits with icicles."

"I didn't want to know that," I chided. "When we find this vault, remind me to lock you back in it."

"Har har har!" Rumple fake laughed. "Just you wait to see who's locking who in what, girly."

"You don't have hands," I pointed out.

"Stop reminding me!"

We continued our trek for hours. My stomach growled, but I ignored it as I pressed on, knowing that I had to reach my destination.

But I couldn't outrun exhaustion, and I needed to sleep. Curling up next to an outcropping, I rested with my head against my arms and tried to rest while Rumple kept watch.

"Something is following us." Rumple woke me a candle mark later.

"What?" Startled, I lifted my head and searched the darkness. "Where?"

"I wasn't sure, but it's been on our tail for a while, staying just among the shadows."

"Do you know what it is?" I asked.

"I don't, but it is stealthy. I almost didn't catch it."

"Then how did you notice at all?"

"Uh, that's the problem."

I looked to my side to where I had laid the axe. He was missing.

"I didn't catch it. *It* caught me," Rumple said apologetically as I saw the great axe rise into the air above me, the holder cast in shadow. I blinked and wanted to run, but I was cornered, pressed into the stone wall at my back.

The axe turned and swung, coming right for my head.

I turned, closing my eyes, waiting for the death strike, but felt the drift of air as it passed right by me.

Opening my eyes, I saw the golden axe return as the wielder expertly spun it in their hands and took a few more practice swings.

"This is amazing craftsmanship," the stranger said in awe. "It has to be some of your best work."

"Put me down, you thief," Rumple cried indignantly. "I don't care—what are you doing? Don't do that. It tickles."

Honor stood in the cavern next to me, her dark hair braided down her back, a cloak made of wolf's fur covered her shoulders, and she looked completely at home wielding my battle axe.

She spun Rumple above her head and then bent forward, easily passing it behind her back before bringing it back up. Using both hands, she tossed it over her head, aiming at the root of a tree that had grown through the roof of the cavern.

It stuck with a thud.

"I think I'm in love," Rumple cooed. "I've never been handled with such strength, such dexterity."

Honor grinned and turned to me, the dimple in her cheek showing her amusement. She tossed out a hand, and

I grasped it. She pulled me to my feet before wrapping me in a hug.

"How are you here?" I asked, burying my face in her cloak, breathing in the scent of the woods and outdoors.

"You called me," she said.

"No, I didn't." I pulled back in puzzlement.

"You used the mirror and scried for me."

"We never even spoke. How could you know?"

Honor grasped my shoulder, and she gave it a squeeze. "I may be the outcast of the family, but it doesn't mean that I don't recognize your magical signature. I could feel your desire for help. And since Lorn and I were in the Northern Woods, it was easy for me to take a break and seek you out."

The Northern Woods. Where the elves lived in secret.

Northern wasn't even an apt description because that was somewhere between Rya and Kiln, but no one actually knew where it was unless an elf escorted you.

Of all my sisters, I felt it was Honor that I was the closest too. It was because of her I'd discovered my gift for alchemy and blacksmithing. When one of her throwing knives broke, I'd taken it and reforged the metal, but along with it, I'd attempted my first spell. I'd created a knife with a seeking spell, and accidentally created a deadly weapon that always hit the target.

It was Honor's favorite gift, and even though it was my first attempt at blacksmithing, she loved it. Even now, I could see the hilt of her throwing knife sticking out of the hidden pocket in the black vest she wore over her black shirt and pants.

"I'm so glad you're here," I breathed out, giving her another hug. I quickly relayed to her everything that had happened over the last few weeks, and her expression never changed. It was neutral, her feelings hidden behind years of training.

"Sounds like a challenge," she said, walking forward. She pulled the axe out of the root. "And you really talk?" she asked.

"Talk? Who needs to talk? Just hold me," Rumple purred, and I knew he was completely smitten in my sister's hands.

"He never shuts up," I added.

"Really?" Honor smirked. "That sounds like he can be a pain in the axe."

I laughed hard, my voice echoing in the cavern.

Even Rumple roared at her joke. "I like her. Can we keep her?"

I just shrugged. Honor strapped Rumple back into the bandolier and handed him back to me so I could slip him over my shoulders. Honor took the lead as we continued our trek. When we came to a juncture with two paths, she looked down into the caves, her eyes closed as she listened, and then she took a sniff of the air.

"I believe it's the left cave." She pointed and looked back at me for confirmation. "Am I right?"

"How did you know?" Rumple asked suspiciously.

"Rhea said the mines were working again, and I can smell a faint sulfur and dioxide scent coming from this cave."

"Marry me!" Rumple yelled out.

"Stop it," I snapped. "You're a dwarf, and she was raised by elves. Aren't you supposed to be enemies?"

"Hey, we can't all be perfect."

Honor shook her head. "He is a handful."

"You haven't even taken me into battle yet. I'll show you a handful," he boasted.

Honor stilled; her eyes going wide, her nostrils flaring, and she reached for the daggers in her left pocket.

With quick successive throws, she let the throwing knives fly over my shoulder. I turned just as one imbedded into the shoulder of a goblin, the other into a skull. They fell over dead.

Honor raced over, quickly searching their bodies, her face grim as she held up an arm to see a branded red mark.

"Scouts. We are definitely close. If they don't come back, that means hundreds will be on our tail."

My mouth went dry. How could Honor and I fight off hundreds of goblins? In short—we couldn't.

"How much farther to Ter Dell?" I asked Rumple.

"Not far at all, but if Honor is right, we won't make it. Goblins are fast. They can scale the walls."

Honor dragged the dead bodies over to a pit and pushed them over with her foot. They fell—and I never heard them hit the bottom.

"Rumple, can you guide my sister to Ter Dell? I'm going to slow them down."

"Honor, you can't do it alone. You're going to need an army."

She pulled two more deadly looking daggers from her leg sheaths. "Don't worry, I've got more than enough help with these blades."

Without another word, she ran back up the tunnel, her boots silent along the stone steps as she dissolved into the shadows.

As her form disappeared, I heard Rumple's audible

sigh at her departure. "Hey, you," I grumbled. "Get your head on straight. We've got a job to do."

"Right." He cleared his throat. "Let's go."

When I ran, I wasn't graceful like my sister. My footsteps slapped the earth like a wooden paddle beating a rug. I didn't know how to adjust my gait or properly pace, and I soon found myself out of breath and panting. I slowed when I came to a stone half wall that overlooked a drop off. My hand going to my side as I focused on breathing to relieve the side stitch.

"Where to?" I asked, sucking in my air between my teeth as sweat was running down my face.

"We're here. The once glorious city of Ter Dell, the resting place of our high king," Rumple said, his voice filled with emotion.

It was exactly like my vision. The waterfall flowing from the ceiling into the water wheels that were creaking slowly. The only building still standing was that of the warning bell. The tower stood like a beacon over the silent city. I looked down to see a crumbling set of stairs was the only way down into the streets.

"You never told me how the city was destroyed."

As I spoke, we passed by an alley and saw the bones of a dwarf laying in the street, his helm still covering his skull, and in his belly area—a dwarven axe. More bodies lay strewn about, and each one we passed was a dwarf with the symbol of Ter Dell on their pauldron. A war hammer and axe crossed on a field of green.

"Rumple, what happened here? I don't see any goblins, or . . ." I trailed off as I saw more evidence of fighting. As a blacksmith, my eyes focused on the weapons, searching for signs of goblins. Their blades were cruder, curved, and had less artistry. Every weapon had an echo of their owner, and goblin blades had a feeling of vileness when touched.

I kneeled and touched the edge of a short sword; the ore sang a familiar note. It was made of silven, like my necklace.

"Don't," Rumple warned.

Getting up, I pinched my lips together to hide my feelings as I touched an arrow, running my finger over the arrowhead. It sang. I could feel Rumple's impatience with me as I kept slowing to brush my fingers across the metals and I continued to hear the ore sing to me. Each weapon was made of silven mined within the mountain.

I closed my eyes and my chest constricted.

"You weren't attacked," I breathed out in accusation.

Rumple was frustrated. "We were."

I grabbed a small throwing axe and held it up. The feeling inside was making me sick. "Not from an outside enemy." I dropped the axe onto the ground and looked around. My eyes opened to the scene before me, their memories flooding back into my body. A bloody war was fought, but it was not between the goblins and dwarves.

I gasped, my hand covering my mouth. "The dwarves of Ter Dell went mad and killed each other."

CHAPTER TWENTY~SIX

"Sometimes our greatest enemies are those within," Rumple said softly.

I sighed. "Greed."

"Greed had infiltrated our guards, then our blacksmiths. Even myself and our king. His vileness leeched into all our weapons, and we turned against each other. Ter Dell fell not by goblins, or by war with another guild. We fell by each other's hand, guided by none other than Greed himself. That is how your friends became cursed. Someone dug through the bodies of the fallen, found the cursed blades and carried them to the surface."

"Molneer," I said angrily.

I saw the city with fresh eyes, and I couldn't help but feel for them. Feel Rumple's loss of his family, his brethren, and kin. No one should have to live through this kind of destruction.

"But you survived," I said.

Rumple sighed. "I wished I hadn't. When the last dwarf fell, the spell on me was gone. I opened my eyes to see I was the last one standing, and the dwarf on the other end of my blade was none other than the king himself."

A painful silence followed as Rumple waited for me to

condemn him, to blame him for losing the city. But I didn't see it that way. I knew the influence Greed had over a person. I saw it with Kash, Damon and Spencer. It was a battle not everyone could overcome alone.

"Why do you think he let you live?" I asked.

"Let me live." Rumple snorted. "There was no one else he could control to kill me. It was just dumb luck, but that set a fire within me. With the death of my kingdom, he was strong enough to take on a physical form. I'd chased him down for years and he always escaped my grasp. I knew I would do everything in my power to trap him, and I did. Past the city of Ter Dell, below even the lowest level of our mines, is the vault. No one can go there except the very strongest of my lines of Stiltskins. That is where we will find Greed."

I licked my lips in nervousness as we continued through the city. My heart ached as I saw the once glorious kingdom, now nothing more than ash and bone. The beautiful banners faded and deteriorated into dust. The furniture within the homes, cracked and eroded by the moisture in the air or eaten away by bugs.

We had come to a central fountain, and it surprised me to see the clear water running within. My lips were dry and cracked, my clothes damp from the heat. The fountain was a gift.

I immediately ran my hands through the water.

"It's cold," I said in surprise.

"It's a natural mountain spring. It's safe to drink."

And I did, slurping noisily from my hands. I scooped more, brushing it over the back of my neck, cooling myself off. I would have dunked my whole body in if I hadn't heard the whispers of danger.

I looked up just as a shadow disappeared over the edge of a building and an arrow sliced through the air, embedding into the stone ledge inches from my face. *Goblins.*

"Watch out!" Rumple flung me backwards until I was on the ground, pressed against the fountain's base. "How dare they enter our sacred home!" Rumple grumbled beneath his breath. "I will not let their kind desecrate my lands."

I felt myself pulled upright as though I were lifted by an unseen hand.

"Unharness me, let me at them!" Rumple pulled against the ties.

With him pulling at my back, I tried to reach up to remove him. Another arrow loosed, and I saw it streak out of the sky. Rumple did not, and I was a perfect target with my hands struggling behind my back. I tried to duck, but I couldn't with the weight of him thrashing behind me.

I closed my eyes and waited for the arrow to strike.

Instead, it ricocheted off metal, and I opened my eyes to see the dragon blade standing over me. His eyes glowed red within the black helm.

He leaned down, the black swirling mist drawing closer to me. I heard the voice within, his thoughts clear as day.

Mine.

"Kash?"

For a second, the mist cleared as Kash fought for control and I could see his golden eyes.

Another arrow struck his armor, and Kash pushed me down, spinning to protect me.

My heart raced as I crouched and glanced up to see the goblins swarming out of the alley and across the roofs of the buildings as they zeroed in on us. The goblin's armor was silver, ill-fitting and clearly made for a much larger warrior.

"They're wearing our armor!" Rumple roared in frustration. "Stealing from the dead! I will kill them for desecrating my brethren."

I finally unleashed Rumple from his holster and held him out before me. "Okay, let's do this."

I stepped to the side of the blade, clearing the way for him to take a goblin's head off instead of mine. Their feet pounded the street, the rhythm thrumming through the mountain and matching the racing of my heart.

A throng of them were cut off as the hawk blade appeared, his long rapier slicing and dicing as he redirected them around and right into the path of another blade.

The lion blade stepped into their path, his great two-handed sword gliding through the air and cutting them down. One escaped his blade by racing up the side of the building and was quickly silenced by Honor's dagger.

My sister raced to my side, her face filled with excitement.

"What did you do?" I asked.

"I needed more blades to fight the goblins." She winked at me. "I didn't necessarily mean my blades."

"There's no guaranteeing that they won't kill us after they save us," I added.

"I'd like to see them try. After all, we are the daughters of Eville. We won't go down without a fight."

More goblins attacked us from another direction, meeting their fate as they collided with my Rumple-axe and the deadly dragon blade.

Even though Kash's dagger was the shortest of the

weapons, it was the fastest. The strikes were quick and clean. He never looked back as he moved to the next target.

I couldn't understand what was going on.

Kash didn't remember the goblin attack in the castle. It had been the blade controlling him. And I now knew that Greed controlled the blade, but how was it that Greed would destroy his own minions?

Was this really Kash fighting for me, underneath the spell, in the darkness? Some part of him had to know it was me, or was it something else?

It only fueled my fighting spirit. I couldn't let what Greed had done here in Ter Dell happen to the human kingdom. Already, I could see that he was working towards his own goal.

Three goblins jumped on Kash and he fell to his knees. They scratched and dug with their claws in the crevices of his armor.

He jerked, and I saw blood seep through and spill onto the white stone.

The blades couldn't be killed, but even I was able to eventually penetrate the armor with a chisel.

Swinging the axe on my accord, I cut down two of the goblins while Kash grabbed the third around the neck and tossed him against the closest building. The goblin hit with a thud and fell to the ground, unmoving.

It seemed the other goblins had watched the group on Kash and they began to attack in packs. They knocked Spencer to the ground in a swarm, biting and digging at the crevices in his plating.

"Rhea!" Honor screamed. "Do something!"

"I'm open to suggestions," I cried out.

"Your earth magic," she yelled. "Use it."

"Shake and bake," Rumple crowed again.

"I can't," I said. "What if I bring the whole cavern down?"

"Then we will die and take them with us," Rumple yelled in return.

Easy to say when you're an enchanted axe.

I kneeled and reached into the earth, searching for the ley line of magic. But then I heard it. The song of the silven ore, and I knew now what my gift really was. I didn't reach for the ley line. Instead, I reached deep into the mines themselves, searching for the magic ore and feeling its familiar makeup—then I called it to me. The ground shook; the dwarf buildings that hadn't been cared for in a century slowly toppled over.

Goblins scattered, running to the shadows, freeing the three blades as they retreated. Only some regrouped and charged right for me. One leapt into the air, his mace coming straight for my head. The goblin choked out a grunt as he met a swift death from the dragon's own blade.

Another snuck up behind me and tried to wrench the axe from me. I swung, knocking him back.

"They're after Rumple!" I yelled as the dragon took down another goblin.

I curled my fingers into fists and felt the earthquake beneath my feet, the ore rumbling and shifting as it moved through the ground. The armor rattled and danced in the street, pulling toward me as if by a giant magnet.

The show of magic caused the goblin hordes to pause, but they were not to be deterred, for greed was driving them.

I screamed as I pulled even harder on my magic. The city crumbled as I drew from the ore, hearing the mines screech to a halt down below the ground. Now, every head turned toward the waterfall, and the giant wheels that turned the mine.

"Run!" I yelled over the din of the great wheel's creaking. They would hear my warning. Damon was buried beneath a pile of goblins that were trying to scratch at his face. I used my magic to fling the empty dwarven armor around like projectiles, knocking the goblins off his body.

Spencer and Honor ran toward the edge of the city.

I tried to keep control of the ore as Honor ran next to me, but my magic was stilted, and it was like I was stuck in mud. I strained, and sweat beaded across my forehead. I flung another helmet at a goblin, but it slowed and stalled midair, then fell.

My knees buckled under the stress as I struggled to call the magic. It wasn't coming as easily and I couldn't understand why.

Honor watched me, her face filling with sorrow.

That's when I heard the sound; the clanging of the mine and the rushing roar of water as we came to the edge of the city and the cliff. It was just like the dream. My vision of Ter Dell. A single bridge only a few feet wide ran over a giant chasm. On the other side were the tunnels that led down to the passageways below the mines, and what I assumed to be the vault.

But unlike my vision, on one side of the chasm, the water rushed down the wall that fed to the various water wheels that hung above the city. When I turned my head to the right, I saw the other side. Molten lava was slowly coming down the other. Chutes had been built to direct the volcano's flow to the city and when the two elements met under the bridge, burning hot steam rose, creating a searing hot fog.

I understood now what they meant when they said not every dwarf could go this far into the mountain. Even now, my skin was sweating with moisture, and I had a feeling that if I crossed that bridge, I would boil to death.

Honor looked for an answer but found none. "There's no way to get across."

"Not unless you're a Stiltskin," Rumple said.

"We need to cross it," I cried out.

Honor leaned forward, and the steam blasted upward, and she backed away. "That's hot! I've never felt anything like that. It'll kill us."

Kash leaned forward and rested his hand over the steam. He pulled it back and shook his head.

We were trapped between instant death or a goblin horde.

The water churned, and I looked up at the giant water wheel and an idea formed in my head. I quickly calculated how many pounds of water rushed over the falls and into the wheel. Could it be redirected into the city?

Using my gifts, I closed my eyes and dug into the mountain, feeling the ore within. If I pulled on it, I could use them like projectiles to knock the wheel off and send the waterfall into the city.

"Honor, I'm going to flood the streets. Everyone, hold on to something." I inclined my head toward the wheel, and she nodded.

I closed my eyes and focused on pulling, using the ley lines as backup, but once again I was stilted. My magic was slow to respond, like it was being pulled elsewhere. A few stones came loose from the wall, and they shot out, but it wasn't enough.

The giant waterwheel didn't budge.

The enemy howled, and I looked behind me to see a mass of goblins bearing down on us. Damon had hung back and was fighting them, buying us time, but even he couldn't fight off a hundred by himself.

Honor looked at me, her beautiful eyes filled with guilt. "I'm sorry, Rheanon, this is all my fault."

"What is?"

She shook her head, pulled out her knives, shifted her weight, her feet digging into the earth, and she took off running down the street to help Damon.

She yelled in challenge.

"Honor, no! No," I screamed, seeing her jump into the mass of goblins.

As soon as she did, the band holding back my magic snapped, and it rushed out like a typhoon. Enormous boulders of ore crashed up through the earth, breaking the water wheel. The waterfall backed up, and then the wheel rolled over the dam—breaking—and water came rushing down into the city.

"Now you've done it, girl!" Rumple said as a wall of water rushed toward us.

Squeals of terror echoed as the goblins pulled back and raced to higher ground, leaving their prey. Then I saw her. Honor's body spread out on the stone. Unmoving.

Damon stood, staring at Honor's prone form. He looked up at the rushing wave, then back toward our group.

He sheathed his sword and turned to face the surge, racing toward Honor. He grabbed her under the arms.

"Damon!" I cried out in warning, but my voice was

silenced by the roar of the water swallowing him with its massive power.

Spencer turned and ran toward the cliff. He made a motion with his hands and Kash nodded.

With the water licking at Spencer's feet, he sheathed his rapier and pulled out two knives. Kash ripped Rumple from my grasp and pushed me backward off the edge. I screamed as I fell into the dark abyss.

"What a dumb way to die!" Rumple yelled, his voice echoing as we fell.

CHAPTER TWENTY-SEVEN

"I take that back. This was genius," Rumple said smugly as we clung to the cliff side. "I saved you both!"

Kash was clinging to the axe with one hand and me with the other, and Rumple's blade dug into the rock.

What felt like a push had been Kash taking us both over. He'd turned midair and swung the axe into the cliff as an anchor. Spencer had done the same using two daggers. Above us, water rushed over our heads, arching like a wave, leaving us dry and safe.

I could see Kash's hands trembling to support our weight. He slipped, and I gasped.

"You know. That ore. It's all in this cliff as well," Rumple said casually.

I put my hands to the earth and felt it shift and move, creating steppingstones for both the blades to stand on. When he transferred his position to the outcropping, Kash still didn't release his hold on the axe or me. His body was still vibrating, and I saw the signs. It was likely after nightfall, and he should have transferred back, but he was fighting it. I knew why. He wanted to protect me, and he thought it would be better in this form.

As the water crested over us, I pressed my forehead to

his chest and felt him quiver. He wrapped an arm around me, and I leaned into him for silent strength.

We had both lost someone. Damon and Honor. Why would she do that? Why would she run toward danger?

It's because of who she was. She was a fighter, through and through. Honor, like her name, was never one to cast spells or used sigils, and now I felt robbed. Robbed of knowing her better, of growing closer to my sister.

She, more than any of us, lived up to her name.

Honor.

I let my tears fall freely. Soon, the heat pelted us as the waves died down.

Spencer tapped my shoulder and motioned to the water that was trickling.

"We need to move now while the temperature has dropped. We've only got minutes." Rumple's warning cut through my grief.

I nodded and pulled away. Kash lifted me up over his shoulders and pushed me back over the cliff. I laid on my stomach and reached over to help pull him up, but his hand shot up, his armored fingers piercing the stone, and he raised himself up with no help.

"Show off," I griped.

The bladesman's shoulders shook.

Spencer almost flew up and over the ledge like a bird, his grace and quickness clear.

"Go! Go!" Rumple called out as we looked at the small walkway and froze. The wave had destroyed part of the bridge and now there was a twelve-foot gap.

"We can't jump that!" I said, staring at it with fear.

As I said it, Spencer had backed up. He ran, easily

making the jump, while I stood staring below into the abyss.

"Nope," I backed away. "I'm not jumping."

Kash picked me up around the waist and I screamed as Spencer leaned forward as if to catch me.

"Kash, don't you throw me. If you throw me, and I fall, I'll die and haunt your sorry Aaaahhh!" He flung me into the air, and my arms flailed as the ground disappeared beneath my feet.

But once I went up, I felt myself falling down. The throw was short.

"No, no, no!" I cried.

But I didn't fall far. Spencer snatched me out of the air and pulled me backward just as Kash came leaping across the gap, almost floating, a screaming Rumple in tow. When he landed, he pointed toward the other side, and we turned and ran. I could feel it. Feel the heat seeping up through the bottom of my soles. The temperature in the room was rising by the minute.

We ran, and even as we neared the other side, I couldn't help but look over my shoulder at the desolate city, searching for a shadow of my sister. We crossed the bridge and headed into a tunnel where it was cooler, but not by much.

"Where to?" I breathed out, wiping the sweat off my brow.

"This way, but it will not get easier," Rumple said from Kash's hand, tugging toward a set of stairs.

"Of course not," I mumbled

He was right. He led us through a maze of tunnels, and we continued to travel downward toward the wall of molten lava.

My knees buckled, and I collapsed against the wall, but quickly pulled away because it was so hot to the touch.

Even now, I could feel my skin dry out and my lips crack.

"There's no way anyone could survive getting to the vault," I said.

"Only dwarves of the Stiltskin line can survive this trip. But good thinking knocking the water wheel down. The waterfall is pouring in through the upper tunnels and is working like a cooling system."

Cool. *This* was cool. I didn't want to imagine trespassing in these passageways without them being as 'cool' as they were now.

My vision started to fade out, and I knew I was at a dangerous level of dehydration. I just wanted to get to the vault, but then I realized we had a serious problem.

"Rumple, how do we kill Greed?" I asked.

Rumple was silent, and I looked up at Spencer, who watched me with interest. I hoped and prayed that he was awake for this. I couldn't fully read Kash. I only guessed, based on his actions, that he was trying to save me.

"We *can't* kill Greed," he said sadly. "We can only re-imprison him."

A moan came from the darkness, and Kash pulled his blade. We turned to see a battered and bruised form on the ground.

"Grimkeep?" I kneeled by the dwarf. He still had a goblin arrow in his shoulder. I pressed my hand to the wound and jumped back as he lashed out with a blade in his right hand.

"Get back! I'll kill you all, you filthy goblins!"

"Grimkeep, you're safe. It's me, Rhea."

The dwarf's head fell back, and he passed out.

I felt along the wound; the arrow wasn't deep.

"Knife," I called out, and Kash handed me one of his. Carefully, I dug out the arrow and cursed under my breath. I could smell the infection. He needed more than healing; he needed a poultice. And we didn't have time or the resources for either.

I said his name, pressing my palm to his forehead, and it was burning hot from fever.

"Grimkeep," I said again, but received no answer.

"Grimkeep, you wake up right now, dwarf! You have a duty to uphold."

Grimkeep rolled his head and opened his eyes. "That's funny, I thought I heard my Uncle Rumple. But that's not possible. He died years ago."

"I'm not dead yet, you ninny. Now get off your arse and pick up your weapon. Dwarves don't lay down on the job."

Grimkeep's eyes widened, and he dragged himself up, reaching for the halberd next to him. His eyes were glassy with fever, and I knew he didn't have long if we didn't get him help.

"You've done well guarding the vault, nephew," Rumple said with encouragement. "I'll take it from here."

Tears fell from Grimkeep's eyes, and he wiped at them with the collar of his jerkin. "I tried, Uncle. I tried to keep the vault guarded, but there were just too many of them. And they kept digging and digging."

"I know." Rumple sighed. We continued down the tunnel and stopped in front of a pile of debris. I looked for a door. Even now, I could see bits of gold through the floor.

"Where is it?" I asked, climbing on the rubble and looking up and around.

"You're standing on it."

"Where's the door?"

"There is no door."

"But I thought it was a vault? I thought that you'd locked Greed in a vault."

"No. A vault is something that can be opened and closed. This is a grave." Rumple's voice lowered with sadness.

"It's your grave," I whispered.

"'Tis, and I took hold of the world's greatest enemy and buried him with me, but slowly he slipped through my fingers."

I moved toward a dirt pile. Kneeling, I shifted the soil away to see a half melted golden cup. Farther down the cavern was evidence of large holes cut through the earth.

"Molneer," I said.

"Yes," Grimkeep muttered, his hand holding his side. He grimaced and tried to hide the pain from his wound. "He's been digging here for months, and I didn't know it. I can't guard the tomb all the time."

"But how? I thought he couldn't get this low in the tunnels. We made it this far because I collapsed the waterfall."

"He didn't. He dug from the upper tunnels." Grimkeep pointed up, and I saw the giant holes in the ceiling, hundreds of feet up, coupled with a mass of pulley systems and levers. Even now, a giant metal contraption hung from the ceiling that looked like a jaw. "They've been sending a giant mechanical shovel down and pulling up hundreds of pounds of dirt at a time. They take it to the old dwarf mine that is now run by goblins. Every time, I break apart their operation. They rebuild."

Rumple panicked. "Rhea, do you feel him? Is he still here?"

"What do you mean?"

"Is Greed still here?"

I didn't need to even touch the ground. I could feel the gold coins, the iron, ores, and metal beneath the earth. But I sensed none of the vileness that I felt when I touched the cursed treasure.

The tomb was empty, but it wasn't recent.

Greed had escaped a long time ago.

"No," I whispered, turning to look at the golden axe that was still in Kash's hand. "Greed isn't buried in the earth. He's in this room."

As I spoke the words, Kash laughed. A deep, horrendous laugh that shook me to my core. I had thought the blades couldn't speak, and I'm glad they never did because the voice that came out was pure evil.

"That's right, Rumple. I'm not dead, but alive."

The two blades twitched and shook.

A black shadow, the shadow that I had seen many times swirling around the helm, slipped out of their bodies and formed a dark cloud in front of us.

Kash screamed. He curled inward, his body cracking as if his bones were fighting against what was coming next. I cringed as Spencer and Kash fell to their knees. Kash's dragon helm fell on the ground. The rest of their armor, made from shadow and gold, ripped from their skin, moving to the center of the room where it formed into a blurry mass. The rapier and golden knife crumbled into dust.

"Greed!" Rumple cried out in challenge, still in Kash's grip.

The shadow entity continued to laugh as the cloud grew, then the armor shifted and morphed into scales, each one attaching to Greed. Kash's fallen helm lifted off the ground as it elongated and turned more lifelike before attaching to Greed's body. The shadow shifted and left its spiritual shape. What stood in front of us was a golden dragon.

"At last," Greed breathed out. "I've found you. I've waited a hundred years to be reunited, brother. But your form leaves much to be desired. Unlike me," Greed chuckled. The dragon pulled back his long neck and body, stretching.

I rushed over and kneeled between Kash and Spencer. Spencer was out cold, the transformation too much for his mind, and I wasn't sure if he would awaken. Kash was shaking, covered in cold sweat, his eyes wide and clear, his hand gripping the axe.

"I'm not your brother, you ugly beast!" Rumple cried out.

"You are the only one who has ever been a challenge for me. Each time I weasel my way into the heart of the innocent, it is you that finds me. But this time, when I escaped, I took control of a village. I made them disappear, and no one turned up to stop me." Greed snaked across the top of the cavern and disappeared into one of the mining holes.

I thought he was escaping, but he popped out of another one and clawed his way back down the wall, bringing his massive head eye level with us.

"With ease, I infiltrated another village and then

another. I went to larger towns. Like playthings, town after town, village after village. I even appeared at the high court of kings. Wreaked some havoc with the princes. I could have easily had them kill each other, but what was the point?" Greed sighed. "It would have all been over with too soon. I didn't have a worthy opponent. I needed you."

"The king wasn't obsessed with searching for golden treasure," I said, moving to stand in front of Kash. "It was you, controlling the king, searching for your nemesis."

"Very smart." Greed let out a breath of fiery air. I cringed as the hot air brushed past my cheek, drying out my already chapped lips. "I knew he wasn't truly gone. For all great heroes never truly die. Their spirit lives to fight on. I could *feel* his. I just needed someone strong enough to bring him back. A magic user with exceptional power. So the search began . . . until I found you," Greed chuckled, his head swinging toward me. "I had *so* hoped you would have learned something from my blades and given him a form like that, but I'll live with my disappointment. An axe, however. Truly unexpected."

"That's the reason you let me experiment on you?" I said, aghast. "Because you wanted me to turn Rumple into a *cursed blade*?"

"Why else would I let you take a part of my essence?" Greed snorted.

I looked at him in disgust. "I would never make a weapon like that."

Kash rolled over and got to his knees. Using the axe, he pushed himself upright. Spinning the axe head, he gripped his fingers on the handle. "You've stolen my life. Used my body like a puppet. If you want to fight, fight me."

"We can take him, you and I!" Rumple roared encouragingly.

"Oh, little prince," Greed almost purred. "You were so easy, so spoiled. You were the easiest one to control because you had the most to lose. You couldn't fight my control then. What makes you think you can win now?"

Kash cast his golden eyes toward me and I saw his pain, the doubt that was plaguing him.

"Ah, I see. You're confused," Greed said with mock sympathy. "You want to know if your feelings are true toward the one called Rhea. Was it you who desired her, or I? Did you only want her because I felt her power first and I claimed her as my own?" The dragon disappeared into a dark, misty cloud and moved closer to Kash. Swirling around him like a cloud of doubt. Kash waved at the shadow, and it swirled around his hand like a bracelet.

I feared it would reattach itself as armor, but Greed seemed to be toying with Kash, trying to make him a fool.

Kash's head lowered. His dark curls shook as he gripped the handle. His weight shifted, and he dug his boots into the soil.

"It was *my* desire, you felt," Greed said. "I wanted her power; *desired* her power. You felt nothing toward her. You're just an empty shell, unable to feel anything other than what I want you to. After all, it was I that protected her from the Goblins, not you."

"That's a lie," I said, speaking up.

"Is it?" The shadow moved toward me, and I could see two red eyes.

"You feared me. Feared what I could do. It wasn't protection. You needed me to turn Rumple's essence from gold into a tangible form. You only defeated the goblins so they wouldn't steal him. They sensed him too, but they would've destroyed the artifact. Even though you pretend you're all powerful, you couldn't truly control the king. You'd fed him so much greed he became lost in that agenda, coveting gold and notoriety."

"True, I didn't keep quite a firm hold on the king as I would have liked. Unlike Kash, here. He truly was my puppet. He felt nothing for you."

"No," I said quietly. "It's a lie. I know you. When I touched the ley line under the mountain, I got glimpses of you, Greed. And I know your true secret."

"It's gold," Rumple whispered knowingly.

I shook my head and smirked, taking a step back toward the cloud that moved away from me. As if to protect itself, it shifted back into a dragon, hiding behind golden scales and a mouth full of teeth.

Unafraid, I moved closer and raised my hand up to touch Greed's giant maw. "I know *why*."

The dragon's nose twitched, his red eyes flinched, and I pressed my palm to the scales between each nostril. Then I did something daring.

"Get away from him, girl," Rumple hissed.

Ignoring his warning, I leaned forward and pressed my cheek against his snout. In my periphery, I could see Kash's shocked face. He took a step forward as if to protect me.

"I know your *true* name," I whispered. "And it's not Greed."

I felt it. A gush of pain that flowed out of Greed like a dam had broken. A river of emotion that burst forth. Greed tried to pull away from my touch, but I held on, wrapping my arms around his snout. He snarled and snorted, but I gripped harder, staring up into his eyes that I knew were not truly red.

"You were abandoned as a child," I said as I relayed his memories. The echo of his past that I saw in him.

"Stop it," Greed growled a warning.

"You grew up an outcast, always watching others, wishing you could have what they did. So you took it by force, and you grew to be a great conqueror. You led your people, gaining respect, but still you were never satisfied. Because you could not take by force what must be earned —what you never had. Friendship."

Greed's eyes were wild. He tried to pull away, but I reached out and placed my hand on his snout and shushed under my breath.

"Your true name means loneliness."

He hissed and pulled out of my grasp. "Stop, your words hurt."

"They hurt because it's the truth," I said. "I read your dwarven name in the Book of Eld. Loneliness. It just took me being in this mountain to piece it together. To feel the connection and hear the echoes. Truth breaks all lies, even the ones that we tell ourselves. Isn't that right, Einsamall?"

Grimkeep, who had been silent, pulled himself up. He leaned on the halberd and came to stand in front of the dragon. "As in *King* Einsamall, the first king of the dwarves of Ragnar?"

I nodded. "And the very first of the Stiltskin line."

"*You!*" Rumple growled out. "I don't believe it. Our first king. You caused us to destroy each other. For what? Let me at him! I'll chop his head off. He doesn't deserve to be king. I will destroy you!" Rumple almost swung himself right out of Kash's hands.

"You don't have to be named loneliness, or greed. Because we can be your friend. You can pick a new name, one that is honorable."

Tears stung my eyes as I thought of my sister.

Greed let out a roar of pain. He clawed at his golden scales as if they burned him. I let go as the great dragon flung his head about, lashing and fighting the darkness within. He continued to claw at his own skin and the darkness leaked into the air. Greed's red eyes focused on me, and I watched as the red dissipated and I stared into eyes of black and gold, like burning coals.

The dragon fought the darkness within him. His long tail lashed out, accidentally smashing into the giant claw shovel hanging from the ceiling.

A rusty groan caught our attention right before we heard a snap above us.

"Watch out!" Kash yelled as the chain holding the suspended mining contraption broke. The metal hooks of the shovel opened wide like teeth, and they fell from the ceiling. Kash raced for me as a golden claw reached out and knocked him back.

I stared as death rushed toward me, and my last thought was how much that open shovel looked like a dragon's mouth.

CHAPTER TWENTY-EIGHT

My chest exploded with pain. Breathing was impossible. I was trapped beneath what felt like a hot, burning coal, except it was a dragon's head. I pushed against his body and already his scales felt cooler.

"Kash," I cried out weakly, unable to take a deep breath.

"It's okay. We've got you." Kash and Spencer were by my side, both pressing their backs into Greed's head, their feet leveraged against a wall.

"Push!" Kash yelled.

The brothers strained and moved Greed's head upward a few inches, but it was only enough room for me to inhale before it dropped back down on me, and I heard a rib crack.

I gasped, unable to breathe. I could feel my vision going dark as I was slowly suffocating.

"I'll get you out. I promise." Kash's voice was warm and soothing as I looked up into his gold eyes.

"Move over," Grimkeep commanded, pushing the princes to the side and taking up the spot closest to me. "You need a dwarf for this."

He leaned down, gripped Greed's jaw, and roared as he lifted the dragon's head by himself. Doing so reopened his wounds, sending fresh blood running down his side and onto his pants.

"Now!" Grimkeep yelled.

Kash and Spencer each grabbed a wrist and dragged me from under the dragon. Grimkeep lost his grip, and it fell with a thud, scattering a cloud of dirt.

"What happened?" I asked, clutching my side.

Kash's eyes filled with pain as he pulled me close and tried to shelter my view of Greed. "Don't look, Rhea."

"No, let me up. I need to see."

Kash pulled me into a sitting position, his arms wrapped around me for strength and support as I looked at a golden dragon that lay unmoving across a pile of dirt and gold. The metal claw mining contraption's teeth were embedded in Greed's neck, his once fiery eyes cold and dead.

"I don't understand." I felt a giant knot of emotion that was forming in my throat.

"He saved you," Kash said. "When the shovel dislodged, Greed knocked me out of the way and covered you with his body, sheltering you."

"Rumple," I murmured, turning toward the axe in Spencer's hand. "You said Greed was invincible. That he couldn't die."

"I didn't think he could," he said softly.

Spencer brought Rumple near and kneeled next to me and Kash, his eyes filled with sadness. "I think I know what occurred. *Greed* couldn't die."

"Then what happened?" I could feel my frustration

building. How little control I had over the situation made me feel inadequate. All the emotions I had picked up from Greed, and losing Damon and Honor were too much. I couldn't hold them back anymore and I let the tears of heartbreak fall.

"I think it was because you found his true name," Spencer said. "When you did, you made him mortal. So I guess he died from loneliness."

"But he wasn't alone," I said, feeling my heart ache. "He had us."

"No," Spencer corrected. "He never had us. We would never forgive him for what he stole from us."

I looked between Grimkeep, Kash, Spencer and the silent Rumple. They agreed. They never would have forgiven Greed. But I had gotten through to him. I think somehow, in his dark soul, he really was searching for a friend.

Kash brushed the hair out of my eyes and placed a kiss on my forehead. "Despite how we thought of him, I think he cared for you as a friend. I think he saw how you treated me and he wanted that."

"I knew you were still you." I leaned against Kash, pressing my face into his shoulder. "I knew you wouldn't hurt me."

"And it's that absolute trust that I think won over Greed. At first, he didn't like you. He thought you made him weak because of my intense feelings for you. He didn't like the fact that you outsmarted him. Then he became jealous of how I felt about you. In some ways, I think he cared for you too. He died protecting you."

"Now what do we do?" Spencer asked, looking at Greed's golden carcass.

With Kash's help, I stood and sucked in a breath at the intense pain in my side and chest.

"Leave it to me." Feeling more confidant in my abilities than ever before, I used my magic and reached into the earth, calling the singing ore to me. The shovel was knocked away as I encased the entity once known as Greed in the sparking silven ore. Using my forging magic, I created a memorial plaque at the bottom.

Here lies Einsamall. Never Alone.

Grimkeep nodded. "It'll do."

"Rumple?" I asked.

He was silent for a long moment before answering. "If only I knew. I could have saved him, prevented all of this from happening."

"You can't blame yourself," Grimkeep said. "We all battle inner demons."

Sweat beaded across my brow, and I could feel my dress sticking to my back. Too much time had passed, and the tunnels were no longer cooling. "We need to go."

We ran back up the passageways, Spencer doing his best to carry Grimkeep, who yelled at him the whole way. "Put me down, I'm not a baby!"

"Stop squirming!" Spencer gritted his teeth as he hauled the dwarf up the steps and then we came to the bridge and the twelve-foot gap.

"How are we going to get across that?" Grimkeep grimaced.

"I can't throw you," Kash said. "I'm not as strong without the cursed blade."

I bit the inside of my cheek. "Well, how about a cursed axe?" I pointed to Rumple.

"What did you do, girl?" Rumple said in shock.

"I did exactly what Greed wanted, just not the way he expected me to. I saw the methods Molneer used when creating the cursed blades. It was in the Book of Eld. After studying Greed's cursed armor, I just adjusted the technique. I created another cursed blade, but it's not really cursed. More like enhanced. It's not to control or manipulate someone, and it's not tied to day or night. Sorry Grimkeep, I don't think you should attempt it with your injuries."

The dwarf nodded and looked relieved.

"What are you saying?" Kash asked.

"She's saying I'm awesome! Get over here, big boy, and let me turn you into a real dwarf warrior!" Rumple was overly eager to give it a try.

Spencer shook his head. "Nope, I'm not going through that again. This guy seems more unstable than Greed."

I looked at Kash, and he knew what I was asking. I could see the fear in his eyes. He didn't want to lose control again, but he also wanted to save us.

"I love you." He turned, gave me a crooked smile, and his eyes lit up again when they met mine. "I'm saying this now, just in case I don't come back."

"You will," I said with assurance. "And I love you too."

"Gimme! Gimme Gimme!" Rumple chanted. "I'm gonna have me some hands!"

Spencer handed Kash the axe, and he gave me a confused look. There wasn't a way to activate it.

"What do I do?"

"Say his name," I smiled. "That's it."

"Not just 'that's it'," Rumple argued. "You need to say 'Rumple Stiltskin of Kiln, please make me a great dwarf warrior'."

"I'm not saying that."

"We don't have time for this," Grimkeep growled.

Kash bit his lip and looked at the axe with trepidation. "I trust you," he told me, before raising the axe and saying, "Rumple Stiltskin."

This time the axe melded with Kash's skin, wrapping around him with golden plated armor. His helm was a double-horned helmet like Grimkeep's, and when he looked up at me, his eyes were clear and golden, twinkling with mischief.

"I'm still me," Kash said in relief.

"And I've got hands!" Rumple's voice came from the helmet. "Sort of. They're kind of sissy hands."

Kash frowned. "They're not sissy." He tested his strength by reaching down and crushing a small boulder to dust.

"I'm a blade."

"Not a blade, a dwarf axe. Even better," Rumple said smugly.

"I'm ready. Let's do this." Kash flexed his muscles and reached for Grimkeep.

"No, brother, me first. Someone should be on the other side to help catch." Spencer stepped forward.

Rumple as a blade gave Kash more strength than he'd ever had as a dragon blade. I figured it was because Greed was split three ways, never sending his full potential to one person.

Kash tossed Spencer farther than the cliff, and he landed four feet past the edge.

One by one, we flew. Grimkeep, then me, and Spencer tried his best to catch us, but we more or less bowled him over. Kash jumped last, landing with a loud thud, the earth shaking beneath his feet.

"Do you think the goblins will come back?" Grimkeep asked, his voice quiet as he looked among the rooftops and alleys.

"I'd like to see them try," Rumple yelled. "Now that I've got big sissy hands, I'll cut all of them down to size."

"Do you ever stop talking?" Kash groaned.

"Come over here, you ugly goblins!" Rumple was a little too thrilled to be Kash's armor.

"You okay?" I asked Kash, secretly searching his eyes, looking for the dark cloud. When I touched the armor, I didn't have the same feeling of foreboding as I did when touching the cursed gold.

"It's fine." Kash winced as Rumple yelled another challenge. "He's loud, and he is kind of a pain—"

"Don't say it," Rumple warned.

"In the axe." Kash laughed.

"Sissy hands," Rumple shot back.

"That's it. Rumple Stiltskin." Kash held up the weapon.

"Wait, no, I didn't mean to," Rumple wailed as he was pulled from Kash, the armor flying off to form an axe once again. Kash took the bandolier and strapped the axe onto his back.

"Oh, son of the Terst Bjorn ," Rumple cursed before falling silent to a pout. As we left the city and headed up the stone steps to the upper tunnels, he finally apologized. "They're not really sissy hands. I take that back."

"I'm not saying your name again," Kash said with a sigh.

"Puh-lease say my name," Rumple begged.

"Nope." Kash grinned and shot me a look.

I laughed as the majority of our trek back to the surface level was Rumple begging for someone to say his name.

"I don't know what you're talking about?" I teased. "Rumple who?"

CHAPTER TWENTY-NINE

I t was still daylight when we stumbled out of the mines, dirty, cold, and tired. Grimkeep was on his last legs of energy and had to be carried out by Spencer and Kash. When we collapsed in the snow, I cried out, grasping my cracked ribs.

"Let us help!" A familiar voice cut through the air.

I looked up to see Brenna, Benton, Annette, Fezik, and Taffy. Fezik raced to Grimkeep's side.

Brenna kneeled by me and reached for my injured side.

"No." I shooed her away and motioned to Grimkeep. "He's far worse. But wait—" I slipped my hand into my satchel and gave her an energy charm. "You should be able to heal longer now."

Her face brightened, and she immediately went to see to Grimkeep.

"What are you doing here?" I asked Annette.

Annette grinned and wiped soot from her dress and hands. "You didn't expect us to just leave you here, did you? As soon as we got to Verdan, we told Fezik and Taffy what happened, and we came back to rescue you."

Benton went to the mine entrance. "That was the last

of them, right, Annette?"

"Yes," she clapped her hands together. "There's no one else down there."

"Honor," I whispered, my heart breaking.

Using his magic, Benton folded the entrance in on itself, collapsing the glamour.

As the sunlight poured through the tops of the trees, Spencer and Kash froze in awe. It was a beautiful thing to see them step into the light and look up, letting the sun's rays cross their face.

"It's been years," Spencer said, tears flowing down his cheeks.

"I never thought I would see the sun again," Kash added, rubbing his hands through his hair and over his face. "I thought we would be cursed forever."

"Not forever," Damon said from the back of the wagon.

"What?" Spencer cried out and ran over to his brother.

"Not too hard." Damon grimaced and pulled away to reveal the long bandages on his side.

"I thought you were dead," Kash said.

"Well, we might have been if not for that one." Damon pointed to Annette. "She led me out."

Annette grinned. "I am a seeker, after all. It's my job to find people. By the way, Rhea. I think this one belongs to you." She motioned to the back of the wagon, and curled up sleeping on a makeshift bed was Honor, her arm and forehead bandaged.

"Is she?" I asked, fearfully.

"Just sleeping," Damon said, his eyes casting a soft look toward my sister. "I've never seen bravery like hers. Distancing herself from you so your magic could work to save your friends. That is honorable."

"What?" I said in a loud whisper and narrowed my eyes. "What are you talking about?"

"Rhea, I'm awake," Honor said hoarsely. She sat up and winced. She was favoring her left arm.

"What does he mean you distanced yourself so my magic would work?" I asked her.

She looked down. "I'm so sorry, we never told you."

"Told me what?" As I moved to sit on the bed across from Honor, I reached for her hand, and she pulled back. "There's a reason they separated me from all of you our whole life." Honor licked her lips, tucking her stray hair from her braid behind her ear. "It's because I'm an antimage."

"What?" I shook my head. "That's wrong. I've never heard of that."

Her blue eyes looked up at me, and she pleaded for me to believe her. "I am. I'm more than that. It's like I'm an unlucky coin. We don't know the effect I will have. I will either drain you of your magic or block it. Neither one is healthy for the training of six teenage sorceresses. In fact, I'm the worst person to have near you in a battle of magic. Knives. I can do that, though." Her head dropped low, and I saw the tears in her eyes.

"So when I was trying to use magic and couldn't . . ."

"I knew it was me. I was draining you. I had to get as far away from you as possible."

"But to run into a horde of goblins?" I raised my eyebrow at her and gave her a look my mother would be proud of.

She shrugged. "I've dealt with worse." Honor fidgeted with the blanket on her lap. "The good thing about my gift is I heal really fast."

"So that explains everything."

"I'm like a magic vampire. Except I'm drawing your magic, not blood. Mother said it was best to stay far away from all of you. So Lorn took me, and we always tracked the ley lines because they are like a never-ending supply of magic."

I reached across and pulled her into a hug, and she stiffened in my grasp. I tried to think back to the times we were together. She never wanted to touch us, and there was hardly any contact. I always thought it was because she was cold and aloof. Now I realized she was scared of hurting us. I underestimated Honor. She really was the most dangerous of us all.

"But what about Damon?"

A slight blush fed her cheeks, and she pinched her lips together. "He chased me down and pulled me into a building right before the wave swept over me. But then the weirdest thing happened."

"What?"

Honor bit her lip. "As the water rushed inside the room, I thought he was trying to drown me, and I panicked. He held my head above water, and we were tossed around. In my terror, I accidentally drained him of magic and removed the curse. He changed before me. The armor fell off like paint chipping off an old wall, and the sword he carried crumbled into nothing. I thought I'd killed him."

"When, in fact, *she* saved me." Damon leaned against the doorframe, his green eyes settling on Honor. "She really is something."

Honor blushed and went speechless.

We spent the next candle mark catching up on things we'd missed. I learned her boundaries and the signals that followed her uncontrollable magic. When she got tired, her magic would reach for mine, and I could feel myself draining. I moved to the far side of the room, out of her reach. Then I felt the pull stop.

Her face fell in horror, but I shook my head and told her, "It's all right. I won't leave you."

Honor's face crumpled, and tears fell from her eyes. "I can't tell you how much I needed to hear those words. I thought you would resent me when you knew."

"I could never resent you," I said. "In fact, I'm sorry that you've been isolated for so long. That we didn't reach out sooner. But Honor, your power makes you special, not something to be feared."

"That's my greatest fear," she whispered. "Of being alone."

"You're never alone," I smiled. "I'll always be here for you."

"Thank you," she sniffed. "I came to help you, but it looks like you were the one who helped me."

With Greed's death, the plague on the kingdom had finally lifted, though his influence remained. Pieces of the cursed treasure still existed, and those in possession were held under a veil of selfishness.

Even King Goddrick had changed. When I was brought before him, I didn't see a cold and cruel king, but a weary and worn old man. The hard glint in his eyes was gone, the ugly, downturned mouth was replaced by the warm and kindhearted smile of a generous king.

"Are you Rheanon Eville?" King Goddrick asked. He

was sitting on a humble throne of redwood, his golden crown replaced by a silver circlet, his fingers unadorned.

"I am, Your Highness," I said nervously, unsure whether to curtsy or bow.

"It seems I have significant gaps in my memory. I think I'm getting old. But I've been told I have you to thank for saving our kingdom from falling further into the curse of selfishness and greed." He got up from his seat and looked over at his three sons for confirmation.

Kash stood tall and proud, his dark hair still damp, making his curls seem even more unruly. He was extremely dashing in his red velvet jacket and white pants tucked into polished boots—and not a single hint of gold on his uniform. On his hip, I noticed an empty sheath.

I looked toward Spencer and Damon. They were all in similar uniforms. Spencer kept pulling at his collar, and his keen blue eyes focused on the exit. I knew he wanted to leave and delve back into the library and his stack of books.

Damon's green eyes met mine, and he bowed his head, his long hair brushing the edge of his collar. I once again felt like I was looking into one of the noblest hearts. The curse of the blade really chose their personas well.

I gazed back at Kash, whose eyes locked onto mine, and I felt the heat within them as he focused on my lips.

My mouth parted, and I sucked in my breath. Kash smiled knowingly.

There was no way he could have heard my breathing from that far away . . . could he?

Oh stars, I had completely lost focus on what King Goddrick was saying. Bringing my attention back to the king, he was just finishing up with his plan on how to give back to his people and redistribute the extreme wealth he'd recently gained.

I couldn't help but think about what Greed had done to the king. King Goddrick's aspiration as a ruler was to be the most generous. Somehow, Greed had warped his heart and amplified it, turning his desire inward instead of outward.

"Your Highness, may I ask what has happened to Freya?" I knew she deserved punishment, but a part of my heart ached for her. She'd protected the princes' secret and cared for them. Like so many others, she'd succumbed to greed and paid the ultimate price when she lost her son.

The king inclined his head. "Freya and Captain Adams have caused much suffering. They're in prison for now, but like the rest of us who have hurt others, they will work for the remainder of their lives to make amends."

"And Molneer?" I asked.

"Ah, yes. Molneer will stand trial with his own people. His fate is in their hands. I've offered our services to the dwarven guild of the plains to help them rebuild after the damage caused by the earthquakes and avalanches. Mines should never be run by goblins. The underground explosions have ceased, and our land should be safer now."

The kingdom has found peace from greed. All it needed was time, and that made me smile. "I'm happy to hear that, Your Highness."

"So that's everything, I guess." King Goddrick grinned and clapped his hands to his thigh in excitement.

I blinked and took a step back, looking at the ground.

Keeping my eyes focused on the long red runner in the throne.

"So what can I offer you, Rheanon Eville?" King Goddrick asked, his face beaming with pride. "What prize can I offer to the girl who can turn straw into gold? There must be something that you want." He held his palms open wide and gestured to the room.

Kash straightened, his shoulders tensed, and he looked right at me.

"Prize?" I said, confusion filling my tone.

"Yes, I was told I bluntly offered a marriage contract to the person who could spin gold. Is that something that would interest you?" the king asked. "A wedding that would include a kingdom?"

My mouth gaped open in surprise, and I tried to rack my brain for his wording. He did offer marriage to himself. I felt my stomach roil at the thought of marrying King Goddrick.

"Um . . . no. I uh, think I'm good." I felt my voice rise as I began to chatter nervously. "I don't think I'm ready to settle down and run a kingdom . . . like, ever. Even though you are a most handsome king."

Kash and his brothers frowned. I slowly backed away from the king and his three sons.

"In fact," I added, "I think a few years of solitude would do me good. I can't express my gratitude enough, King Goddrick, but I will have to decline the formal invitation of a marriage contract or proposal." As I said my final word, I felt my boot hit the end of the runner and I knew I was only a few feet away from the exit. I did my best attempt at bowing and curtseying before I ran out the door.

CHAPTER THIRTY

"What did that knife ever do to you?" Rumple chastised as I let my hammer ring against the metal.

"Nothing." I gritted my teeth and heated the silven ore in the furnace.

"Could have fooled me. I would have thought it killed your dog or something, the way you're beating it to death."

"Shut it," I snapped. "Sol, I need it hotter."

My salamander spun around in the forge and I saw my metal turn white. I drew it out and laid it on my anvil where I worked on the metal again.

After my disgraceful exit from the palace, I couldn't find the strength to return home to Nihill. Instead, I went back to the manor, but this time I remembered to put the ward back up, making it impossible for anyone to find it.

Honor had stayed for a few weeks and helped me repair most of the house. She'd been the one to go into town to get me supplies. I just wanted to avoid everyone. The shame I felt for how I treated the king and the princes weighed heavily on me.

The weeks passed, and winter's icy grip gave way to spring, and I found tending to a large house by myself was becoming daunting. My presence had attracted many of the fae. The Eville lands were filled with sprites, undines, and I now had an army of salamanders at my beck and call. They loved it when I fed them magic. They wrestled in the orchards, burping fire at each other. I'd banned them from wrestling in the manor after they'd almost burned the house down . . . twice.

"You know, living in the castle would have had its perks," Rumple grumbled from his hook on the wall. "Servants . . . food . . . servants."

"You are welcome to go march yourself back up to the princes and offer yourself as their new blade. Who knows? The king still needs a bodyguard and there are benefits of having you as the next blade."

"I might just do that. I miss sissy hands," Rumple snapped back at me, showing his impatience. I knew he was tired of talking to me, and I hadn't been the most amiable. In fact, I was downright grumpy.

"Go ahead, use your feet and walk up there." I held the blazing hot knife I was working on and pointed it right at the middle of the axe head where I assumed Rumple's face would be. "Oh, that's right. You don't have any."

Rumple grew quiet, and I knew I had upset him. He'd never once complained that I'd brought him back as an axe. Except for the hands thing. I figured he just wanted to bring Kash back into the conversation. There were times I thought he missed him as much as I did.

For the next hour I worked at the forge, pounding out the metal into a blade before moving to the grinding wheel. Late into the night I continued, sanding and finally attaching a silver handle. I didn't know why, but I etched in bits of scales as an homage to Einsamall.

When I was done, I had a beautiful blade. All it needed was a sheath.

A tree branch cracked, and I looked warily into the darkness. Sol came to the front of the furnace, and he stomped his feet and growled.

"Come out and face my wrath!" Rumple screamed from his hook on the post. "I'm not scared of you, for I am the mighty—,"

"Rumple Stiltskin!" A voice in the woods called.

"Wait, what?" Rumple cried out as his golden form dissolved and floated across my face and into the woods. Seconds later, a golden warrior stepped into view.

"Hey look!" Rumple cried out in excitement. "It's sissy hands!"

I couldn't move as my golden knight walked confidently toward me. He removed the helmet, setting it aside to stare down at me.

Kash's curly hair had grown longer over the last few months. His unshaven jaw made him look dangerous. Those gorgeous eyes I usually associated with laughter were filled with pain.

"Why?" he asked, stopping in front of me. "Why couldn't you accept me?"

"Accept you?" I said. "I do."

"Then why did you run away from me? And hide behind the darn ward!" He raised his hands and pointed back up the path where I saw two people waving jovially at me. Marco stood behind Velora, his arms wrapped around her waist.

"He still had the seeking spell from my sister?" I guessed.

Kash's brows furrowed. "I found Honor and tried to

follow her back here, but she's too good. Even as good as I am, I couldn't follow her. Annette refused to help me. She said you didn't want to be found. So, I spent weeks tracking these two down instead. Then I begged them to help me find you. And you're here, living life, like you don't even miss me."

"That's not true," I whispered. "I do miss you."

Kash spotted the blade I had finished and picked it up.

It fit perfectly in his hands. He tested the weight and then flipped it around, into the air, and under his wrist. "It's like it's made for me."

"Because it is," I breathed out watching in awe as he and my blade became one. I had dreamed of this moment, and I almost cried when I saw that he still had the empty sheath by his side.

He slipped my knife into the sheath, and he closed his eyes. "Now, I feel whole again." When his eyes opened, he grabbed my hands and held them close. "Even though we were no longer the king's blades, and I wasn't cursed, I felt alone. Lost. Like a part of me was missing." He tapped the blade at his hip. "I was right. It's you. I need you by my side to make me whole."

Kash cupped my face and leaned down, his eyes watching me carefully, waiting—and when I didn't hold my breath, he frowned.

"Is there someone else?"

"No," I said evenly, proud that I had learned to control my emotions.

"I no longer take your breath away." He sounded like his pride was hurt.

"I think you do; you just might have to work a little harder than giving me a look," I said.

He grinned in challenge. Kash leaned down and kissed me, his lips claiming mine as I reached up and wrapped my arms around him.

When his pulled away, my heart was racing, and I was indeed breathless.

"I still got it." He kissed the tip of my nose. "Please, Rhea. I've only ever spent nights with you, please promise to live your days by my side."

"For how long?" I asked.

"For as many days as I take your breath away," he promised.

"So, in other words, forever," I said and grinned.

"If you will marry me."

"As long as I don't have to marry your father," I muttered, exhaling loudly.

Kash frowned, "My father?" Then his head fell back, and he let out a boisterous belly laugh. "Did you think my father was offering you his hand in marriage?"

"Uh, yeah," I said sheepishly.

He chuckled. "No wonder you ran away. Oh Rhea, he was offering you the chance to choose one of us to marry. One of the princes of Kiln, and then you chose none of us. Spencer was hurt a bit, Damon took it in good stride, but I also threatened to beat them within an inch of death if they even joked and offered their hand to you.

"So it's either marry you, or . . ."

"There is no 'or'. Marry me. We can help rebuild the kingdom, and with your gifts, we can help bring glory back to Ter Dell."

"Oh yeah!" Rumple cried out, the helmet almost rattling off the table in his excitement. "Sign her up, sissy hands. And sign me up too because I know you're going to need me by your side to fight off those goblins. You and I are going to make a great team." Rumple quieted, and I heard him clear his throat. "I mean, if that's what you want, Rhea." He sounded so polite, but I could almost secretly hear him whispering, *Please. Please. Please.*

"I don't think I'm made out to be a queen," I mumbled, uncertainty creeping in my thoughts. I held my scarred and soiled hands out. "Look at me. I'm made for getting dirty in the forge. It's what I love. It suits me better than setting tea parties."

"Nonsense," Rumple interrupted. "Our women were wicked in the forge. You were considered blessed to get a weapon forged by a warrior maiden. You would make a great dwarf queen despite your lack of beard."

I blinked in surprise and looked at Kash. He pointed to the helmet. "What he said."

My laughter filled the air and Kash dropped to one knee before me, his face filled with pure love. "Rhea, be my warrior queen. I don't care if you don't have a beard."

I sniffled, wiping the tears from eyes. "Yes, Kash. Yes."

"Yahoo! We're getting married," Rumple whooped. "I'm going to be the flower girl!"

"Rumple Stiltskin!" Kash yelled. The armor pulled away and forged back onto the blade of the axe. "You're going to be locked in a trunk if you don't quiet down."

"You wouldn't dare. You need to take me on the honeymoon. Someone needs to protect sissy hands from—wait. Put me down! Help! Rhea! Help!"

Kash took Rumple outside the forge, and with a deft two-handed throw, tossed him overhead across the clearing until he stuck in the trunk of a maple tree.

"Hey, good shot!" Rumple shouted as he settled into the wood.

"Let's just make sure to leave the children at home." Kash leaned down and picked me up in his arm.

"Which ones?" I asked, turning to point at Velora and Marco.

Velora yelled out in a high-pitched voice, "Hey Rhea, do you have any butt?"

Marco shook his head and headed into the house after Velora.

"All of them." Kash grinned and scooped me up, lifting me high into the air.

As Kash carried me into the manor, Rumple's voice echoed in the forest.

"Hey, Rhea? Sissy hands? . . . hello? Anyone? You forgot me! The glorious Rumple Stil—oh wait. I should probably stop telling people my name or they'll learn of my magic power. It will have to be a secret. I'm good at keeping secrets. I'll need a new name. How about Nancy?"

Coming June 2022

ABOUT THE AUTHOR

Chanda Hahn is a NYT & USA Today Bestselling author of The Unfortunate Fairy Tale series. She uses her experience as a children's pastor, children's librarian and bookseller to write compelling and popular fiction for teens. She was born in Seattle, WA, grew up in Nebraska, and currently resides in Waukesha, WI, with her husband and their twin children; Aiden and Ashley.

Visit Chanda Hahn's website to learn more about her other forthcoming books.
www.chandahahn.com